DWARF IT ALL

DWARF IT ALL

DWARF BOUNTY HUNTER™ BOOK SIX

MARTHA CARR
MICHAEL ANDERLE

DISRUPTIVE IMAGINATION

LMBPN Publishing
PMB 196, 2540 South Maryland Pkwy
Las Vegas, NV 89109

First Version, March 2021
Version 1.01, April 2021
ebook ISBN: 978-1-64971-610-1
Paperback ISBN: 978-1-64971-611-8

THE DWARF IT ALL TEAM

Thanks to our JIT Team:

Dave Hicks
Dorothy Lloyd
Jackey Hankard-Brodie
Peter Manis
Deb Mader
Diane L. Smith
Kelly O'Donnell

If We've missed anyone, please let us know!

Editor
SkyHunter Editing Team

CHAPTER ONE

Johnny Walker sipped his only drink of choice—Johnny Walker Black Label, of course—and nestled into his seat with a grunt of satisfaction.

Right about now, this is the only thing I got goin' for me.

Agent Lisa Breyer sat across the aisle of his private jet and her finger swiped from side to side across the screen of her tablet. She sat hunched over the device in her lap and her frown deepened with every second.

"You might wanna give it a rest on all that swipin', darlin'."

"Uh-huh," she muttered flatly, still completely engrossed. "Give me a sec."

"Lisa."

The half-Light Elf federal agent nodded vaguely but didn't stop.

Johnny wadded the napkin the flight attendant had brought him with his drink and lobbed it across the aisle at her.

She jumped when it bounced beneath the seat in front of her and turned her head slowly to glare at him. "Now's not the time for target practice."

"Hell, I know that." When she didn't smile in response, he

wiped the smirk off his face and fixed her with a stern expression. "But you ain't gonna find the answers you're lookin' for in that fancy piece of tech."

"We're about to walk into a meeting of a hive-mind of brainwashed magicals who spoke to us through a giant worm's mouth like it was an intercom, Johnny. Forgive me for wanting to learn as much as I can about such a potentially deadly trap before we land in Albuquerque." She returned her attention to the tablet and picked up where she'd left off, although her one-fingered swipes seemed to have considerably more anger behind them now.

He studied her profile for a long moment as he sipped his whiskey. "Do you think it's a trap?"

"I have no idea what to think. Whoever that voice belonged to mentioned us by name and gave us an open invitation to join the collective or whatever. That means they're expecting us."

Sprawled along the aisle between them, Luther whipped his head off his forepaws and looked at Johnny, panting. "They didn't call us by name, Johnny. The hive-mind doesn't even know we exist."

Rex stretched his back legs with a canine yawn and finished with a low whine as he licked his chops. "Yeah, Johnny. We'll be your element of surprise."

The dwarf snorted into his drink and muttered, "That's the best you can come up with?"

"Excuse me?" Lisa's wide-eyed gaze locked onto him again.

He shook his head. "I'm talkin' to the hounds."

"Huh." She studied him as if absorbing what he'd said, then returned to her tablet.

The bounty hunter sighed inwardly and tried to give her the space she needed for whatever kind of research she could possibly be doing right now.

Sit back and enjoy the silence. There ain't gonna be much more of it where we're headin'.

Five seconds later, the obnoxiously sticky-wet sound of one of the hounds licking themselves rose even over the drone of the jet engines. Johnny tried to tune it out but it seemed the hounds wouldn't let him have his peace and quiet.

"Hey, Rex. When we're talking about a hive-mind, is that, like...everyone gets turned into bugs?"

"What?"

Luther shuffled in the aisle to face his brother and shifted from licking his paw to licking Rex's muzzle. "Hive. That's for bees and stuff, right?"

"Huh. Or naked mole rats."

"Wait, we're gonna go fight rats? Hey, what makes 'em naked, anyway? I've never seen a rat in pants."

Rex yawned again, and Luther took the opportunity to lick inside his brother's open mouth before the larger hound pulled away. "Will you cut it out?"

"What? I thought you maybe left crumbs there for later."

Johnny scowled at the back of the seat in front of him, slid his hand over the armrest, and snapped his fingers.

Both hounds looked at their master. "Aw, come on, Johnny. You said you'd have dog snacks here for us."

"Yeah, what happened to the treats?"

He snapped his fingers again. "Stop."

With a heavy sigh, Lisa dropped the tablet on the seat beside her and turned another scowl onto the dwarf. "You know, just because you prefer the company of your dogs over everyone else does not give you an excuse to snap at me and bark out one-word commands."

The hounds jerked their heads toward her. "Uh-oh, Johnny."

"Yeah, your lady two-legs is pissed. Wait—what happened?"

Johnny stared at Lisa and tilted his head slowly. "I think someone's a little too focused on that tablet."

"I'm over here minding my own business, Johnny. And you—"

"I was talkin' to the hounds. Again."

"Oh." She glanced at Rex and Luther—who both stared at her and panted with their tongues hanging out of their mouths—then closed her eyes. "The dogs."

"I know you're itchin' to find a way to storm the bastards who are kidnappin' shifters all over the place—"

"Not only shifters, Johnny."

"Sure. Not only shifters. But diggin' yourself into a hole without any actual answers ain't gonna make you feel better." The bounty hunter raised an eyebrow and pointed at the tablet. "The best way to ease a troubled mind is to get off the damn tech."

With a frown, Lisa snatched her tablet off the seat and stood. The hounds didn't move a muscle to get out of her way, so she stepped slowly over their outstretched legs to cross the aisle toward Johnny. He scooted his feet back beneath him to give her space to ease past him.

She paused, glanced at his black boots tucked beneath the seat, and smirked before she sat beside him at the window.

Yeah, I got manners, darlin'. When I want 'em.

"Do you think I've been scouring the Internet from your private jet for hits about the hive-mind kidnappers?"

He shrugged. "I'm fairly sure there ain't much more that would get you all twisted up like you are."

With a humorless chuckle, she opened her tablet again, placed it in his lap, and ignored him when he raised both hands in a quiet but pointed refusal to play with her fancy device. "Nelson sent me a briefing of what the other agents are doing on the ground in New Mexico before we took off."

"Huh." He looked at the tablet but didn't bother to read the information. "Yeah, I get pissed when Nelson sends me his damn files too. Which ain't possible if I leave the tablet at home."

"You don't even own a tablet, Johnny."

The dwarf raised his glass toward her and took another sip. "Even better."

Lisa rolled her eyes but couldn't completely hide the small smile that crept through her concern. "Okay. Well, take a look at this anyway. No? Fine. I'll brief you then."

"Oh-ho, Johnny!" Luther uttered a short yip and the young blonde flight attendant at the front of the jet jumped slightly in her seat. "She's getting down to business now. Maybe you should get a room—"

"We're in a flying can, bro," Rex interjected. "A small one. And why would they need a room?"

"She's gonna brief him. That's what he wears under his pants, right?"

"Oh, I get it..." Rex snorted and sat to lick between his legs. "Hey, Johnny. You want us to go hang out with that other lady two-legs up front? I bet she has treats—"

The bounty hunter snapped his fingers a third time. "That's enough, boys."

The hounds stared at him for a moment before they hunkered down on their bellies and licked their chops.

Lisa leaned forward to look curiously at them, then smiled warily at the dwarf. "Do they have much say about where we're headed?"

He cleared his throat and muttered, "Only about you briefing me."

Luther sniggered.

"So what has you all shook up about these other agents, darlin'?" he said quickly to end that line of questioning.

She returned her attention to the tablet, leaned her elbow on the armrest between their seats, and positioned her device so both of them could see clearly—so much so that her shoulder pressed lightly against Johnny's and stayed there. He glanced at it briefly before he sipped his whiskey again.

"It's not much, honestly," she said and the frustration crept into her voice. "Three agents were sent to Albuquerque by the department about two months ago. It involved a racketeering case from what I can see, but almost every damn thing's been redacted in the file. At least the one he emailed me, surprise, surprise. But I did get a contact number for Agent Ellis Paulson."

"Uh-huh. Have you given him a call yet?"

"No, I didn't have time before we had to leave so I thought we'd reach out once we landed—or maybe once we get to a hotel. I think it's a good idea for us to hole up for the rest of the day before we head to Gallup, right?"

"After the day we had makin' friends with shifters and hearin' our names come out of a monster's mouth with an announcer's voice? You bet." Johnny studied her frown as she scoured the annoyingly redacted case file again. "We can go into this central hive weirdness with fresh minds. I think you have the right idea."

"Great. Whoever invited us there, Johnny—the crazy hive-mind leader or whatever who mentioned our names and knew exactly what we were up to? He said we didn't need an address. That we'd know the location when we saw it."

"Uh-huh. Is that a problem?"

Lisa wrinkled her nose. "I'm not sure. It sounded almost like he knew we'd stumble across it somehow."

"It's bound to happen sooner or later. I don't see why that has you all jittery like this."

"I'm not jittery." She elbowed him in the side. "There's something here that doesn't quite add up but I can't put my finger on it."

"This whole damn thing ain't addin' up, darlin'. We took an indie case from a Blue Heeler and assumed we were only fixin' to find Nina Williams. It turned out to be a helluva party with two shifter packs and a geek squad from Philly. Plus, the big bad brainwashing boss is out in the middle of Bumfuck, New Mexico. It ain't supposed to make sense when the hole goes this deep."

For a moment, Lisa merely flipped through the pages of the case file on her screen. Then, with a soft click, the tablet screen turned off and she placed it in her lap with a sigh. "Yeah, you're right."

"I know."

"So am I, though."

"I never said you weren't." Johnny drained the rest of his whiskey, leaned sideways into the aisle, and wiggled the empty glass at the gorgeous flight attendant who'd watched them during the entire flight in case she was needed for something like this. She stood immediately and went to pour him another drink.

"Whatever we're steppin' into when we reach that ware-house," he continued, "and all them re-programmed magicals kidnappin' others to grow their ranks, I ain't worried about it. We'll find the answers."

"Right." Lisa gave him a small smile and leaned into him a little more. "That's what we do, isn't it?"

"You bet. I ain't fixin' to break that winnin' streak neither." Johnny cleared his throat and made a show of stretching both arms high before he kicked his legs out in front of him and lowered his arm around her shoulders. She snorted but didn't move away.

When the flight attendant returned with a fresh glass of whiskey and saw the dwarf and the half-Light Elf so close together, her brilliant smile faded. "Here's your whiskey, Johnny. Can I take your empty glass?"

"That's fine, darlin'. Thank you." They traded glasses, and he sipped slowly on another four fingers of the only drink he ever needed. "Ah... The perks of havin' my own jet with my own damn crew on payroll."

Lisa snorted. "The free refills? I'm very sure you got those on every first-class flight before your little arrangement with the Department."

"Naw. That ain't it, darlin'. You know, I ain't realized how much I hated folks callin' me Mr. Walker until I got the feds to start payin' folks not to."

"Oh, I see." With a chuckle, she plucked the glass from his hand and took a tentative sip. A small cough escaped her after she swallowed and she handed the drink to him with a grimace. "That's all I need."

"Uh-huh. Say that again when we get to the hotel."

CHAPTER TWO

They touched down at Albuquerque International Sunport before dinnertime and once they'd checked into the Hilton Garden Inn in Albuquerque Uptown, Lisa made the call to Agent Paulson using the number provided by Nelson. No one answered and voicemail picked up with a generic, robotic recording to leave a message after the beep. She scowled and left her contact info and their hotel room number.

Johnny stopped beside the small table against the wall, which was a third of the size of the massive desk at the back of the main living room their separate bedrooms shared. "What did you go and do that for, huh?"

"Do you mean call the contact we may or may not get some help from with this whole hive-mind business?"

"No, I mean give him our room number. If I wanted feds knockin' on my hotel door, you coulda called Nelson instead."

"Relax. Paulson's undercover." Lisa leaned back in the chair and drew a deep breath. "Meeting us at the airport or out for a public 'Hey, we're FBI agents' stroll isn't exactly an option."

"You ain't."

"What?"

He opened the untouched bottle of Black Label he'd removed from his duffel bag and stretched into the cabinet above the sink to grab a glass. "You ain't an FBI agent."

"Okay, Johnny. Technically, I still am—"

"You have your salary and a few contacts but the way I see it, you're my business partner first. We haven't taken a federal case since we started the whole indie PI business, anyhow."

"Because you made a deal with the Department to not take any more federal cases—" With a sigh, she shook her head. "You know what? It doesn't matter. We could still use all the help we can get and if Ellis Paulson delivers, I certainly won't complain. And will you stop calling it 'indie PI'?"

"Why? That's what it is."

"You're an independent contractor, Johnny."

"That's what I said. Indie—what?" He turned with two glasses of whiskey in hand, one of them with less than half his usual four-finger pour. "Why are you lookin' at me like that?"

Despite her irritation, she laughed quickly and folded her arms. "Probably because I know I'm about to down that drink and ask you for another."

"So you're feelin' that optimistic, huh?" He placed her glass beside her, tipped another splash of whiskey into it before he put the bottle on the table, and joined her. "We'll get the answers we need, darlin'. All we need now is a little more time to unwind like we ain't had in the last few days. And maybe a tip from this Paulson fella. Other than that, I ain't gonna let you—"

"Get it!" Luther shouted as he barreled out of Johnny's bedroom and through the center of the small living area. "Johnny, Johnny, Johnny! We got incoming!"

Rex raced after his brother and they both barked madly as they skidded to a halt in front of the door. "If it's that unkillable worm, Johnny, Luther's gonna shit himself."

"I would never."

Lisa frowned at the hounds. "Is everything okay?"

"I'm askin' myself the same thing." The dwarf turned in his chair, ready to reprimand the hounds into silence. "Boys, y'all need to—"

Three sharp, swift knocks came at the door and the animals raised their voices in two curdling bays.

"Told you, Johnny!"

"Open it. Let us at 'em!"

"You call room service or somethin'?" he asked Lisa.

She shook her head. "It might be Paulson."

"Then he's damn fast." After a huge swig of whiskey, Johnny stood, placed his glass on the table, and strode to the door. When he snapped and raised his index finger, both hounds sat immediately on either side of him.

"Who is it, Johnny?"

"Yeah, someone following us? Some brainwashed jerkface trying to get to us first?"

"Dunno." Through the peephole, he saw the distorted head and upper torso of an incredibly tall woman in a bomber jacket, her blonde hair pulled into a high ponytail. When she raised her fist to knock again, he slid the lock quickly and jerked the door open. "What?"

She didn't even flinch at his rough greeting. "I'm looking for Lisa."

"For what?" He squinted and scrutinized her warily. She appeared to be nothing more than another tall, leggy blonde and wore olive-green chinos beneath the bomber jacket and a pair of striped hiking sandals.

"Lisa Breyer." The woman raised an eyebrow at him and tilted her head to return his study. "A mutual friend of ours gave her my number. Let me guess. You're Mr. Walker."

"Johnny?" Lisa called as she rose slowly and her hand inched toward the service pistol in her shoulder holster.

"I ain't Mr. Walker," the bounty hunter grumbled, unwilling to confirm or deny her assumption by correcting her as to how to address him. "And I reckon we ain't got no mutual friends. Who are you?"

The visitor grinned. "Ellis. I received a call and was given this room number, so—"

"Ellis Paulson?"

"The very same. Do you mind if I come in or should we have the entire conversation in a public hall?"

Johnny grunted and stepped back. He opened the door barely enough for the woman to squeeze through although her shoulders bumped against the doorframe and the door. The second she was inside, he shoved the door closed again and slammed the lock into place.

"Whoa, Johnny." Luther sniffed around Ellis' hiking sandals and his tail wagged as he followed her slow steps into the hotel room. "You might wanna get your head checked. This Paulson guy is not a guy."

"He's a lady two-legs, Johnny," Rex agreed and chanced a quick lick at the woman's exposed ankle beneath her three-quarter pants leg. "I think you might be starting to lose your touch."

"I ain't."

"What was that?" Ellis looked up from the hounds and studied the dwarf's scowl.

"Nothin'." He subjected her to another hasty study and gestured toward Lisa with an open arm. "Lisa Breyer. Ellis Paulson."

"Oh. Hi." Lisa pulled the open edge of her cardigan over her shoulder holster again and stepped forward with her hand extended. "Thanks for stopping by on such short notice."

"I was in the area." Ellis nodded firmly and the handshake was brisk and ridiculously short. When she released Lisa's hand, she wiped hers quickly on her pants and gazed around the hotel room.

It's like a nervous tic. Great. Nelson sent us an undercover agent with hygiene paranoia.

"And I assume Nelson gave you my contact info."

"Yeah. Um…sorry." Lisa pulled out one of the three chairs around the dining table and gestured for the woman to sit. "Have a seat. We have a couple of questions for this case we're on here if you have a few minutes."

"I can't stay, I'm afraid. I have a meeting downtown in a little under an hour."

"Then why are you even here?" Johnny grumbled.

The agent tossed her wispy bangs out of her face and slid both hands into her jacket pockets as she spared him a sidelong glance. "Like I said, I was in the area. And on the off-chance that you hadn't left the hotel on your own, I thought I'd invite you to join me."

"Invite us to your meetin'?" He snorted. "You're undercover, ain'tcha?"

The woman pursed her lips but looked at Lisa.

"What are you gonna do? Show up with a coupla magicals and two hounds and say you thought you'd bring some friends along for the ride?"

"It won't take longer than five minutes but I can't be late for this one."

"Uh-huh." The bounty hunter folded his arms and scowled even harder when Lisa gave him a warning glance.

"Unless you have somewhere else to be tonight."

"No, we don't." His partner swallowed what was left of her whiskey and placed the glass gently on the table. "Five minutes is a small price to pay for your time."

"Wonderful." Ellis' smile was brief and tight-lipped. "My car's out front. I'm happy to drive you here when we're finished."

"The hell you will." Johnny folded his arms. "I always drive."

The undercover agent turned slowly toward him and raised an eyebrow. "You can follow me then."

"Yep."

Ellis stood, turned quickly and walked to the door, and let herself out of their hotel suite. "I do have to be on time for this meeting, though, so if you don't mind…"

"Come on." Lisa nudged the dwarf in the elbow and nodded toward the door. "This is why we stopped here for the night."

"We stopped to get a little R&R before we barge into the belly of the beast, darlin'."

"I don't know about you, Johnny, but getting whatever information she has for us will certainly make me feel far more rested and relaxed. I'm sure it's not a long drive."

He slugged the rest of his whiskey and turned toward the door. "You ain't ridin' with her on your own."

"No, that would be weird."

I know that sarcasm. She thinks I'm overreactin' but somethin' don't feel right about another fed bargin' into our hotel and our business.

Johnny snapped his fingers. "Git on, boys. We're goin' into town."

"You got it, Johnny." Rex trotted dutifully at his master's side and paused while Johnny waited for Lisa to step into the hallway first. "Where are we going again?"

"To the naked mole rat hive," Luther added, physically incapable of cutting off his rapid, thumping ear-scratching until the job was complete. "Duh."

"Luther," Johnny snapped.

"Yeah, yeah, Johnny. I'm coming. Wait—so this other two-legs has a meeting with rats?"

"Downtown rats, Johnny?"

The dwarf closed the door behind Luther and scowled down the hall at Agent Paulson, who waited for the elevator doors to open. "We're waitin' for that fed to do her undercover business, and then she'd better help us with ours."

"Oh, yeah. Good plan." The hounds trotted beside him and

Luther sneezed violently, which made him stumble into his brother.

"Watch it."

"Come on, bro. You know sneezing with your eyes open makes 'em pop out of your head. I need my eyes. Hey, Rex, you notice that weird smell?"

"On the lady two-legs with holes in her shoes?" Rex pressed his nose against the carpeted hallway as they joined Lisa and Ellis at the elevators.

"Uh-huh."

"Yeah. Smells funny. Magic but not, right?"

"Oh, yeah." Luther sat at the bounty hunter's feet and fixed his attention on Ellis. "Hey, Johnny. I think that's what undercover smells like."

Johnny hooked his thumbs through his belt loops and squinted at Agent Paulson. The woman looked at him with the hint of a smile and raised her eyebrows when the elevator doors opened.

I can't say nothin' about it where she can hear but I know somethin' ain't right.

CHAPTER THREE

Agent Paulson's meeting did, in fact, last only five minutes. From a table at the window inside the Flying Star Café on Menaul Boulevard, Johnny watched the woman talk to a short man in basketball shorts, both of them seated on a bench across the street. Ellis nodded. The man shrugged. Nothing was exchanged with a quick pass of a hand or secreted within a rolled-up newspaper.

Still, somethin's up with that one.

"You know, I bet if you glare at her long enough and hard enough, you might end up with x-ray vision." Lisa took a sip of her water and placed it on the table.

"It's not a bad idea," Johnny muttered. Engineering an extra lens on his night-vision goggles would probably come in handy at some point.

I'm sure I can find out how to add x-ray vision to the gear.

She snorted. "That was sarcasm, Johnny."

"I know. But now I'm gettin' ideas."

"Oh, great. Hey, I'm very sure we didn't come here to dig into Agent Paulson's case. Only to meet her." When he didn't reply, she leaned back in her chair and folded her arms. "So why are you watching her like she's part of ours?"

"The woman's hidin' somethin'," he grumbled.

"Of course she is. She's undercover."

"I ain't talkin' about her job." With a frown, Johnny pointed at Rex and Luther who lay quietly at his feet beneath the table. "The boys said somethin' don't smell right about her."

Lisa rolled her eyes. "I don't think they know what they smell half the time, Johnny."

Rex snorted. "She doesn't know anything about coonhounds, Johnny."

"Yeah. Like how stinky she is when she's nervous and sweatin'," Luther added. "Go on, Johnny. Tell her."

"They said, 'like magic but not.'" Johnny turned away from the window long enough to dart her a sidelong glance before he zeroed in on Agent Paulson again. "I ain't ignorin' somethin' like that."

"Huh." She narrowed her eyes. "But that could mean anything."

"Did Nelson say anythin' about what kinda magical she is?"

"Right. Because a full write-up of every agent's past and Oriceran bloodline is included with contact info."

He scowled at her and leaned back with a smirk. "It's startin' to sound like I'm talkin' to myself, darlin'."

A sharp laugh escaped her. "Probably because you're as on-edge as I am, but you won't let yourself admit it. No, Johnny. I have no idea what kind of magical she is."

"Go ahead and check."

"Right now?" She glanced around the café, which was starting to fill up with Albuquerque's elderly population who preferred to eat early and get back home and in bed before the younger generations even considered dinner. "Come on."

"Ain't no one gonna see, darlin'. Just do it."

"If you want to find out so badly, why don't you check?"

"I...can't." He looked quickly out the window again. *She'd better leave it at that.*

"I have no idea what that means, Johnny."

"I mean I can't, all right. I ain't playin' with magic 'cept for what I can build up and blow up with my gear. So go ahead." When she remained silent, he gestured toward the window. "For cryin' out loud, darlin'. She's on her way here, so cast the damn spell and check, will ya?"

Lisa cleared her throat.

He drew a deep breath through his nose, closed his eyes, and added a mumbled, "Please."

She finally muttered the spell he had never taken the time to learn—despite most magicals being able to do it on their own—and waited. Five seconds later, she leaned back in her chair again and shrugged. "Okay. Maybe you're right."

The bounty hunter turned away from the window with wide eyes. *That ain't good.* "About what?"

Lisa leaned toward him and lowered her voice. "She's a shifter, I think."

"What do you mean you think? Either she is or she ain't."

"Yeah, that's the thing. Something else is messing with her trail. It doesn't block it but seems to flash in all different colors that don't belong to a shifter." She sighed. "It makes it hard to tell."

"A shifter in the FBI..." Johnny rubbed his bristly red beard with short, irritated strokes. *Like the bastards wanted more of Amanda. They don't get everythin' they want.* "See? I ain't paranoid."

She pointed at him. "No, those are your words, not mine."

"Do you have any idea what's blockin' it like that?"

"Johnny, if I did, I would've said exactly—"

The café door opened and the little bell jingled as Ellis stepped inside and scanned the front room for her newest contacts. She found them immediately and nodded before she moved toward the table.

Lisa pleaded silently with him to not make a big deal out of it. He pursed his lips and gave her a brief nod that said, "I got this."

She didn't look convinced.

"I appreciate you waiting for me." The agent pulled out the empty chair between the two partners and sat. "With that out of the way, how can I help you?"

Agent Breyer leaned forward and picked her glass up. "We're looking into—"

"Whatcha got swimmin' around you right now?" Johnny wiggled his fingers toward Ellis and sniffed.

Lisa closed her eyes.

"I'm sorry?" The woman looked from one to the other in confusion.

"What's the block?"

"I'm…not sure I follow."

"FBI shifter Paulson. We got that far. But somethin' else is messin' with your signature. I'm askin' right now what that is. It's time to cough up."

The woman snatched the third glass of water from the table and sipped slowly. She held her composure incredibly well beneath the bounty hunter's bold scrutiny before she graced him with another tight smile. "I told you I'm undercover."

"Uh-huh. Are you tryin' to hide bein' a shifter or somethin' else?"

"Johnny—" Lisa protested.

"No, it's fine." Ellis tossed her bangs out of her face again. "You've turned out to be very much what I expected, Johnny."

He snorted. "That there's your first mistake. Expectin' anythin' from me."

"But Agent Nelson certainly does paint a vivid picture. Honestly, I expected you to have noticed this sooner."

Beneath the table, his hand balled into a fist. "So what's the block?"

"My partner and I took extra precautions for this current

case. If Nelson didn't tell you what we're doing here, neither will I. Another precaution. I'm sure you understand."

The bounty hunter stared at her until she felt the time was right to continue.

"It's merely a few layers of cloaking enchantments. We are two undercover agents moving through some highly influential circles in New Mexico, and we can't leave more of a trail than what we want our targets to see."

"That makes no sense. Someone could still track the wiggly trail that says you're all kindsa magicals jammed into one."

Ellis inclined her head. "It doesn't have to make sense to you, Johnny. We know what we're doing."

"You and your partner."

She nodded.

"Is he a shifter too?"

Lisa cleared her throat. "Why don't we change gears here and—"

"No." Still staring at the dwarf, Ellis folded her muscular arms and raised her eyebrows.

"Uh-huh. Where is he?"

"She is currently in a meeting discussing public trading options with the board of the company we're investigating. And I promise you she's very good at her job—exactly like I was told you are. Now, though, I'm starting to wonder what you bring to the table besides paranoid scrutiny and an attitude I frankly can't stand."

He pointed a finger at her and opened his mouth. It took a moment to realize he had nothing to say to that, so he gestured at Lisa and slumped in his seat. "Go ahead, darlin'. Shift gears."

"Thank you." Her gaze settled on him a little longer than it should have before she focused on Agent Paulson and moved on with the whole purpose of their meeting. "In a nutshell, this is a kidnapping case. It became a little complicated in Florida, but the pieces came together and led us here."

MARTHA CARR & MICHAEL ANDERLE

"How many victims?"

"Three that we know of. Specifically."

Johnny snorted. "Add another thousand to that and we might be closer to the mark."

Ellis' eyes widened. "That's a big case."

"Like I said, it's complicated. Nelson thought that since you and your partner are on the ground here, you might have heard something about what's going on. An organization centered in Gallup has a longer reach than we realized at first. The…network stretches fairly wide all over the country and—"

"They've been snatchin' shifters left and right," Johnny added. "Brainwashin' 'em to build a mindless army tryin' to screw with the gates."

"To Oriceran?"

"Uh-huh."

"Not only shifters," Lisa clarified. "Although they are the majority of the victims this group targets. Is there anything you can tell us about kidnappings here? Large groups of shifters coming into the state maybe or the surrounding areas? An increase in crime?"

Ellis looked thoughtful and shook her head. "I've been focused on my case here for the last few months and haven't even thought about looking around for something else. Especially not something this big. Is this a federal case?"

Breyer wrinkled her nose. "Not exactly."

"Well, that explains why we weren't told about it. I'm sorry I can't help you with this. Nothing's crossed my radar about kidnapped shifters and"—the woman turned to Johnny with a half-curious, half-mocking frown—" brainwashing them, did you say?"

He grunted. "You heard me."

"Huh. And Nelson still sent you to me?"

"We're merely trying to pick up what we can before we head

to this organization's central location tomorrow." Lisa shrugged. "But I guess we'll have to wait until then."

Ellis stared at the table and slid her finger up and down the paper menu in front of her. The seconds ticked past and Johnny exchanged a glance with Lisa before he leaned toward the other woman and cleared his throat.

She startled and refocused to look at him. "What was that?"

"I ain't said nothin' yet but now, I'm wonderin' if you have all your ducks in a row."

"Sorry. I was thinking."

Sure. I bet she's thinkin' how to get rid of us as quickly as she can.

With a sharp breath, Ellis turned toward Lisa. "Where did you say this location was?"

"Gallup. Honestly, all the information we have to go on is that we're looking for an…underground warehouse out there, presumably with considerable activity in and out. Other than that, our sources didn't exactly offer more detail."

"Underground…" The woman's brow furrowed before she rapped her knuckles on the table. "I think I might know the place you're talking about."

"You don't say." Johnny smirked but she ignored him.

"Well, it's not entirely underground but we were out there last week to look at a few factories." Ellis shrugged. "There was a fair amount of activity at a building we'd been told was empty at that point. Honestly, I assumed it was part of another inspection."

Lisa took another sip of her water and watched the dwarf over the rim of the glass. "It sounds like something we might be able to use—at the very least, we could look into it."

"Uh-huh." He narrowed his eyes at Agent Paulson. "Then how about you give us the address and we'll mosey on in on our own?"

"I'm happy to take you in the morning."

"Uh-uh. Nope." He shook his head and sliced a hand decisively as if to quell any argument. "We have our case and you have yours. An address will be fine."

"Don't be ridiculous." Ellis crossed one leg over the other and glanced at the hounds. "I'm meeting the foreman at one of these newer factories anyway. And I have no problem letting you follow me in your car if that makes you feel better about it."

"We don't need a chaperone—"

"Johnny." Lisa leaned toward him. "She already has connections. We might as well use them."

"Connections for what, huh? Parking a rental outside the hive's damn warehouse and walking through the front door?"

The other woman folded her hands on the table. "I think you hit the nail on the head with that one."

"Say what now?"

"If the building I'm thinking about is the right one, the front entrance has been boarded up for almost a decade now."

Johnny dismissed her with a wave. "A couple o' boards ain't nothin'. I can get through anythin'."

"That was a figure of speech, Johnny." Ellis glanced at him and her lips twitched in and out of a smirk.

I like this fed even less than her cockamamie excuses for everythin' under the sun.

"What I should have said was the warehouse was closed and the entrance filled in. There is no front entrance."

"You said you thought there was an inspection."

"Yeah, of the property. But if this organization you're looking for is housing hundreds or thousands of kidnapped magicals somewhere, yes. It's most likely underground and below an abandoned warehouse would be the perfect place. My partner and I did an assessment of the entire property about three weeks ago. One of the perks of going undercover, right? Menial, useless work to keep playing the part. But we found another entrance into the actual warehouse. I can show you exactly where to go and which corridors to avoid."

"Why would we need to avoid parts of the building?" Lisa asked.

Agent Paulson raised her eyebrows. "Faulty structure. We mapped as much as we could before we had to focus on a few other leads. I can save you time if you'll let me help."

Johnny frowned at her for a long moment, his suspicion etched on his face. "And why would you wanna help when you have your work cut out for ya with your case?"

She stared at him for what felt like forever before her smile completely disappeared. "You told me they're kidnapping shifters from all over the country and brainwashing them in huge numbers, Johnny. I can't exactly stand aside and let that continue. And I don't enjoy the idea of letting the two of you take longer than necessary to find these assholes."

So she's callin' this loyalty to her kind. Fair enough.

"It sounds like a plan to me," Lisa said firmly, which left no room for argument.

But if the truth be told, he hadn't intended to argue against this little team-up with a fed shifter who seemed to have all the answers they needed.

Still, it feels too easy.

"All right. We'll meet again tomorrow and you can show us how to get in. We'll handle the rest on our own." Johnny started to stand but Ellis put a surprisingly strong hand on his arm.

"We just got here."

"Huh?"

"Johnny, we haven't even ordered our food yet." Lisa raised her eyebrows. "That's why we're here. For dinner."

"Right." He dropped into his seat again and ran a hand through his auburn hair. "Where's the damn waiter?"

"I told him to wait until we were ready." Ellis turned and signaled to their server with a raised hand.

He could feel Lisa's gaze on him as he scowled at the table. *This ain't how it's supposed to work. We meet the contact, get the info, and get out. This here feels like sittin' down for a three-way dinner date and I ain't on board.*

A lull in the already low conversation around them in the café was interrupted by a low growl from beneath the table.

"Luther," Rex complained with a snort. "You can't hunker down here with me and stink the whole place up."

"I didn't do it."

"Your tail lifted in my face, bro." Rex slunk out from under the table with a huff and sat at Johnny's side.

"Oh, come on. It's not that bad. I'm hungry. Hey, Johnny—" Luther's head thumped against the underside of the table and he uttered a sharp yelp. Ellis glanced at the water that sloshed in their glasses and frowned. "Johnny, hey. We're gonna get food now, right? You'll get us a snack?"

"Find something that doesn't make him stink, huh, Johnny?" Rex lay down again and rested his head on his forepaws with a low whine. "I think I lost my appetite."

The server finally reached their table with his notepad and pen and a chipper smile. "Welcome to the Flying Star Café. My name's Andre, and I'll be…" He paused and wrinkled his nose. "I'll be…"

Lisa tried to covertly cover her nose with her hand and darted Johnny an accusatory stare.

"I'm sorry, folks. I—" The man tried desperately to not look disgusted. "They must be cleaning the grease traps in the kitchen. It's the wrong time of day for it, but—"

"I don't smell nothin'." Johnny's eye twitched when the smell hit him too. It wasn't the worst he'd experienced since he'd adopted the two coonhound pups and raised them. He waved at Lisa and Ellis. "We're fine. Come on. Y'all put in your orders and we can get a move on."

CHAPTER FOUR

The meal was unremarkable, even for the hounds, and when they finished, Agent Paulson said she'd meet them at their hotel the next morning so they could follow her to the location.

"I'm honestly flattered that you came all the way to Albuquerque to check with me," she said as she headed toward her light-green Subaru Outback that was most likely part of the undercover gig. "Gallup's a long drive."

"Feel free to not come then." Johnny stood with his hands on his hips and watched the hounds sniff the small patch of grass beside the café and do their business.

"We assumed you wouldn't want to have a conversation like this over the phone," Lisa said and tried to smooth over Johnny's animosity.

"I appreciate that. See you tomorrow then. Oh." Ellis turned and pointed at them. "You two look like you could use a little pick-me-up. Have you ever been to Albuquerque?"

She shook her head.

"Then you should try the Night Walk at the Botanic Garden. After dark, that is. Many couples head down there at the end of August. I wouldn't know but I heard it sets the mood."

"Say what?" Johnny jerked his head up but still didn't look at her.

"Oh." Lisa cleared her throat. "We're not—"

"Enjoy yourselves. This city has more to offer than you might think." Ellis crossed the street and headed to her car.

The dwarf hooked his thumbs through his belt loops and squinted at the faded green grass. *We ain't what, exactly?*

"Yeah, good riddance," Luther shouted as he lowered his leg again beside a small scrubby bush. "She smells too weird, Johnny, I'm tellin' ya."

"Not nearly as bad as you, bro."

"That's the enchantment," Johnny muttered and turned to watch Agent Paulson slip behind the wheel and drive off. He glanced at Luther and smirked. "What's your excuse?"

"Oh, come on, Johnny. I'm a hound."

Lisa approached him with a stern frown. "Did you have to make that so difficult?"

"I thought you'd worked it out by now."

"Worked what out?"

"I don't like feds."

She rolled her eyes. "Johnny—"

"'Cept for you, darlin'. But you ain't exactly livin' the life currently. I don't trust the woman and now, I gotta drive down the highway with her for seven hours tomorrow to see if the place she thinks we're goin' is the place we oughtta be."

With her hands on her hips, she tilted her head and smirked at him. "Did you forget about the private jet already?"

"'Course not."

"So…we could simply fly there."

"Nope." He snapped his fingers as the hounds finished their business and turned toward their rental car.

"Because you don't want to share it with another fed. Okay, I get it."

"That ain't it, darlin'." He glanced at her with a sheepish expression. "The pilot refused to fly there."

"What?" Lisa burst out laughing.

"It ain't funny. He wouldn't do it even for a bonus and said somethin' about native spirits doin' funny stuff to his controls. Trust me, I tried."

"Wow. So you have your own jet but it only goes so far."

"It looks like it. And now we have a long drive ahead of us." He scratched the side of his face in irritation, paused at the driver's door, and turned to study Menaul Boulevard. "It's time for that R&R now."

Lisa shut the back door of the SUV after the hounds and climbed into the passenger seat. "Okay. Agent Paulson mentioned—"

"No."

"Johnny, you didn't even let me finish."

"You wanna go strollin' down some lit-up garden after dark. The hotel's better."

"It's something to do. To get our minds off…you know." Lisa strapped her seatbelt on as he started the car. "Being personally invited to join a hive-mind intent on taking over Earth and permanently messing with the flow of magic from Oriceran."

He snorted. "I ain't a fan of garden strolls."

"Seriously? When was the last time you tried it?"

"Never."

She laughed. "If you wanted to stay in the hotel for the rest of the night, that was the wrong answer."

"What? Do you want me to lie to you?" He shifted into drive and darted her a sidelong glance.

"No." She grinned. "I want you to go to the Night Walk with me."

"You were about to tell that shifter fed we ain't…somethin'. What'd you mean?"

"What?" She looked away quickly and leaned back. "Oh, I only meant we didn't come here for sightseeing. I know that's not exactly your thing."

"Uh-huh. And now you're beggin' me to let you drag me along to a giant garden in the middle of the desert in the dark for fun."

"Yes, Johnny. Because I'm into sightseeing. Come on, I didn't make a list this time if that's what you're worried about."

He shook his head as he pulled away from the curb and headed down Menaul Boulevard, unable to hold back a chuckle. "I'll drink to that."

"Okay, sure, but after the Botanic Garden."

Two hours later, they walked through the gates of Albuquerque's Botanic Garden with their Night Walk tickets in hand. It was packed with people of all ages, including several families with what seemed like swarms of school-age children running around them and the occasional senior citizen who hobbled along the path or scooted step by slow step behind a walker.

"All right. If you thought this was gonna be some kinda romantic walk between the flowerbeds, it looks like you chose the wrong night."

Lisa laughed and her eyes lit up at the hundreds of light displays along the walkway. "I didn't say anything about a romantic walk, Johnny."

"Huh. Well, good thing this ain't it."

She smiled and slipped her arm through his, and they moved down the path behind the crowd of people taking in the sights during one of the last warm nights of the summer.

Rex and Luther trotted quietly behind them. They whipped their heads from one side to another to stare at the lights or sniff passersby and yip random greetings to strangers who couldn't hear a word they said. Finally, Luther uttered a low growl and yipped, his tail sticking straight up in the air. "Johnny. I think I found the mole rats."

"The what?"

"The hive. They're buzzing." Luther yipped again, and Johnny snapped his fingers.

"Hush up, boy. I convinced the ticket fella ya'll were well-behaved and wouldn't cause any trouble for these folks. Don't make him come out here with his walkie-talkie and prove me wrong." Despite what he'd said, Johnny stiffened and scanned the darkness around the intricate light displays that blazed in every color. "What do you see?"

"The swarm, Johnny."

Rex snorted. "You're so—oh, yeah. Johnny, they're here."

"To me, boys. And stay sharp."

"What's wrong?" Lisa asked, her smile fading.

"The hounds said they see the hive."

"Here?" She lowered her voice and scanned the lights and all the pedestrians milling through the Garden. "That wasn't supposed to be part of this stop."

"I know." Johnny swept his gaze through the crowd. "Where'd you see 'em, boys?"

"Straight ahead, Johnny. Wait—no. Two-o'clock."

"You don't even know how to read a clock," Rex muttered.

Luther let out a low whine. "Shit. You're right. Hey, there's another one, Johnny! Right behind the giant light-up dinosaur."

The dinosaur of lights was impossible to miss and Johnny frowned as he and Lisa strolled casually along the path and searched for anyone who might be watching them. With luck, they would screw up and the partners could locate them.

"Oh, wait!" Rex yipped this time. "It disappeared again."

"Naw, I think I see." Johnny zeroed in on two men who stood beside the dinosaur covered in green and orange neon lights. They both stared at him and Lisa before the shorter one—with his shirt undone by too many buttons and a puff of chest hair peeking over the top—leaned toward the taller one and muttered something. "Lisa. The two guys beside the dinosaur."

"What?"

He turned toward her and nodded subtly in that direction. "They've been starin' at us, and I recon—"

"Daddy!" An earsplitting scream of delight ripped through the air behind them. One of the men lit up in a dazzling smile beside the dinosaur as a five-year-old girl raced toward him past the bounty hunter and his hounds, her arms outstretched.

"Look at you!" He rumbled a laugh and picked her up, threw the giggling kid into the air, then caught her and pretended the dinosaur would eat them both.

Oh, sure. Kids can run and scream all they want but I get a warnin' to keep my hounds quiet.

Lisa harrumphed in confusion. "You thought the guy waiting for his family was part of the hive-mind?"

Johnny cleared his throat. "They were starin' at us."

"Johnny, Johnny! There's another one!" Luther lunged toward the side of the path but stopped short and waited for his master, his tail wagging furiously. "Right there at those weird, dangly flowers. See it?"

"Oh…" Lisa stifled a laugh and leaned toward the dwarf to point across the walkway at the flowerbeds. "Is that what got the dogs all excited?"

He caught sight of a shimmering blue light that darted around the nocturnal flowers that opened beneath the decorative lights and sighed.

"I'll rip 'em apart, Johnny!"

"Yeah, let us at 'em! We'll teach 'em not to mess with—"

The dwarf snapped his fingers and grunted. "Boys."

"Can we, Johnny? Can we?"

He bit down hard on his bottom lip and looked slowly at his trusty hounds. "You said swarm."

"Uh-huh."

"Yep. That's right."

"And y'all thought the tiny pixies flyin' around playin' Mother

Nature with those flowers were the same bastards who sent an armored, respawnin' worm against us in the swamp?"

A woman in her twenties pushing a stroller scowled at him as she passed. "There are children here, you know."

"Yeah, hounds too."

"Please watch your language." Her eyes widened and she increased her pace down the pathway to get away from the foul-mouthed dwarf.

"What?" Johnny looked at Lisa and shrugged. "I ain't allowed to say pixie?"

"Um…" Luther's tail lowered slowly between his legs. "What?"

Rex nibbled at the fur on his brother's neck. "You messed that one up, bro."

"Hey, wait. You thought they were the hive too! Johnny never told us not to look for pixies. Whatever the heck those are."

Johnny let out a long, heavy sigh and shook his head. "Keep movin', boys."

"But Johnny—"

He snapped his fingers. "No. You ain't chasin' after pixies in a public garden." *And I ain't convinced any of us know what we're doin' with this bastard of a case.*

"So no hive-mind," Lisa muttered. Her smile returned slowly as she scanned the pedestrians' faces around them, still a little tense.

"I guess not." The dwarf cleared his throat. "Sorry."

"Don't be. I'm merely glad we didn't get this far only to realize we had this whole thing wrong from the get-go." She squeezed his arm in hers a little tighter. "You know, now that I think about it, the website for the gardens did mention night-blooming flowers and nocturnal pollinators."

"Huh. Is that what they're callin' pixies these days?"

"Well, I'm not sure that would exactly draw people in. But New Mexico is the Land of Enchantment, after all. Right?"

Johnny steered them away from two small children who chased each other up and down the path and laughed shrilly. "If you say so. I'm fixin' to enchant us the hell outta here in the mornin'." *It'd be far more magical if I didn't have a superstitious pilot flyin' my jet.*

CHAPTER FIVE

The plan was to arrive in Gallup after dark the next day, which gave them more than enough time for pitstops and a relatively casual dinner to finish the seven-hour drive from Albuquerque. Johnny refused to eat with the federal agent he still didn't trust and opted to take his meals in the back of their rental SUV with the hounds.

When they reached Gallup, New Mexico a little after seven pm, the sun had almost completely set. Ellis led them through terrain that looked incredibly familiar for a state he had never intended to visit in the first place.

He tightened his hold on the steering wheel and grumbled, "This looks too much like goddamn Arizona."

"Huh. Maybe that's because we're almost on the border of New Mexico and Arizona."

"I don't like it. There's too much desert and not enough green."

Lisa fought back a smirk. "You seemed to take it in stride when we were in Arizona."

"Sure, 'cause Sedona has an old hermit named Otis living in a cave and that hermit had somethin' I wanted."

"Gallup has something we want too, Johnny. The heart of this hive-mind—or whatever we're supposed to call it."

The dwarf grunted. "If that shifter fed's even right about her little hunch."

"She's going out of her way to help us." She gazed at the sprawling landscape under the last of the sunset. "It is possible for someone to help simply because they want to, you know, with no ulterior motives."

"That might be. But I think that ain't exactly why she's helpin'."

"Why? Because you don't like feds?"

"No, I don't trust feds." He shrugged. "Or like 'em. But all this came together too easily, darlin'. Nelson knows of some agents sent out here for a different case and this one just so happens to think she knows exactly where we need to be 'cause she did some diggin' on her own with a partner we ain't seen? It smells fishy."

In the back seat, Luther lowered his head, his ears flat against his head. "Sorry."

"Okay, Johnny." Lisa folded her arms. "So either this whole thing is a giant FBI conspiracy and both Nelson and Agent Paulson are in on it with the hive-mind and whoever that creepy voice we heard from the unkillable worm was. In which case, we can't trust anyone ever. Or you can admit that it's still beneficial for you to have friends in the Bureau, and she's doing us a favor because she doesn't want to see shifters or any other magicals kidnapped and brainwashed. Which, if I had to guess, is part of the reason she became a federal agent in the first place."

He didn't say another word on the matter because she was right.

Nothin' in the Glades turned out anythin' like we expected on this case. I guess it's gonna keep goin' that way until we eliminate these bastards.

They followed Ellis' Subaru through a maze of low, squat, incredibly long factory buildings erected in the middle of nowhere. Despite all the properties around them, they continued with no indication that they would stop anytime soon. They kicked clouds of dust up behind them as the paved road grew bumpier and more worn away.

"Christ. Have these folks ever heard of road maintenance?"

"If the warehouse has been shut down for the last decade, I don't think the state's looking to spend tax dollars on repairing a road no one uses."

"We're usin' it."

Lisa took a deep breath and steeled herself.

At the end of the unbearable road, Ellis pulled off into a derelict, pot-holed parking lot halfway covered with sand and dirt blown in from the desert and never removed. When she got out, the echo of her car door shutting sounded far louder than it should have.

Johnny, Lisa, and the hounds joined her in the center and took a moment to view the front of the abandoned warehouse— or, at least, what they could see of it.

A huge section of the roof at the front of the building had collapsed some time before, half the roof shingles had been stripped away by the weather, and the rest of the supporting structure sagged in on itself in the middle. There used to be a ventilation shaft at the side of the building, but the huge metal pipe had been filled in with cement, as had what Johnny assumed was a staircase inside what would have been the front doors if they'd existed.

"You said faulty structure."

Ellis nodded.

"This looks more like a cheap coverup for biohazard. Do you know anythin' about what happened here?" The two partners both waited for her response as the hounds sniffed the gravel-strewn parking lot.

The agent stared at the collapsed front of the warehouse and her eyes narrowed as she rubbed absently at the center of her chest.

"Agent Paulson?" Lisa asked.

"Hmm?"

"Are you thinkin' that hard again?" Johnny rubbed his chin in irritation. "Listen, if you can't remember where this entrance is, go back to Albuquerque. We'll find it—"

"No, no. It'll take you hours. Probably longer without any light. Come on."

"You ain't answered my question."

"What question?"

"Do you know what happened here? Why they filled part of the empty buildin' with concrete?"

"No." Ellis darted him a small, humorless smile. "We were out here for an inspection, not an archaeological dig."

She turned and walked parallel to the building and toward the open desert surrounding this small huddle of factories and not much else.

Johnny rolled his eyes. "Someone has a smart mouth."

"Oh, come on." Lisa elbowed him in the side as they followed the agent onto the sand and dirt between the scattered, scrubby bushes and rock formations that studded the desert. "You're peeved because you're not the only one."

"Huh. Peeved. It's not the word I would have chosen, darlin'."

"Call it whatever you want."

He whistled for the hounds and they raced across the parking lot to catch up to their master.

Ellis led them farther into the desert than he thought was necessary. By now, the sun had long since set and given way to darkness.

"I ain't sayin' it simply to say it," he called ahead to her. "If you don't remember where this other entrance is, we'll find our own way in."

"No, it's here." The woman stopped at a prickly bush much

larger than the others around it and glanced at the clear sky studded with stars and a moon a little past full. "We chose a good night to come out here without a light."

She stooped to clear dirt away at the base of the bush, then pulled a huge section of the ground up and out of place using a handle. The bush toppled and the three stood over a gaping hole in the desert lined with rebar rungs that extended far deeper than they could see.

Johnny snorted. "You put this in your report to your fake employers?"

"Yes, I did. It's a racketeering case, Johnny, among other things. The corporations we're investigating look good on paper but some individuals at the top see the value in secret entrances to abandoned warehouses. You know, to conduct illegal activities where no one can see."

"Oh, sure. Eloquently put, by the way."

Lisa sent him a warning glance he couldn't see and took a small flashlight from her back pocket. "Whatever this is here for, there's a reason. So let's go take a look."

"You said this was as busy as all get-out the last time you saw it." Johnny scowled at the shifter agent. "I ain't seen a soul out here. It's as quiet as a grave."

"Maybe being shown the best path down through these tunnels out here will soothe some of that criticism," Ellis said flatly. "I can take you as far as my partner and I mapped out but then I'll have to leave."

"That suits me fine."

"Okay, I'll go first." Lisa rolled her eyes and stepped between them. She clicked her flashlight on and stuck it in her mouth to start the climb down the secret entrance.

The other two gave her sufficient time to descend before the shifter woman nodded at the belt of explosive disks slung around the dwarf's hips. "What are those?"

"Extra power cells. I made 'em myself."

"I don't think we'll need batteries this far underground."

"You never know." He squinted at her as the echoes of Lisa descending the rebar ladder grew fainter. *I'm not tellin' this one a thing about my gear. Not when she looks like she's fixin' to snatch one off me and chuck it at—*

The hounds.

"Aw, shit."

"What's wrong?" Lisa called from the tunnel.

"Last time I checked, these ain't flyin' hounds."

"Why do we need to fly, Johnny?" Rex trotted toward his master and snorted as he shook dirt out of his nose. "I thought we were going down?"

"Yeah, hey. We can dig. You want us to dig, Johnny? We can—" Luther stopped at the edge of the hole and peered into the darkness. "Oh... Hey, Johnny? How are we supposed to get down there?"

"I shoulda kept those damn duffel bags from New York," the dwarf muttered.

"Do you need help?" Ellis asked with a smirk.

"Yeah, you're enjoyin' this, ain'tcha?"

"Or you could leave the dogs up here. It might be safer."

"Yeah, for the bastards I'm hopin' we find down in this hole." Johnny rubbed his mouth and chin vigorously, then capitulated with a grunt of frustration. "Sure. Fine. I could use some help."

"No problem." Ellis looked questioningly at the hounds and pointed from one to the other.

"Luther."

"Yeah, Johnny." The hound whipped his head up from the dark hole in the ground and Lisa's moving flashlight at the bottom.

"Paulson's gonna carry you down."

"What? Why?"

"You're squirmier. Go on."

He gazed at Ellis with wide eyes. "Am not."

Rex sniggered as he trotted toward Johnny. "Hey, it's like the other day at the shifter den, right? Johnny rode a shifter. Now it's your turn."

The agent glanced sharply at the dwarf and he looked away quickly and cleared his throat. *Yeah, she can hear 'em. I gotta keep playin' like I don't.*

"Come on, boy. I ain't fixin' to take all night."

With a low whine, Luther shuffled toward the woman, who settled into a crouch to let him sniff her hand before she gave him a good pet. "We'll wait for them to go down first, buddy. No problem."

Luther stared at her. "Johnny, this is weird."

"Better luck next time, bro—whoa! Hey!" Rex squirmed in Johnny's arms as the dwarf pulled him toward the edge of the hole and tucked him awkwardly under one arm. "Johnny. Johnny! There has to be a better way—"

"Hold still."

"Ha-ha. Look who's squirmy now, Rex."

His brother growled at him as they began the descent.

The dwarf paused to scowl at Ellis and waited until he was sure she saw him. "If anythin' happens to that hound—"

"Yeah, I know. You'll come after my entire family, all my friends, and wipe everything I ever loved off the face of the Earth. What, you think I haven't seen *John Wick?*"

Johnny grunted and as he continued down the ladder, he caught a glimpse of the agent rubbing her chest again with a little wince before she disappeared past the edge of the hole.

"Hey, lady," Luther said. "You should get that checked. I heard a doc friend telling Johnny all about chest pains. Could be a heart attack or somethin'." He sniggered. "Yeah, Johnny thought he was havin' a heart attack two years ago. Turned out he'd eaten too much fried catfish. But still…"

Yeah, she can hear him, all right. I can give her points for not talkin' back but that's all she gets.

CHAPTER SIX

With the hounds safely on the ground at the bottom of the shaft in the New Mexico desert, Johnny and Lisa followed Agent Paulson through a series of branching tunnels. Some were carved out of the harder rock bed around them. Others had been constructed with cement and looked considerably sturdier.

Ellis had brought a flashlight too and she swung it from left to right as they moved. She scrutinized the various tunnels and chose each consecutive one with barely any hesitation.

"You memorized this place real quick, didn't ya?" Johnny muttered.

"It pays to be an undercover overachiever on a case like mine." The shifter woman swung her flashlight toward the righthand tunnel and continued. "The better I know this property, the better chance we'll have of apprehending anyone who decides to use it in ways they shouldn't."

"Like the guys we're lookin' for."

For a brief moment, her back stiffened before she sighed heavily and rubbed her chest again. "I didn't think heartburn would set in for another twenty years at least."

The dwarf snorted. "Tell me about it."

Lisa glanced questioningly at him but he shook his head and waved her off.

"It sure smells like rats down here, Johnny." Luther zigzagged across the tunnel floor behind his master, his nose pressed against the concrete. "And dirt."

"And weird magic that's not magi—oh." Rex chuckled. "Yeah, that's the shifter lady."

Johnny wanted to ask the hounds if they'd picked up on anything else but he still didn't want to disclose his translating-dog-collar secret in front of Paulson. So far, the only fed who knew anything about his communication with his hounds was Lisa, and she wasn't even technically a fed. Not the way he saw them.

It's best to keep it that way or I'll end up with Nelson's friends all over my ass askin' me and the boys to do a few tricks.

A tiny shiver ran through him at the thought.

"Okay, here we go. It should be right..." Ellis turned around the bend. "Yep. Here it is. This is as far as we got."

Johnny and Lisa joined her in an open room that seemed to be half bunker and half gigantic storage closet. Boxes and crates were stacked along the concrete walls, and a table in the center of the room held a dusty halogen lamp and a crowbar. A steel door was positioned in the far wall, presumably leading into the expanse of the abandoned warehouse that also extended underground.

As long as the rest of it ain't filled in too. If it is, we've reached another dead end.

"That door leads to the rest of the warehouse?" Lisa asked.

"That's my guess, yeah." Ellis scanned the room and rubbed her chest again.

"You and your partner didn't think it was a good idea to keep goin' past this part, huh?"

Agent Paulson sighed. "I told you. We didn't have enough time to keep going. So if anyone is down here running the horror show you described, it's most likely on the other side of that door. Good luck and…be careful, huh?"

"Yeah, thanks for getting us this far," Lisa said as she stepped across the room.

Johnny turned as Ellis reached the entrance to the tunnel again. "That's it?"

She paused and placed a hand on the doorway while the other one moved to her chest. "I told you I'd—"

"Yeah, that you'd get us this far and you had to split. I know. But you also said you wanted to help. Shifters lookin' after shifters and all that, right? I saw that pistol on your hip, Paulson. You ain't unarmed."

"Johnny…" Lisa muttered.

"Plus, I ain't exactly fixin' to climb that ladder up to the desert two more times to get my hounds out when we're done."

The woman sighed heavily, then straightened slowly and removed her hand from the doorway. "Okay. Sure. You got me."

"Good." The bounty hunter spun toward the steel door and nodded for Lisa to keep moving with him. "I'm not sayin' we need the backup, but if these assholes are scuttlin' around here in the big numbers I expect, I ain't gonna pass up—"

A grating shriek of metal on metal and pebbles dropping rose behind them. The two partners spun to where Agent Paulson hauled another steel door mounted on a rolling track across the exit of the storage room and the entrance to the tunnel—and their way out.

The door met the other side with a boom and jolted more pebbles to rain around the doorway before a lock clicked into place.

"What the hell are you doin'?" Johnny demanded.

Ellis turned slowly to face them and a sneering grin spread across her lips. "You don't want to pass up this opportunity, Johnny Walker."

Her eyes flashed with silver light and a brief flicker of multi-colored waves.

"To be locked in these tunnels with you? I don't think so."

"Johnny…" Lisa brushed her hand against his arm and stared at Agent Paulson. "Her chest."

A faint glow of reddish light seeped from beneath the tank top barely showing under Ellis' partially unzipped bomber jacket. It wasn't visible when he looked directly at it but if he stared at her shoulder, it was unmistakable.

Damn. I'd bet my rifle collection there's an Oriceran mind-control sigil burned into her skin. And she was givin' us her tell the whole damn time. How did I miss it?

"Johnny." Luther uttered a low growl and bared his teeth, his response echoed by Rex who stood perfectly still beside him. "The shifter lady smells crazy now."

"Yeah, Johnny." Rex flattened his ears. "Like the shifter who kicked the bucket in the back yard."

They're confirmin' what I already know.

The dwarf gritted his teeth. "Shit, Paulson. They already got to you too?"

Ellis laughed and it most certainly didn't sound like her voice. "We said you'd know the place when you saw it, dwarf. Come. We have so much to share with you. We're waiting."

"Goddammit." He rolled his eyes, stormed past the woman who'd clearly already been turned by the hive-mind who knew how long before, and stopped at the storm door she'd slid into place to block their exit. With a grunt of effort, he yanked the steel latch handle up but it wouldn't budge.

"We wouldn't recommend that way out," Ellis crooned. "The tunnels are old. Who knows how long they'll last even without added pressure?"

And the asshole runnin' this show played his next card. I can't blow this door down. I'll be blowin' us sky-high with it.

He turned and pointed sharply at her. "Is there anythin' left of that woman in there?"

"So much." Ellis grinned. "But much more of us now."

"I swear to everythin' good and green on this planet, if you've turned Paulson into some walkin' talkin' husk and there ain't nothin' left, I'll—"

"Yes." She inclined her head and studied him avidly. Her eyes glinted with excitement and greed as her grin widened. "That's the kind of fire we've been searching for. We're very much looking forward to everything you have to offer us, Johnny. And you, Lisa Breyer."

When Ellis turned toward her, the half-Light Elf leaned away and shook her head. "Don't."

"You'll understand soon enough. We're waiting." Paulson gestured toward the door but no one moved. "It's in your best interest to follow, you know. Believe me, we understand your hesitation. It was in all of us at first. But if you didn't want to be here, you wouldn't have come."

She strode across the room, her gaze focused intently on the steel door at the other side. With a quick jerk and a shriek of rusty metal being forced to move, she opened the door and stepped through into more darkness. "Take as long as you need. But there's no going back now that you're here."

The hive-mind shifter disappeared into the hallway beyond and the storage room fell completely silent.

"Johnny…" Lisa swallowed.

"Yeah, I know, darlin'." He approached and stopped beside her to scowl at the open doorway. "We saw the goddamn signs and didn't put two and two together."

She glanced at him, her eyes a little panicked. "This is the part where you say 'I told you so,' isn't it?"

The dwarf shrugged and ran his fingers lightly along the edges of the explosive disks hooked to his utility belt. "I ain't sayin' nothin' except we gotta keep goin'. Paulson wasn't wrong. This is where we wanted to be."

"That wasn't Paulson, Johnny. Not after she closed that door."

"Sure, but what the hell else am I supposed to call her?"

Lisa's hand hovered over the grip of her pistol in its shoulder holster and she gave him a thin smile. "Paulson. That's who she is. Who she'll still be when we finish this."

"You took the words right outta my mouth, darlin'. Let's go burn this hive to the ground." Johnny stepped through the doorway to the dark hallway beyond. "Look alive, boys. We're headin' into the heart of this whole fucked-up situation."

The hounds trotted after him and sniffed the air and the floor with their tails straight up. "We're on it, Johnny."

"Yeah. Let them try to brainwash us." Luther looked at his master. "We going after the rats now, Johnny?"

"Yeah." He snorted. "Big ones."

CHAPTER SEVEN

They moved quickly down an incredibly long corridor lined with doors every ten feet on either side. Johnny and Lisa checked each one and they were all locked. She turned her flashlight off and slid it into her pocket. It wasn't necessary now that the track lighting along the ceiling gave off a weak, flickering glow. Up ahead at the end of the hall, brighter light spilled through the door left open only a few inches after Agent Paulson had passed through it.

A low hum grew steadily louder as they headed down the hallway toward that door. That was the only sound besides their footsteps and the hounds' nails clicking across the hard surface beneath their feet.

"It's too quiet," she whispered.

"Yep. Maybe we'll step into a fancy office. The folks stuck in this hive-mind bullshit can go anywhere around the world, right?"

"That's what it sounded like."

The bounty hunter nodded. "It might be they're all out on their screwed-up missions. Then again, it might not. Be ready for anythin', darlin'."

"That about sums up the last few months, yeah."

He glanced at her with a small smile as they reached the door. "We find the heart of this—what's drivin' the magic behind it—and we cut it out, you hear?"

"I couldn't have said it better myself."

Very slowly, Johnny took hold of the edge of the door and pulled it open.

Light flooded the hallway and blinded them momentarily, and they shielded their eyes until their vision adjusted. When it did, Johnny stared for a moment before he scowled at the main room of the underground warehouse. "Huh."

"Uh...Johnny?" Rex crouched and growled low. "These aren't pixies too, right?"

"Not even close."

They stood at the top platform of an open staircase that descended on their left along the wall. But the height gave them a perfect vantage point to view the entire room filled wall-to-wall with magicals. And yes, the majority of them were shifters but none of them acted the way they were supposed to.

Naw, this is what the hive is all about. They're actin' like insects.

At first, the movement within the warehouse seemed scattered and erratic, which made sense with hundreds—if not thousands—of bodies crammed into the same space together with barely enough room for any of the captured magicals to move. But after ten seconds of staring at the grotesque sight of what could only be described as a hive, Johnny noticed a pattern.

The victims moved in five different concentric circles—at least as far as he could see. Each circle moved in the opposite direction of those on either side of it. The magicals shuffled slowly side by side and occasionally jostled against each other without seeming to notice or care. None of them spoke and every single face held the blank, vacant expression of someone walking in their sleep.

All of 'em all at once, walkin' in their sleep.

A buzzing tingle of intensely strong, concentrated magic filled the air, prickled along the back of Johnny's neck, and made his nose itch. The musky smell of so many bodies packed together was overwhelming, but even the hounds didn't comment on it. Luther sneezed and shook his head vigorously, but that was the only reaction.

"How are we supposed to find the heart in all this?" Lisa whispered, her nostrils flared.

"Do you see the circles?" He nodded toward the center of the massive warehouse room and the small inner ring of shuffling, brainwashed magicals. From where they stood, it was impossible to see what existed at the heart of that circle, but he didn't need to see it to know they would find their answers there. "I assume that's where we need to get to."

"So let's go." Lisa nodded firmly and moved toward the stairs. She seemed unable to look away from the grotesquely packed bodies, none of which seemed to notice the two un-brainwashed magicals and two coonhounds who entered their midst.

"Welcome!" The voice boomed across the warehouse—the same voice that had blasted from the armored worm's open mouth in Johnny's back yard.

She froze at the top of the stairs.

All the milling, vapid victims of the hive-mind froze as well. They all turned at the same time wherever they stood to face the staircase and looked at the bounty hunter and his federal-agent partner.

"Isn't it glorious?" It came from every mouth at once but seemed to be spoken directly into their minds, so deafeningly loud that Lisa staggered away from the top of the stairs and pressed her back against the wall. The eerily happy and unmistakable announcer's voice was in there, louder than any single voice on its own but partially drowned by the thousands of others that joined it. "We didn't expect you so soon. But there's no time like the present, right?"

"Jesus Christ." Johnny squinted at the automaton created by so many magicals acting and speaking as one. He marched across the metal mesh of the platform and thumped his hands down on the metal railing that separated it from the twenty-foot drop to the warehouse floor. "You're done, asshole. This ends right now."

"Of course it does," the hive-mind droned. *"But not in the way you think, Johnny. Come. Join us."*

"Not fuckin' likely."

A shrieking laugh burst from the center of the warehouse for two seconds before the rest of the hive-mind opened their mouths and laughed too. The dead-sounding cadence of "ha-ha-ha" without any real humor whatsoever triggered a wave of goosebumps to tingle across every inch of his flesh.

"By the ancestors," Lisa whispered, her face ashen beneath the bright overhead lights.

"Johnny." Rex growled, whined, and growled again. "Johnny, this is—"

"Make it stop, Johnny." Luther crouched low beside his brother. "My ears are gonna explode."

So are mine. Probably.

The dwarf smacked the iron railing again. "Hey!"

The laughter cut off abruptly but his ears were now ringing.

"Come down from your high tower, Johnny Walker." It was the announcer's voice again and it spoke with perfect clarity across the massive room. "Come and see what we're doing. You have questions, I know. I have all the answers you require."

That's the first time the bastard said 'I.' Johnny and Lisa shared a glance. She'd picked up on it too. *It means someone is down there runnin' this show—the heart of this goddamn Frankenstein's monster.*

"We don't bite," the gleeful voice added with a chuckle. "Not here and not you. Come, come."

"Boys." Johnny glared at the dark pit at the center of the smallest circle in the warehouse. "Y'all stay close. Don't make a move until I say so, understand?"

"All good, Johnny," Luther muttered. "I can stay right here if you want."

"Yeah, we can look for a way out—"

The dwarf snapped his fingers and turned away from the railing. "We need you with us. Let's go."

Lisa looked at him with wide eyes and set her lips grimly, but she didn't hesitate to join him at the top of the stairs and they descended together. Each footstep on the metal-mesh steps clanged and echoed around them. The hive-mind still stared at them with thousands of pairs of eyes, and the farther they moved down the staircase, the stronger the humming buzz grew.

When they reached the bottom, the closest magicals backed away to give them space. The others followed suit until the victims made a pathway for the bounty hunter and his team that led toward the center of the final circle. They closed the gap behind them once the newcomers passed and turned to watch their slow but steady progress.

The hum grew stronger.

"Join us."

"What?" Johnny glared at the closest magical—a Wood Elf woman with a pale face and matted hair. The glaze over her eyes cleared for an instant before she said it again.

"Join us." He noticed that her mouth didn't move, which confirmed his perception that they could somehow speak into his mind. The thought was chilling.

"Share it all with us."

He whirled to where a giant of a shifter man loomed over him, although the guy didn't step into the open path. His eyes were covered in a thin film of white but they stared directly at the dwarf.

"And we will share it all with you—"

"All right, cut that shit out." Johnny flipped him the bird and kept moving.

"Do you hear it too?" Lisa muttered.

"In my damn head, yeah. Don't listen to it."

Rex snorted. "What are you talking about?"

Luther skittered away from the magicals who closed in behind them as they moved forward. "Yeah, I don't hear anything, Johnny. Except for all these mouth-breathers."

The bounty hunter didn't want to say anything to the hounds and risk giving away what might be the only card up their sleeves at this point. *It's exactly like with Portland's demon witch. Her fear potion wasn't meant for hounds. This magic ain't either.*

The tingle of strong magic grew even stronger with each slow step across the warehouse—like pins and needles that pricked Johnny's flesh and his mind.

"Join us."

"The grand design has room for you too."

"Share your mind."

"Give us what you have."

The voices crowded around him from every side and he cleared his throat as he pressed on.

"Johnny, wait…" Lisa's voice sounded far away and she'd paused and now stared blankly ahead. "There's something—"

"Bad idea, darlin'." He had to fight against the growing urge to simply give in as he placed a hand on her back and guided her forward and muttered in her ear, "Remember Portland?"

"Yes. The witch would have been a good addition—"

"No. Wrong." Johnny caught her hands, slid his fingers through hers, and gave her a little shake. "The part about it not bein' real, darlin'."

"Not real…" She sucked in a sharp breath and shook her head. "Shit."

"It's all right. If you see me slippin', feel free to repeat the scathin' review you gave me at that Johnny-hater meetin'. Snap me right out of it."

With a wry chuckle, she regained her senses and squeezed his hand. "It shouldn't be too hard."

They proceeded in silence and the path opened and closed around them until they reached their destination. The magicals stood perfectly still and stared at them, their eyes completely white although they occasionally flashed with green or orange light.

This ain't the end.

"Do you wanna move aside?" Johnny snapped.

They didn't.

"You'll have to forgive them." That announcer's voice came from behind the final defense of brainwashed magicals. "They're new."

The low hum in the air rose in volume until the white-eyed magicals stepped aside like robots and cleared the way for the partners to finally reach the heart of the hive.

A hole had either been dug or blasted into the floor—three feet deep and six feet in diameter. Tattered pillows and half-ripped cushions lined the bottom of the hole and an Azrakan was seated on a particularly large pile of them toward the rear.

The magical was incredibly old and decrepit-looking and sprawled across the stack of pillows. His curved, forked horns looked like they were molting, or perhaps that was simply the dankness of the warehouse and so many bodies pressed together. Folds of skin covered in patches of withering hair drooped in every crevice and dip of the Azrakan's features. The only part of him that didn't look like it was rotting away with age and the use of so much magic were his eyes.

These were bright green and incredibly lucid. They flicked from one to the other as the bastard studied Johnny and Lisa with an intensity that was disconcerting.

And I thought Grady had it bad by blending magic with tech and his body. This guy's been drainin' himself dry for way too long.

CHAPTER EIGHT

"There." The Azrakan's drooping lips peeled back to reveal stained, crooked teeth. More than a few were missing. "In time, they'll be better able to respond to the collective energy without direct orders. The process is, of course, still fresh in their minds. But it always comes through in the end. Please. Sit."

He raised a gnarled, claw-like hand and gestured at the mounds of pillows around him in the pit he'd turned into his throne. Johnny stared at the three-inch nails that curled in on themselves at the ends of the being's fingers, exactly like his molting horns.

"Naw. If your personal hygiene is any indication, I aim to stand right where I am."

The Azrakan's eyes widened, and every magical in the warehouse turned at once to face their hive-mind leader and the strangers in their midst.

"*Sit!*"

The shouted command was powerful enough by sheer volume alone. But with it came an intensifying surge of the low hum that persisted and the buzzing tingle that rippled across Johnny's flesh. The power of it even seemed to prickle under his skin.

As if shoved by invisible hands, both partners stumbled forward over the edge of the pit in the concrete floor, although none of the hive-mind victims had moved. They landed on their hands and knees and Lisa choked out a gasp.

"Now what the—" The bounty hunter gritted his teeth against the immense pressure that bore down on him from every direction and the rising hum of magic aimed with precision against him. "What the hell kinda message do you think this sends to your guests?"

"It's only a taste of what we can do together, Johnny." The Azrakan chuckled. "You walked into our home where our connection is strongest. What else did you expect?"

"This ain't a home, it's a—" With immense effort, he pushed off his hands and knees and slumped against the rim of the hole lined with cushions. "A damn prison."

"Oh, no, no, no." The being raised both arms from the pillows and gestured at the entirety of the warehouse and beyond. His arms began to shake before he lowered them again quickly. "This is freedom, Johnny. That's what you have to understand. Freedom from pain and isolation and confusion. From the agonizing debasement of struggling simply to survive, only to make one poor decision after another. And from knowing deep down in your heart of hearts that you're a failure."

"Nice try." He glanced at Lisa, who struggled to lean back against the pillows as well. He wanted to reach out to her but he couldn't move beneath the weight of the hive-mind's combined magic and their intention to force him to sit. "But you're barkin' up the wrong tree with that shit." He met the Azrakan's green gaze again squarely. "You don't know anythin' about me."

"We know enough. But please, why don't you tell us more?"

Lisa clenched her eyes tightly shut and uttered a low groan.

"That ain't gonna happen." The dwarf had to throw himself sideways to lean an inch toward his partner. "Portland, Lisa. It ain't real."

"And you...you're a bounty hunter with your head so far up your ass, you still think you're Oriceran's gift to Earth."

She said the same thing at that Johnny-hater meetin', didn't she? Good. She's still fightin' it.

"Hey, Johnny," Rex whispered. "You guys keep, uh...sitting there and having your little chat."

"Yeah," Luther added. "We'll sniff around. There's something behind those pillows next to the talking moose."

Johnny grunted and hoped that was enough for the hounds.

The Azrakan's gaze flicked toward Rex and Luther. "We would have advised against bringing your pets with you, Johnny. They won't last long once you and Lisa decide to stay."

"They'll be fine."

"Such loyalty goes both ways, doesn't it?" The horned magical ignored the hounds and focused instead on his newest victims. "Exactly like with us—here in our home and out there, scattered across this new world. It's new for Oricerans, of course, when you look at the larger timeline."

"We know what you're...trying to do," Lisa muttered and the veins in her neck and temple pulsed as she struggled against the force of the collective magic that bore down on them.

"Ah, yes. It's a larger concept. You will, of course, understand much more of it when you give in."

Johnny snarled. "We ain't—"

"Bup, bup, bup." The Azrakan lifted one knobby, hooked finger with a curved, cracked nail at the end. "Let me finish."

Despite the fact that Johnny Walker didn't let anyone finish when he had no interest in hearing what they had to say, he found himself unable to utter a sound when he opened his mouth to say so.

Shit. This brainwashin' crap's stronger than I expected.

"Allow me to explain the process to you both." The rotten-toothed smile appeared again and pulled at the corners of the mouth almost buried beneath so many folds of skin. "You'll spend the first few months within our inner circle—right here, close to me. That's where the most important work begins. Unraveling all those cobwebs within your mind that keep you closed-off and disconnected from those around you. Then, as you elevate yourself within our consciousness, you will move slowly away from us as any child moves away from their parent when they're ready to leave the nest."

The crazy fucker thinks he's nurturin' an army of progeny. My folks had their issues but he makes 'em look like superheroes.

"And then," the Azrakan continued, "when you finally join us completely—when you merge with that freedom I can feel you longing for, Johnny—you will leave this place. You and every other convert will go out to fulfill your duty to the collective. You will bring us more and you will make us stronger."

Luther hopped into the pit halfway between Johnny and the crazy-ass magical who controlled everyone's minds. The hound sniffed around the pillows and remained close to the side of the hole in the ground. "I think we're close, Johnny."

Rex sniffed the floor at the edge of the pit and glanced warily at a brainwashed Crystal who stood motionlessly. "Same kinda coverup as the shifter fed, Johnny. Hard to track. But we got it."

The Azrakan glanced at the hounds with a sneer but still chose to ignore them. "Oh, and there's no need to fear the sigil work, if that's what you're worried about. When I said we offer freedom, I did mean in its entirety. There's no pain, but it does allow our righteous soldiers to continue receiving what they need from us as they travel farther from home."

"To do what?" Lisa snapped.

Johnny grunted. *Oh, sure. He ain't turned off her chatterbox.*

The being's forked tongue flicked between his rotting teeth as he studied her with renewed interest. "To make us stronger."

"And then what? When you…bring everyone else in against their will—"

"Oh, it's never against their will, Lisa." He chuckled again.

"Everyone always comes around, exactly like you will. What we offer is impossible to refuse. You'll see. It's all a matter of time."

"You can't keep the gates open forever," she muttered. "There are still hundreds of years left until they close. Maybe..." She scrunched her face up and swallowed. "Maybe thousands. You won't even be here when they close again."

"Wrong." The Azrakan pointed a curling nail at her. "I have lived through one other cycle of open gates between Earth and Oriceran, Light Elf. I don't intend to disappear during a second. And time becomes so inconsequential when it ceases to exist within this collective power we all share. You will see."

Johnny wanted to scream at the magical and throttle the wrinkled old throat. Unfortunately, he could do neither.

"Yes, Johnny? Was there something you wished to say?"

The dwarf hadn't noticed the pressure growing tighter around his throat until it released and he said the first thing that came to mind. "Fuck you."

The Azrakan didn't bat an eyelid. "Yes, I understand that it's confusing to you now. But you'll understand eventually. You'll comprehend everything in ways you can't possibly conceive now within the limited scope of a single—"

With a hiss, the horned magical swept a weak hand toward Luther, who'd sniffed the cushions two feet away.

"Shoo. Get out!"

The hound whipped his head up and growled. "Found it, Johnny."

"It's there in the pillows, all right," Rex added and also growled at the horned magical from the edge of the pit. "Hard to find in all the stink, Johnny. This goat smells worse than that skunk Luther only half-buried—"

"Hey, I buried it all the way. I'm sure the squirrels dug it up."

"Squirrels don't—"

"Out!" A flickering swirl of dark green light conjured around the Azrakan's cracked nail pointed at the hounds.

Rex backed away a few steps and Luther crouched low before he stepped away along the curve of the pit.

"Don't even think about it," Johnny warned.

"I despise dogs." The Azrakan sneered at him and the green light at his fingertip snuffed out. "Of all the stupid, mindless creatures on this planet, they're the worst. No question."

"What?" Luther uttered a low chuff. "Rex, did the two-legged reindeer call us stupid?"

"That's what I heard."

"Johnny, he's gonna pay for that."

"They have their uses," the dwarf said. *If they don't pick up on this next part, we're all screwed.*

"Well, whatever relationship you think you've cultivated with a couple of dumb animals, Johnny, it's best you let go of it now. That will make this whole process easier for you." The Azrakan's eyes flickered to Lisa, who rocked slightly, her mouth open as she stared at the cushions in front of her. "Well, look at that. It seems Lisa's a natural. We'll do very well with her skills in—"

"You should get yourself a hound."

"I'm sorry?"

Johnny grunted and his eyelids fluttered as the buzzing hum drowned everything out but the sound of his voice and the Azrakan's. *Hang in there, darlin'. Only a little longer.*

"They ain't stupid, you know." He forced himself to stare at the crazy magical's eyes and not look at the hounds. "And they're real good for huntin'."

"Hmm. I hear you did an excellent job of hunting all your own, Johnny. Before the dogs and before you holed yourself up in your little bunker of a home in the Everglades. Isn't that right?"

The bastard did his homework.

"Sure. I'm good. The thing is, though, a hound can track simply by instinct. They're real good at findin' what they need and *goin' after it.*" He waited and prayed to whatever forces might be listening that Rex and Luther didn't take this moment as an opportunity to be complete boneheads. Unfortunately, nothing happened.

"I see you have strong feelings for them." The Azrakan hissed and closed his eyes as he raised his wrinkled chin. "Ah, yes. You're starting to fall in with us now. Lisa's almost there as well—"

"Yeah, but these here hounds," Johnny continued and fought against the fog that swept in quickly to drown his mind out. "These hounds can...get where I can't."

"Oh, shit, Luther. He's talking about us."

"Wait, that's the signal?" Luther stared at the Azrakan. "Can't he say—"

"Like right now!" Johnny roared.

CHAPTER NINE

"Go!" Rex shouted as he launched himself off the edge of the pit and directly at the Azrakan. The hound narrowly missed the sharp prongs of the magical's curved antlers and barreled into his shoulder instead to hurl him sideways.

The withered being screamed with rage and every single magical connected to the hive-mind screamed with him.

Johnny and Lisa screamed too.

That stupid dog! I'll rip his—

The dwarf snapped his mouth shut and shook himself vigorously.

The damn freak almost had me.

"Luther!" he shouted. "Get it!"

"What does it look like I'm doing, Johnny?" The hound pawed at the smaller pile of cushions beside the Azrakan, whose claw-like hands flapped wildly as he shrieked and tried to bat Rex away.

"You'll never make it out of here on your own, Johnny! You won't survive without us!" Green light bloomed around his finger, intended as an attack against the coonhound.

The dwarf slapped his numb hand against the explosive disks

at his belt and fumbled to pull one free. "If you lay a goddamn finger on my hound— What the—"

Hands clawed at his shoulders and he threw himself forward onto the pillows. The brainwashed magicals with all-white eyes continued to stretch toward him and took slow, shuffling steps. Some of them were jostled closer by those behind as the circles of their hive-mind members pushed them forward.

One of them stumbled into the cushioned pit and knocked Lisa over. She gasped as her eyes opened wide and she scrambled away from the dead-eyed wizard who clawed at her from where he'd landed. "Johnny—"

"Almost there, darlin'." The feeling had begun to return to his fingers now.

"Get back!" The Azrakan finally managed to shove Rex away as Luther tossed the last cushion aside and snatched up a small black item that somehow still glinted in the light.

"I got it, Johnny! I got the thing!"

Rex raced with his brother toward their master as the magicals closed in and pushed against each other to reach the pit and the bounty hunter. "What thing?"

"I don't know. The not-magic smell!" Luther dropped a small black box with rounded edges into his master's lap.

The dwarf clamped his hand around it instead of the uncooperative explosive disks.

When he did so, the commotion at the edge of the pit stopped instantly. The Azrakan struggled to pull his sagging body off the cushions and gasped. "No. Give it to us."

"You mean this?" Johnny tossed the box in his hand, glad to see his reflexes were finally returning. "I can't do that, bud. I can't let you keep runnin' this creepshow here neither."

"That is not for you!" the being screeched. "It's ours!"

The dwarf struggled to his feet and glared at the horned magical. "Not anymore it ain't."

I gotta find a way to get rid of this without killin' the folks here who don't know any better. If I—

"Johnny, look out!" Lisa shouted.

He couldn't turn in time to avoid a clumsy swing and a white-eyed shifter's beefy arm connected with the side of his head. It hurled him across the cushions, and the humming, thrumming black box of old-school Oriceran magic toppled from his hand.

More and more mindless drones stepped into the pit. The hounds snarled and snapped at ankles, feet, dangling hands, and whatever they could reach. None of the magicals seemed to notice or care, even when the animals knocked them over or dragged them down.

Johnny stood again and without thought, delivered an uppercut swing into the shifter's groin. The poor guy wheezed, fell face-first onto the cushions, and didn't move.

"There's nowhere for you to go, Johnny." The Azrakan snarled and his green gaze flicked frantically across the cushion in search of the black box. "If you don't join us now, you'll die down here."

"Nah." He slipped a hand into his pocket and pulled out a small handful of black detonating beads. "There's always another option."

Lisa chose that exact moment to leap to her feet, her consciousness and her strength restored enough to launch a blazing barrage of fireballs toward the ceiling of the warehouse. All eyes looked up to follow the blaze and she landed a blow to the face of a wizard who'd stepped into the pit with them. He fell back into the others behind him, who surged forward again and trampled their unsuspecting fellow victim. She snatched the explosive disk out of Johnny's hand.

"Crush the beads!" she yelled and thrust it toward him.

"Huh?"

"Do it!"

"Johnny, there are too many of 'em," Rex shouted.

"Yeah, you sure these aren't zombies?"

"Johnny!" Lisa shoved the disk under his nose. "The beads."

She had a plan.

He slapped the handful of adhesive explosives onto the side of the disk and lurched forward when two more hive-mind magicals tackled him from behind. The dwarf caught a fleeting glimpse of Lisa plastering something black and shimmering against the gooey side of the disk and her body jerked forward a split second before a Wood Elf with white eyes charged into her and brought her down.

"No!" the Azrakan bellowed and lurched forward off his tattered throne.

Well, there it is. Johnny kicked the chest of the magical behind him and fought toward Lisa. *We're all gettin' blown to—*

A massive explosion wracked the warehouse but surprisingly, he felt only the annoying pain of a brainwashed Kilomea's strong-ass fingers digging into his ankle. The explosion hadn't come from below the writhing mass of hive-mind victims who threatened to swamp them. It came from far, far overhead.

In the next moment, the screams started, although it sounded more like a single scream from thousands of throats. Johnny snatched two cushions up and pressed them against his ears as he growled at the deafening shriek that vibrated through his body. The hold on his ankle slackened and he shuffled on his knees toward Lisa through the magicals who'd fallen on the cushions.

She had her hands clamped tightly over her ears too and her eyes clenched shut.

"Johnny!" Rex shouted and of course, it blasted through the dwarf's head even over the noise. "Johnny, look. It worked!"

"Yeah, she blew up the whole—whoa." As soon as Luther spoke, the unified scream in the warehouse stopped abruptly. The Azrakan's brainwashed minions simply stood motionless.

Lisa pulled her hands slowly away from her ears and glanced from one frozen magical to the next. "What happened? They just stopped."

"Yep." Johnny dropped the cushions from his face and wiggled a finger in his ear. "We either did somethin' right or they're about to come down on us with somethin' even bigger."

"No way, Johnny." Luther sniffed around the far side of the pit.

"Not without their freaky fearless leader," Rex added.

The dwarf turned and snapped his fingers at both hounds, who shoved their snouts into a pile of crumpled Azrakan robes. "Y'all get outta that! There ain't no tellin' what might jump out atcha."

Rex sniggered. "Nothin', Johnny. The talking antelope's gone."

"What?"

"Nothing here, Johnny. Nothing but smelly robes and... Oh, shit. Is that a fingernail?"

"Looks more like a snail shell, bro."

"Huh."

Johnny rubbed his mouth and sighed heavily. "Well, there goes our chance to bring in the asshole behind the hive-mind."

Lisa placed her hand on his arm. "Did you consider bringing a perp in without that expressly being part of a case?"

"Huh?"

She smiled. "You did."

"Well, sure I did, darlin'. That asshole's responsible for kidnappin' all these magicals and forcin' 'em together here like it's a goddamn meat factory."

"Yeah." She turned away from him and looked at the frozen victims who now started to regain their awareness and move on their own. "About that..."

"And how did this piece of shit Azrakan manage to up and disappear when we blew up his shiny little black box?"

"Johnny?"

"Yeah. Nice aim, by the way. I didn't think you had it in ya to throw anythin' that far and high."

Lisa nudged him with the back of her hand. "You should—"

"But this bastard shoulda had to pay for what he did. Shit, how much you wanna bet he didn't give two skunk farts about openin' the gates forever? Naw, that moltin' piece of Oriceran filth was gettin' off on takin' minds over and livin' forever like a sack of—"

"Johnny!" She glanced at him with a frustrated expression. "I'm not saying you're wrong, but we need to save the conjecture for after this."

"After what?"

"Oh, my God!" a woman shrieked.

"Where am I? What is this place?"

"Martin, I swear on my mother's grave if you don't take the trash out, I'll—Martin? *Martin?*"

"I'm not crazy. I'm not crazy. I'm not crazy…"

With wide eyes, Johnny turned slowly to face the throng of the Azrakan's victims, all of whom now seemed to wake at the same time. They were understandably bewildered at being jammed together in a warehouse with no idea how the hell they'd gotten there.

"Shit. There's always fallout, ain't there?"

"Johnny, we have to help them."

"Yeah, I know. Come on." The dwarf wobbled across the uneven cushions before he hoisted himself over the edge of the pit. He stood and spread his arms wide. "All y'all need to listen up!"

"Who are you?" the closest shifter asked, her eyes wide, and her gaze flicked around the warehouse before it settled on him.

"My name's Johnny. And I—"

"Did you do this?" a dirt-smeared wizard shrieked in his face. "Did you do this to us?"

"Hell no, I didn't. Listen, y'all were part of—"

"What is this place?" someone else wailed. "Holy shit, I feel like someone was crawling all over me inside my head!"

Johnny raised his hands even higher. "Now, come on. Settle down—"

"There's no way out!"

"We're gonna die in here!"

"I think I stepped in shit!"

A shifter somewhere in the crowd took it upon himself to freak out and shift with an echoing snarl and all hell broke loose.

The victims newly jarred out of their combined unconsciousness shoved each other, screamed, snarled, and fought to get out of the throng. Attack spells launched wildly and careened through the space. More shifters turned wolf and no one listened to the bounty hunter who bellowed, "Y'all need to get your heads out your asses and calm the f—"

Three quick shots of gunfire cracked, and Johnny almost fell backward into the pit again. A rain of plaster and chipped concrete fell from the high ceiling of the warehouse but fortunately, nothing big enough to squash the hive-mind victims.

It was exactly what was needed to get everyone's attention again.

"Everyone stay calm!" Lisa shouted and holstered her pistol as she stepped out of the pit to join Johnny. The closest magicals backed away with wide eyes until they bumped into their neighbors packed so closely behind them. She drew her ID badge from her pocket and flashed it briefly. "I'm Special Agent Breyer with the FBI. I know what you're experiencing right now is shocking and terrifying, but I promise it's over now. My partner and I are here to help get you all safely home again."

"We are?" Johnny muttered.

She leaned toward him to whisper, "Maybe indirectly, I guess. Go with it." She raised her voice again. "But we can't do our jobs without your help. I need you all to stay calm. Perhaps you should sit. The better you can hold it together for a little while longer, the faster we'll get you out of here."

Someone began to wail—loud, ugly-sounding sobs from the other side of the warehouse. No one bothered to try to soothe whoever it was. They were all on the verge of doing the same thing.

Slowly—one by one at first but then in two and threes and smaller groups—the victims did as she instructed and lowered themselves to the floor. The space filled with a different kind of hum this time. It came from thousands of voices whispering to each other in hushed conversations instead of the tiny black box that had held so much destructive magic.

Lisa nodded and stepped into the pit to give herself some breathing space.

"Damn, darlin'." Johnny hopped down with her. "I half expected you to pull out some fancy gizmo, flash a bright-ass light, and wipe everyone's memories. But I reckon what you did takes the cake."

"Well, the Neuralyzer doesn't exist. But if you want to make life more like *Men in Black*, Johnny, be my guest. You'd be the guy to make it, after all."

He scowled at her. "The men in what?"

"Seriously? Never mind." She shook her head, pulled her phone out, and grimaced. "I guess I shouldn't have expected cell service down here but it's still a let-down."

"Lisa!" Agent Paulson stepped cautiously through the seated magicals with the occasional, "Excuse me," and, "Sorry. Sorry." The woman's eyes were wide and shimmered with tears, and her face had paled to the point where she looked like she'd pass out at any second. "Lisa. I'm so—"

She missed the step into the pit completely and stumbled over the edge onto the cushions.

"Hey, slow down." Lisa helped her to her feet and caught the shifter's shoulders to give them a reassuring squeeze. "Are you okay?"

"No." Ellis shook her head like she'd come out of a dream— which, in some ways, she had, although it was probably better described as a nightmare. "No, I'm not okay. I can't believe this."

"It's not your fault. You had no idea."

"Are you sure about that?" Johnny grumbled. "She seemed awfully aware of what was happenin' before she brought us down here."

"Johnny." Lisa scowled at him.

"No, he's right." Ellis nodded at the dwarf and swallowed thickly. "I was. Mostly. I...I can remember everything. I think it has to do with the fact that I was able to leave this fucked-up place. Oh, Jesus. I don't know who else the bastard got. Other agents. Lisa, this could be all over the Bureau at this point—"

"It ain't." Johnny cleared his throat. "The only reason they didn't sniff you out from the start was 'cause you were already here. Try walkin' into a fed office with that burned into you. See how far it gets you without bein' questioned."

The woman's mouth worked open and closed as her hand lifted slowly toward her chest. She peeled the top of her tank top away, looked down, and sucked in a breath. "It's real."

"Uh-huh. So is everythin' else you remember, I bet." After enduring a long, scathing glare from Lisa, he rolled his eyes and stepped precariously across the cushions to join the agents. "I knew there was somethin' funny when you showed up yesterday. I should've dug deeper, Paulson. It was this asshole's magic throwin' me off. There ain't nothin' wrong with you."

An unsure laugh escaped the shifter woman. "I wouldn't be so quick to make that statement."

"Yeah, well. After a couple of weeks on the sidelines, you'll get your head on straight again." Lisa nudged him again and didn't have to say a thing. He sniffed. "So, uh...sorry for bein' an ass. And everythin'."

"I would have acted the same way." Ellis proffered her hand and nodded. Her eyes shimmered with tears that wouldn't build more than a thin sheen. "We're good, Johnny."

He wrinkled his nose but took her hand anyway. *Lisa's stare might as well be made of those damn fireballs too.* "Yeah, we're good."

When Ellis released his hand, she didn't wipe it on her pants this time but ran it through her blonde hair instead. "I can't believe this. I...I need to call it in and get some of our people out here to help clean up."

"There's no service down here," Lisa said.

"Yeah, I know. But there's a huge server room in the hallway. I don't know how it works exactly, but of all the damn places to get strong Wi-Fi, this is one of them."

Johnny scoffed. "Are you shittin' me?"

The tiny smirk she gave him was much the same as those he'd seen when she was still a pawn for the hive-mind. "How do you think Crazik got that message broadcast to you and that worm?"

"Crazik?" Lisa asked.

At the same time, the dwarf muttered, "Oh, sure. She knows about that too."

"I told you, I remember everything, Johnny." Ellis dialed a number on her phone and raised it to her ear. "And Crazik? That's the bastard's name. Where is he?"

The partners turned slowly toward the pile of empty robes.

"Dammit, boys!" The bounty hunter clapped so hard, the crack echoed through the warehouse and made the confused victims jump. "Hey, sorry about that. Rex! Luther! I told y'all to leave it!"

"We had to check, Johnny."

"Yeah. Gotta make sure there's no more rats. You find any, Rex?"

"Nope."

The hounds trotted toward their master, their tails wagging.

"We did it, Johnny. Right?"

"Yeah. You boys did a hell of a job. I couldn't have done it without y'all." He reached down to scratch behind both hounds' ears before he cleared his throat and raised an index finger for them to sit. "Hell of a job."

"So...we get treats now, right?"

"Whole screwed-up case is over now, Johnny. So, time for treats."

"Not quite yet, boys."

As Agent Paulson stepped away to make the call of her career —and not in a good way—Johnny turned toward the crowd of muttering, whispering, groaning hive-mind victims seated on every square inch of the warehouse floor and stepped out of the pit.

"It might be easier if we call for them by name," Lisa suggested.

"Go ahead, darlin'. We already proved these folks ain't gonna listen to me."

With a snort, she joined him at the edge of the pit and gave his hand another squeeze before she called for the four kidnapped magicals they'd been looking for over the last several days.

CHAPTER TEN

While the extraction team guided the traumatized magicals out of the underground warehouse, Johnny, Lisa, and the hounds stood to one side of the manhole in the fresh air beneath the New Mexico sky. Rex and Luther sniffed enthusiastically, dug up the holes of desert critters, and ignored everything happening around them.

Talking to three shifters and a Wood Elf who'd been kidnapped and dragged across the country to get brainwashed wasn't a particularly easy task.

"Wait—what you mean you came looking for us?" Nina Williams asked and tucked her matted and disheveled dark hair behind her ear.

"Well, that's how it started." Johnny folded his arms. "Boots put the whole thing in motion."

"Oh, my God. Boots." Her eyes widened. "Is she okay?"

"She's doin' fine now, sure. Someone's lookin' after her at home."

"Uh-uh." David shook his head at the bounty hunter and federal agent who tried to explain what was a complicated situation. "You expect us to believe a dog sent you here to find us?"

Lisa shrugged. "Plus a few shifter packs and an armored worm that couldn't be killed."

"What?"

"Listen, those details don't matter right now," the dwarf added. "David, we know Chiron. He's the one told us about you and the other five of your little engineerin' squad goin' missin'."

"Chiron sent you too?"

"In a way. Your tech pals traveled from Philly to the Everglades lookin' for ya. And they're watchin' my cabin until Agent Breyer and I bring all y'all back safe and sound."

"No, forget it." The man gestured toward the small group of cold, hungry, and confused-looking magicals who listened to the discussion. "I'll call Chiron and let him know we're out. But I don't trust anyone."

"David, wait—"

"Let him go, darlin'." Johnny put a hand on Lisa's shoulder and held her back. "It's fine. The poor bastard's been through enough as it is." He nodded at Nina and the shifters from the warring Everglade packs—Magnus and Cassidy. "It's time to get a move on and get y'all home."

"Then why are we still standing here?" Cassidy muttered.

"Huh. That's a good point. Come on." Johnny whistled for the hounds to catch up and led them across the desert toward the parking lot. The freed magicals said nothing during the twenty-minute trek, and Lisa fumed for the first half until Johnny couldn't take it any longer. "What's goin' on, darlin'?"

She scoffed. "That's something of a loaded question, don't you think?"

See, this is why I usually ain't fixin' to date. 'Cause that tone says I'm supposed to already know and I ain't got shit.

He scratched the side of his face and cleared his throat. "Well, it might be if you told me what you wanted, I could do somethin' about it. I already apologized to Paulson—"

"This isn't about Paulson. Not really. Or you, Johnny."

"Huh. Well..." He couldn't think of anything subtle so he went with, "Then why are you so pissed?"

"Because you were right."

"Oh. I didn't know it was a competition."

"No, I mean about the department." She stared directly ahead and sighed heavily through her nose. "Hell, maybe the whole Bureau. I always thought you were blowing smoke up everyone's ass with all your talk about the FBI getting things wrong all the time. Like you were taking it all too personally and it would eventually blow over."

"I did take it personally, Lisa. I still do."

"Yeah, I know. And you have every reason to. Maybe even more reasons now, because I have no idea how I'm supposed to handle this." Lisa turned to look over her shoulder at the last of the victims being wrapped in blankets and given food once they had been examined by medical personnel sent in with the extraction team. "A federal agent, Johnny. Snatched and brainwashed by this Crazik Azrakan, and no one had a clue. Forget that she's a shifter. It could have happened to anyone. Do you have any idea how compromising that is?"

"Yep."

"It's worrying, Johnny. Ellis and I work in the same department—a different division, but still. I thought the department's screwups were specific to you—Dawn's case, the Red Boar, and how they handled it all." She shook her head. "And now with something this big? It's like everyone's become too complacent and they no longer even care."

"Or they have the wrong folks sittin' in those corner offices. Are you gonna talk to Nelson about this?"

"Are you?"

The dwarf gestured somewhat vaguely and shrugged as they reached the beginning of the sand-covered parking lot. "I already had my chance to beef at the whole damn Bureau, darlin'. I thought I'd let you have a chance first. But if you ain't fixin' to—"

"Oh, I'm fixin', all right."

He stopped and turned slowly to look at her.

When she realized what she'd said, she frowned and shook her head. "I mean I'll call him. I have so much to say."

"Yeah, I think you might."

Fortunately, renting an SUV meant they had enough room for three displaced magicals, two hounds in the back, and Johnny and Lisa up front. The dwarf started the engine and Nina cleared her throat. "Um…Mr. Walker?"

"Just Johnny, Nina. Nothin' else."

"Okay. Can we…"

Lisa turned to nod at the Wood Elf. "Go ahead. It's fine."

"It's only…I can't remember the last time I ate."

"Me neither," Cassidy added, folded her arms, and stared out the window at the nighttime desert. "It's freaky."

"Ooh, Johnny! Are they talking about treats?" Luther panted over the edge of the back seat and Cassidy gave him a disgusted glance before she leaned closer to the door.

"Come on, Johnny. She basically said she's starving!"

"Yeah, get Boots' two-legs a burger or somethin'."

"Hey, make it four. She needs four. We'll share."

"It's good to hear y'all still have some kind of appetite." Johnny glanced at the shell-shocked magicals in the rearview mirror but the only one who looked at him was the silent Magnus. "The best thing for ya is a decent meal. Do any of y'all know of a good place still open at…almost ten?"

It was a dumb question given that they'd been trapped underground for the duration of the time in the area. The three on the back seat remained perfectly quiet, the silence broken only by the hounds' excited panting and the thump of their tails against the sides.

"Yeah, I'll look for the closest place," Lisa said as she pulled her phone out again.

"Uh-huh."

They shoulda called this the Land of Disenchantment. I sure ain't comin' back after this.

They stopped at a truck stop outside Gallup to buy food for everyone, the hounds included. It wasn't surprising that the magicals they'd found didn't want to sit so closely together after weeks of being cooped up in the warehouse. Cassidy sat alone at a table in the dining area and stared at the Formica tabletop while she ate a sub sandwich.

What did surprise the bounty hunter—at least enough to make him curious—was that Magnus and Nina sat together at another table. The Wood Elf ate exactly like one would expect from a starving victim, but the shifter man picked at his food while he muttered to her in a low voice.

Johnny elbowed Lisa who was seated beside him in the booth. "What d'ya make of that?"

"What? Of two magicals who've been through hell together taking comfort in each other over a truck-stop dinner?"

"Yeah, that's what I thought." He placed his sandwich on the paper wrapper and stood.

"Johnny…"

"I'll be gentle, darlin', but somethin' feels a little off and I ain't ignorin' that feelin' again today." The two magicals didn't look at him until he pulled a chair noisily out across the table from them and sat. "Do you mind if I sit?"

Nina shook her head. Magnus raised his eyebrows.

"I know y'all have been through a hell of a rough patch over the last week or so. But I see you two sittin' here, talkin', tryin' to eat, and I think back to how we found you went missin' in the first place." He pointed at Magnus.

The shifter continued to chew slowly as he stared at him with a neutral expression. The elf, however, swallowed her mouthful and placed her sandwich down like she'd discovered it was filled with sand.

"Do you know how we found that out, Magnus?"

Nina glanced at the shifter beside her, but he didn't move or speak.

"Huge slashes all over Nina's home. Her blood all over the floor. My hounds sniffed out your scent and led us to your pack."

"Hey," Cassidy said from two tables over. "Leave them alone, will you? We've been through enough without an interrogation from a pissed-off dwarf trying to overcompensate."

Johnny darted the shifter from the Everglades' tourist pack a sidelong glance and sniffed dismissively before he focused on the other two again. "Y'all aren't sayin' somethin' needs to be said."

Nina leaned forward across the table and lowered her voice. "Do you think he kidnapped both of us to lock us up in that…place?"

"Well, that is an idea. Everythin' else the last few days has been as goddamn unlikely." When the Wood Elf's lips pressed firmly together and her eyes blazed with a flash of green-gold light, Johnny shook his head. "But no. I don't reckon Magnus here had anythin' to do with the kidnappin' other than bein' a victim of it. He was in your house before the bastards who snatched you ever stepped through the door and I wanna hear why."

She paled instantly and looked at the shifter beside her.

Finally, Magnus had something to say, but only after he took another bite of his sandwich and made Johnny wait while he chewed. "It ain't none of your business, dwarf."

"See, it is. 'Cause Lisa and I came out here lookin' for the three of y'all specifically. And David and the other magicals from Philly, of course, but they're doin' their own thing and I won't stop 'em. But y'all…" He wagged his finger from one to the other and narrowed his eyes. "Y'all about started a war between your pack and Cassidy's."

The shifter woman frowned when he nodded toward her.

"Now, I aim to finish this case. And that means takin' y'all back home so everyone gets peace of mind."

"We ain't goin' back." Magnus didn't blink.

"And why's that?"

Nina closed her eyes and exhaled a defeated sigh. The shifter looked at her and his eyebrows drew together in a mask of pain. "My pack will rip her apart if they find out."

"Find out what, Magnus?" Johnny leaned back in his chair and folded his arms. "I ain't tryin' to start another war and I sure as shit ain't gonna drop Nina off at home if she's in that kinda danger. But I can't help you if I don't know what I need to know."

Still seated in their booth, Lisa watched the entire exchange with her sandwich half lifted to her mouth while olives and pickles fell out of the end onto the paper wrapper with a splat. She glanced at Cassidy, and the shifter woman raised her eyebrows before she shook her head slowly.

"What did Nina do?" Johnny asked.

"Nothin'." Magnus raised his arm slowly and settled it around the Wood Elf's shoulders to draw her closer. "But I ain't givin' up what I love—not for Reggie, not for the pack, and not for what they want me to do."

Nina looked at her shifter lover with nothing but adoration, although the smile that trembled at the corners of her mouth was dampened by regret.

The dwarf wrinkled his nose as the truth sank in. *It would have been a hell of a lot easier if I'd known the goddamn truth from the start.*

Cassidy laughed and shook her head before she refocused on her meal. "You're screwed, man."

Magnus ignored her and stared intently at Johnny.

"Well." The dwarf sniffed and scratched his cheek through his beard as he thought things through. "I guess you have your mind damn set on what you want."

"There's no question about that," the shifter confirmed quietly.

"All right. Look, Nina still needs to go home. She has a terrified hound waitin' for her, one so loyal she almost gutted herself tryin' to get out and find help."

"Oh, God…" The Wood Elf blinked back tears.

"And I ain't fixin' to go back to Reggie and your pack and explain why the hell their Bearer ain't home where he belongs." He rapped his knuckles on the table and pointed at Magnus. "That's your job."

"They won't listen."

"Have y'all brought this up before?"

The elf shook her head and Magnus stared at his sandwich.

"Then you don't know what's gonna happen. Listen, I have a shitshow to clean up on my property and some smoothin' over to do with two different packs—not to mention the tech nerds campin' out on my lawn."

For the first time, the shifter looked thoroughly confused.

"But I tell you what." Johnny spread his hands in a gesture of reassurance. "If you want a neutral party sittin' in on your meetin' when you tell your shifters exactly what's goin' on—the whole truth—I can be there. And if they try anythin' after that, I'll do what I can to make sure y'all get shipped off on your little… love boat for two."

Cassidy snorted. "I hate sushi."

With a scowl, Johnny leaned forward an inch so Magnus knew he was serious. "But y'all are comin' home with us, one way or another."

The shifter gave him a firm, sharp nod and the bounty hunter stood with a loud scrape of the chair. He strode toward Lisa and took his seat at their table at the booth.

"That was…unexpected."

"Somethin' else we shoulda put together before this whole thing kicked off," he grumbled and lifted his sandwich. "We had our suspicions, yeah, but they were lost in the bigger picture."

"You mean Nina and Magnus? Well, yeah, everything makes more sense now." She smirked and readied to take a bite but paused to continue. "But I was talking about you and your offer to help them out if things go south. I don't know if I would have used 'love boat for two' as the perfect sendoff, though."

He grunted. "It came out, is all."

"Well, the rest of it was inspiring, Johnny."

When he glared at her, she grinned. "Yeah, all right. Whatever. I ain't fixin' to stand by and let the shit rain on any of them all over again. It's complicated enough already."

"True."

Johnny glanced at his hounds who sat obediently beside the table and watched while everyone ate. *There's no way Boots didn't tell 'em about her owner and a shifter.*

"Y'all didn't say anythin' about those two bein' together."

Luther licked his muzzle. "So? Hey, Johnny. You got a piece of ham dangling from that bread. I'll help you."

"We can both help," Rex muttered and his droopy, begging gaze shifted between Lisa's sandwich and his.

"And y'all didn't think that woulda been a good thing for me to know?"

"You didn't ask, Johnny." Rex stood quickly, whined, and sat again. "And Boots didn't tell."

Lisa eyed the dwarf. "Is everything okay?"

"Lotta secrets swimmin' around, darlin'. That's all."

"Right. We're not finished looking into them yet, are we?"

He met her gaze and shook his head as he took another bite of his food, dangling ham and all. *If she has a beef to settle with the feds, I ain't gonna stop her. Hell, I might end up stormin' through HQ at her side.*

CHAPTER ELEVEN

The next afternoon, Johnny and Lisa stood at the back of the half-ring of buildings that comprised the Everglades' local shifter den. They were close enough to hear everything Magnus repeated to his alpha and his entire pack. This included everything Johnny had already told them, the pack who'd come from the city, and the wide-eyed tech junkies from Philly before he released them from their house-sitting duties. They stood far enough away to not be too imposing and so they wouldn't disrupt the ceremonial feel of Magnus giving his statement in front of his pack.

"Have you ever been to Oriceran?" the dwarf muttered and leaned toward Lisa.

She shook her head. "I was born here and never felt the need to go. You?"

"Yeah, I've been there twice. I hated it."

A chuckle escaped her.

He gestured toward the gathered pack. "It's shit like this makes me wanna stay right here on Earth—old-ass Azrakan thinkin' their immortal and stealin' more magic than they should and makin' other folks pay for it. I tell you what, darlin'. I ain't leavin' this planet anytime soon, whether the gates are open or not."

"It's a good thing there's enough here to keep you busy, then."

"You bet."

Nina stood beside the rickety rocking chair someone had pulled out for her to use during the pack's discussions, but she couldn't bring herself to sit. She stared intently at Magnus' broad back on the other side of the compound, nibbled on her bottom lip, and frowned with concern.

These shifters had better get over themselves, or—

A cry of outrage rose from the gathered pack.

"Are you serious?" Reggie snarled. "A Wood Elf?"

"It ain't right!" a woman shouted.

"You can't go runnin' after whoever you want!"

"Get rid of her, Reggie."

"Yeah! That'll get his head straight—"

Magnus whirled and snarled at his shouting packmates behind him and his eyes flashed dangerously silver. "No one lays a hand on her."

"Quiet!" Reggie roared and the pack settled reluctantly. "Magnus, you have responsibilities here. We need our Bearer to—"

"If anyone touches her, I don't care what the hell any of y'all need." He pointed at his alpha who stood on the slanted stage in front of the low, wide main building. "Hurt her, you lose your Bearer. And we all know exactly who's been gunnin' to take my place."

Another round of shouts and growled snarls rose from the shifters. Reggie let them continue for a moment before he raised a hand to quiet them. "Your loyalty is to us first, boy. There ain't a way out."

"If you're tryin' to make me choose, I'll find a way 'cause I already made my mind up."

"She's an outsider."

"You're turnin' against your own, traitor!"

"Y'all shut up," Reggie shouted. "I can't even think. Johnny!"

The bounty hunter sighed heavily when the pack alpha pointed at him. "You know what the hell happened. I need to hear it from you again."

"Yep." He glanced at Lisa and she shrugged.

"You did offer to mediate."

"I didn't think they'd take me up on it, though. It had better be quick." Johnny strode across the packed dirt of the compound toward the gathering and grumbled under his breath.

Lisa approached Nina and put a gentle hand on the Wood Elf's shoulder. "It'll work out."

The elf shook her head. "They won't accept it. They want me dead and Magnus doin' the job he never wanted."

"As the Bearer?"

"Yeah. He doesn't talk about it much but I know it drains him. Whatever he can do that most shifters can't for their ceremony or whatever." The Wood Elf turned toward Lisa with tears in her eyes. "You shouldn't be here. They'll turn on you too."

She couldn't help but chuckle. "Not with Johnny involved. Trust me. He'll make sure everything works out."

"And if he can't?"

"He—"

"Goddammit!" the dwarf shouted from the stage beside Reggie. "Y'all got your heads so far up your asses, it's amazin' y'all can even breathe. For fuck's sake, Reggie. Make the damn deal and put it behind you. I ain't fixin' to draw this out all day. And if any of y'all gets it in your brains to try somethin', go ahead. It ain't been more than a few days since I scuffled with Aldo. I know he remembers how that turned out."

The shifters growled and shuffled their feet, and Reggie looked like he was ready to tear all of them apart himself. But the alpha clapped a hand on Johnny's shoulder instead and lowered his head to confer with the aggravated bounty hunter.

"Yeah, he'll take care of it," Lisa muttered.

"How did a dwarf get in with a shifter pack?" Nina asked. "Especially one out here?"

"Well…" She wrinkled her nose and simply told it how it was. "I think it's because he defeated one of their big guys unarmed."

"How in the world did he do that?"

"He wrestled a wolf. You'd better not bring it up with him again, though, huh?"

After half an hour of shifters shouting at Johnny and him yelling in response, the meeting came to an abrupt end when he leapt off the sagging stage and shoved through the pack toward the two women. "It's time to go."

"What's gonna happen?" The elf hurried after him and darted Lisa terrified glances. "What did they say? Is Magnus—"

"Magnus is fine. So are you."

"Then why are we runnin' outta here like a bomb's about to go off?"

Lisa snorted. "It's not out of the realm of possibility."

"No bombs." They reached Sheila, and Johnny jerked the driver's door open to get in. "Whatever this Glimmering is that's so damn important, they're doin' it right now."

"What?" Nina spun and started to head back, but Lisa caught her arm and shook her head. "He doesn't wanna do that anymore," the woman protested.

"That was the deal, Nina. You're safe. Magnus is safe. They let him off the hook as long as he keeps comin' back for this crazy-ass shifter hoodoo whatever-the-hell. I don't understand half of it but the bottom line is we gotta go."

"Why?"

"We're all outsiders here, darlin', and you have a hound waitin' for you at home. It's best to focus on that until Magnus arrives at your door."

Lisa all but manhandled her into the vehicle and he started the engine. Nina stared at him from the back seat. "They're lettin' him go?"

"It's part of the deal and I ain't fixin' to step foot back here again. They know what will happen if I do."

As Sheila accelerated away from the dirt lot at the end of the compound in a flurry of dust and small pebbles, the elf leaned back and ran a hand through her hair. A surprised laugh escaped her, and she turned to look over her shoulder as the compound buildings faded behind the cloud of dust. When she turned again, Lisa peered over the back of the front passenger seat and grinned.

"It told you Johnny always gets it done."

Boots wouldn't leave her owner's side while Johnny and Lisa enjoyed Nina's offer of iced tea. They sat out on the front porch of the Wood Elf's double-wide trailer, sipped the refreshing beverage slowly, and watched the two coonhounds leap and cavort around the manicured yard.

"Come on, Boots!" Luther shouted and spun in quick circles before he dove toward a bush. "You can't sit there forever."

Rex trotted around the side of the house and sniffed the grass diligently with his tail wagging. "Dude, give it a rest. It was a fling and that's it."

His brother snapped his head up and stared at the porch, where Boots lay beside Nina with her head in the Wood Elf's lap. "Is that what you told him?"

Johnny glanced at the Blue Heeler who was more than content now that her owner was safely returned and he smirked. *These damn hounds have their own drama, and I gotta be the one to listen to it.*

"Yeah, yeah, fine. I get it." Luther sniffed the bush with a little more interest. "I'm not clingy. You let me know when—hey!"

He shoved his head into the leaves, then growled and dug furiously at the base. "Rex! Rex! I found the rabbit!"

Johnny whistled shrilly. "Y'all get outta there. This ain't your yard."

"What?" The hound stopped immediately to look at his master. The rabbit in question scurried across the lawn, and Rex raced after it with a wild bay. "Wait, wait! That's mine!"

"Not if I get it first!"

They disappeared through the bushes lining Nina's yard and he shook his head. "Hounds."

"It's fine." Nina scratched absently behind Boots' ears and chuckled. "They can dig if they want to, Johnny. They deserve it."

"Yeah, that ain't the point." He slurped the tea and exhaled a contented sigh.

"I'm merely glad Boots found them and that they were here to keep her company." She took a deep breath and released it slowly. "Things feel like they might be able to go back to normal—after a while, at least."

"And if they don't, Nina, that's okay." Lisa nodded. "You've been through so much."

"Well, it's over now. I'm home." The Wood Elf looked at her guests and gave them a tight smile. "Thank you. Both of you."

"It's part of the job, darlin'." Johnny gulped the rest of his tea as the hounds barked, howled, and raced through the underbrush and the swamp behind Nina's house. "So if you have any friends who need help findin' someone or whatever—"

Lisa snorted.

"Is that funny, darlin'?"

"I told you this would be easier if you had business cards."

"Oh, sure. So I can slip a case on my belt and throw paper rectangles at folks instead of bombs?"

"What?" Nina stared at him.

"Nothin'. I ain't messin' with cards. But you know where to find me, Nina, if you or anyone you know needs an indie PI."

"I've…never heard that before."

"See?" Lisa smirked at him, then withdrew her buzzing phone from her pocket. "Excuse me. I have to take this."

She walked down the stairs as she answered and stopped only when she reached the center of the yard.

Johnny squinted at her. *Someone she don't want Nina to know about, or me?*

"Yeah," the agent said as she walked in a slow circle. "Yeah, and we told you everything we knew. No, because it didn't come from—hey. That's not our fault. Jesus, Tommy, you need to calm down."

With a grunt, Johnny set his cup down on the porch and stood. "'Scuse me."

"Sure."

He strode down the stairs and pointed at Lisa. "Put him on speaker."

"Johnny, he's—"

"Put him on."

She stabbed the screen of her phone and held it between them with a scowl.

"You got some fuckin' balls callin' her to blow your top like that, Nelson."

"Johnny?" Agent Nelson sighed heavily on the line. "Then you tell me. What the hell did you blow up in New Mexico?"

"My target." He shared a glance with Lisa and she shrugged. "Why? Your shifter agent on the ground out there didn't make a report?"

"No. It wasn't her case."

"It wasn't your case, either, asshole. It was ours. The only thing you did was send Lisa a name and number. You have no skin in this."

"Johnny, I need to know what's going on."

"The hell you do!" The dwarf stabbed a finger at the phone. "I told you to get off my ass, Nelson. I'm doin' this on my own, Lisa's my business partner, and there ain't a goddamn thing you can do about it. Y'all fucked up too many times already and now you done it again!"

After a long pause, Nelson lowered his voice. "What are you talking about?"

"Yeah, the fact that you don't know paints a pretty clear goddamn picture, don't it? Ask Paulson."

"She took immediate leave and won't answer my calls. You need to tell me—"

"I ain't tellin' you shit." Johnny spun away and stormed across the grass, seething. *I thought I was over this. The asshole shouldn't be callin' Lisa to ask what I did, anyhow.*

The agent raised the phone to her ear again. "You should get ahold of Ellis, Tommy. This runs deep. Yeah, I know you need more information, but I'm not the one who— Yeah. You already know what he'll say. Ha. I'm not deluded enough to think otherwise. Sure. I'll tell him. Hey, next time, take a breath before you call me, huh?"

She hung up and shoved her phone in her pocket.

"Tell me what, darlin'?"

"We need to pay HQ a visit. It won't be an official report but at the very least, we should give them a statement—"

"Aw, hell, Lisa. What's he got hangin' over your head, huh?"

She stared at him in warning. "Nothing."

"I ain't steppin' foot in there simply 'cause Nelson's guys are too incompetent to handle their business. I don't work for the feds, and I sure as hell ain't under the department's thumb. He can ask or demand all he wants, darlin'. I ain't doin' it."

"Okay, first of all, everyone knows you were never under the department's thumb, Johnny. Don't blow that out of proportion."

He scoffed and folded his arms.

"And second, I agree with Tommy. No, this wasn't a federal case, but it's a professional courtesy."

"Sure. We're handin' those out like candy now for no reason."

Lisa rolled her eyes. "Look, do you honestly think you can sit here quietly knowing a federal agent was vulnerable enough to get snatched by Crazik like everyone else? That the Bureau had no idea what was going on?"

"It ain't my fault they can't keep tabs on their agents."

"No, but it's our responsibility to tell them what we know so they can avoid it in the future. And if they don't, that's on them."

Johnny wrinkled his nose. "It's on them now."

"You know I'm right, Johnny. We need to give this statement or debriefing or consultation—whatever you want to call it—in person. Who knows how many feds were affected by the hive-mind? Or what kind of side effects there are? Ellis' deserves that much, and if there are others—"

"Shit." He nodded with a fierce scowl. "Fine."

"Thank you."

"But we're doin' this my way."

Lisa's eyes widened. "No. We will not blow FBI Headquarters up."

With a snort, he headed toward Sheila and whistled shrilly. "Get a move on, boys. It's time to head out!"

The hounds raced along the side of Nina's trailer, their tongues lolling. "Where we going now, Johnny?"

"Hunting?"

"Snacks?"

"Digging?"

"Maybe a nap. Yeah, I could use a nap."

The bounty hunter opened the back door of his red Jeep and slammed it again once the hounds had leapt inside.

"Johnny, I'm serious," Lisa called after him. "Johnny? Please tell me that's not what you're trying to do." She turned to the front porch and waved at Nina. "We gotta go. Call us if you need anything, okay?"

"Yeah, all right. Is everything okay?"

"We're about to find out."

"Wait, wait, Johnny." Luther poked his head through the back door as his master started the engine. "I didn't say bye to Boots."

"Then say it," the dwarf muttered.

"But...but I don't know if I'll ever see her again."

"Bro, she walked twelve miles half-starved to find us," Rex said. "If you can't make that work, she doesn't want to see you again."

"Bye, Boots!" Luther howled as Sheila raced away from the double-wide trailer. "Don't forget about me after all—what? Hey!"

Rex burst out laughing. "Oh, shit, bro. She's got some serious attitude issues."

"Yeah, tell me about it." The smaller hound licked his muzzle again. "My kinda bitch."

Johnny glanced at them in the rearview mirror and shook his head. *I don't even wanna know.*

CHAPTER TWELVE

"Okay, Johnny." Luther stood in the aisle of his master's private jet and snorted. "Since you don't even wanna be in DC this time, how about we stop and get snacks first?"

"Come on, Johnny," Rex agreed. "We all know how grumpy you get on an empty stomach. And how distracted Luther and I get when—oh, hey." He shoved his nose under one of the seats, then hunkered down to reach farther. "Bro, I think this is from the last flight."

"Yesterday? Johnny didn't give us snacks on the plane yesterday, either. Oh. Yeah, that's definitely from the last flight."

Johnny snapped his fingers and headed down the aisle as he slung his duffel bag over his shoulder. "Move it, boys. I don't wanna spend any more time here than necessary."

"Which is why we packed for at least a few days," Lisa said blandly as she pulled the handle of her roller carry-on up and followed him.

"Naw, that's 'cause I know Nelson. I told him we were comin' this mornin' but it don't matter. He'll put us up in another hotel, make us wait at least until mornin' to see him, then hem and haw all over the place until maybe we get in for this damn meetin' day after tomorrow. I told you I hate these trips to HQ."

"And you thought landing on a private airstrip that belongs to the FBI was a good way to open the conversation?"

He turned to smirk at her. "Naw. That's me flippin' the jet-sized bird."

The aircraft's captain stood at the front of the cabin with a friendly smile and took the dwarf's offered hand. "Johnny."

"Felix. You had your work cut out for you the last few days, huh?"

"That's what I'm here for."

"Still. You're doin' a fine job."

"Thanks, Johnny. Enjoy your time in Washington."

The dwarf snorted. "Probably not."

The roar of the jet engines filled the air as he, Lisa, and the hounds descended the rolling stairs pushed up against the aircraft. When he reached the bottom, he snorted at the sight of the driver he'd hired who stood in front of a black SUV with a printed sign that read *Johnny and Agent Breyer*.

"Look at this." He gestured toward the sign. "There ain't no one out here on the tarmac and he's still holdin' a sign."

"Did you pay him to hold a sign?" she shouted over the engines.

He shrugged. "Dunno. It was a driver package. At least he got it right and left Mr. Walker outta the picture."

Before he moved toward their hired driver for the stay in DC, he scrutinized the second black SUV almost identical to the first and folded his arms.

Lisa frowned at him. "Okay, I know you're trying to make a statement with the Bureau but I thought always driving was one of your rules."

"If anyone breaks my rules, darlin', it's gonna be me."

"Yeah, but why now?"

The driver's door of the second SUV opened, and Agent

Tommy Nelson stepped out in his usual nondescript fed suit. Black sunglasses hid his eyes.

The bounty hunter darted Lisa a knowing glance and gestured flippantly at the man. "That's why."

"You said he'd ship us off to a hotel."

"It's a good thing I came prepared."

Nelson frowned at the first SUV and the driver holding the sign as he approached the bounty hunter. "What are you doing?"

Johnny shrugged. "What I came here to do, Nelson. That's what you wanted, ain't it?"

"And you had to land your jet on this runway?"

"Yep. It cuts down on all the drivin'. Why are you here?"

The man ran a hand over his receding hairline and sighed. "I came to pick you up since you took the liberty of using the landing access no one expected you to use."

"Now what's the point of askin' for somethin' I don't intend to use?"

"Get in the car, will you?"

"Naw. Sorry, Nelson." The dwarf gestured toward their waiting driver. "We have our own guy. I appreciate you goin' to all the trouble, though."

He snapped his fingers and hurried to the other SUV, the hounds at his heels.

"No, you don't," Nelson muttered and looked at Lisa. "Is he still pissed at me?"

"He's pissed at the Bureau, Tommy." Her grasp tightened around the handle of her suitcase and she shook her head. "After what happened to Ellis, I'm starting to get pissed too."

"Lisa—"

"Save it for the meeting." She strode away in her partner's wake, her teeth gritted.

"I don't get reimbursed for gas, you know," Nelson shouted after them.

Johnny waited for the hounds to jump into the back seat, then turned and flipped Nelson the bird before he joined them. His profile vanished behind the tinted window. The agent sighed and slid into his own SUV to follow the chauffeured vehicle toward D.C.

"Like I'm part of his goddamn entourage. This is gonna be rough."

At FBI headquarters, Johnny burst through the door of the conference room and found Director Zimmerman and two other federal employees seated at the long table. "Well. Ain't this a party?"

No one responded.

Lisa and Nelson entered behind him, and while she took the seat closest to the dwarf at the head of the table, he opted to sit halfway down its length—closer to his colleagues but not exactly pitting himself against the team of independent contractors just in case.

The bounty hunter snorted. *Yeah, he's scared, all right. And he should be.*

The door closed on its own behind the hounds, who chose a corner of the conference room and spun in tight circles before they curled together on the floor. Director Zimmerman opened his mouth—most likely to object to two coonhounds in the room —but the man seated beside him tapped his arm and shook his head slowly. No one said anything about the animals.

"Agent Nelson." Director Zimmerman nodded. "I believe you organized this meeting. The floor's yours."

"Thank you." Nelson stood, stretched to the center of the table, and slid a small handheld audio recorder toward him.

"Huh." Johnny folded his arms. "I gotta hand it to you, Nelson. You beat me on the old-school gear with that one."

"Something tells me I'll regret not recording this," the man said blandly and pressed the record button with a loud click. "This is Special Agent Tommy Nelson, Department of Magicals and Monsters liaison to the Bounty Hunter Division. The time is eleven-oh-three am. Present are Director Zimmerman, Agent Clifford Holmes, and Deputy Assistant Director Jeff Potts. This recorded debriefing of Johnny Walker and Agent Lisa Breyer will serve as an acceptable deposition should the need arise. Johnny, do you consent to this recording?"

The dwarf snorted. "For the first time in over twenty years, you pull out the horse-and-pony show."

Lisa glanced warningly at him.

"I'm here, ain't I?"

"I need verbal consent, Johnny."

"Yeah. Sure. I consent."

"Agent Breyer?"

"Yes, I consent." She mouthed at Johnny, "Be nice."

He sniffed disdainfully and leaned back in the executive office chair.

"Thank you." Nelson placed the recorder on the table and turned toward them. "So. Talk about what happened in New Mexico."

"See?" The dwarf gestured toward the rest of the room with a sweep of his hand. "That's the whole problem. This didn't start in New Mexico."

The director and his aides exchanged confused glances.

"Well, Johnny, that's where it ended. So start at the begi—"

"I wouldn't be so quick to say it ended, either."

Lisa cleared her throat. "Okay, I'll start. Maybe we need a little warmup first."

His teeth gritted, the man nodded for her to continue.

"As I'm sure you all know, Johnny made the decision to start his own business as an independently contracted private investigator. And…bounty hunter."

The dwarf shook his head and glanced at the hounds curled in the corner. *I'd give plenty to be a sleepin' hound on the floor right about now.*

As expected, Lisa did most of the talking to explain the entire case she and Johnny had taken on their own. The others listened intently from the minute Boots appeared at his property to their investigation of Nina Williams' house, the discovery of the disappearances of shifters from two different packs, and how they'd stumbled into Chiron's emergency camp that had been terrorized by the unkillable armored worm.

Nelson stopped them at her description of the Oriceran rune burned into the chest of the shifter who'd pursued them through the swamp. "Hold on. You're saying someone is running around this planet using magic that was banned on Oriceran?"

"Well, he ain't anymore," Johnny muttered.

"We neutralized the source of magic that powered those runes and controlled the victims' minds," Lisa explained. "It appears that we also neutralized the Azrakan named Crazik responsible for it. He told us he'd lived through one other cycle of the gates opening and closing, and I don't see any reason to not believe him. It was very evident that he was extremely old and powerful."

"And he's nothin' but a lump of moldy robes now."

"So there's no proof of this...hive-mind's existence," Agent Holmes said. "Or an actual perpetrator to charge and sentence."

"No." The bounty hunter raised an eyebrow at the man. "But trust me. In this case, it's better the asshole shriveled up when we blew up his—neutralized the source of his magic. That don't mean there ain't proof."

"Such as?" Director Zimmerman asked.

"Such as the thousands of victims simultaneously released from a powerful and traumatizing violation of their minds, Director," Lisa replied. "Not to mention their basic rights. We can't say for sure that every magical involved was taken against their will from the very beginning but watching at least a thousand of them return to consciousness is proof enough."

"It's hearsay, though, Agent Breyer."

"Then talk to some of them."

Johnny grunted. "Like Ellis Paulson."

Nelson stared at him, and the other feds at the table looked completely clueless.

"Jesus, Nelson. You still haven't talked to her?"

"She's still not answering."

"Well, hell. That never stopped you before, did it? Go on and show up at her doorstep like you do mine. That'll get her to talk."

"Johnny," Lisa whispered.

"Right now," the man muttered, "Agent Paulson isn't here for this debriefing. You are. So tell us how she was involved in all this."

"Aw, for the love of—fine. Paulson was doin' her thing in Albuquerque—whatever undercover case she was workin'. She'd been there for a couple of months, right?"

"That's right."

"Yeah, well, she'd been body-snatched for a couple of months by the time we touched down in New Mexico." He leaned forward and thumped a fist on the table, one finger pointed at Nelson. "I knew somethin' was funny when we met. I didn't think it was 'cause the damn hive-mind had gotten to her first."

"That's impossible," Potts said and spoke for the first time. "No federal agent would—"

"It ain't impossible 'cause we were there. Paulson's a shifter. Apparently, shifters are the easiest to brainwash. Who knew?"

Nelson blanched and leaned back in his chair. "Do you have proof of Agent Paulson's...unwilling involvement?"

"It's right there on her chest," Johnny snapped. "The woman has the same damn rune branded into her as the one we found on the guy who thought trespassing on my property was a good idea."

"Is she still under the influence?" the director asked.

"There ain't no more influence. Crazik is gone. So is the hive-mind magic, but y'all have seriously bigger problems."

Nelson opened his mouth, took a quick breath, and shook his head. "We had no idea."

"I think that was the point," Lisa added.

"Every report Ellis sent back was normal—clean. The same as every other time she's been out in the field."

Johnny nodded. "But when she first arrived in New Mexico for this undercover job, you didn't hear from her for a while, right? I'm guessin' somethin' between four and six weeks."

The man's eyes widened. "Yeah. That's part of the process. She worked her way through the ranks and reached out to us when she thought it was safe."

"Yeah, well, guess what? I'd bet my airboat Paulson spent at least the first month not workin' that case but bein' shoved up against a hundred other brainwashed magicals in an underground warehouse seven hours outside Albuquerque."

"That part doesn't make sense," Lisa muttered. "Her partner would have noticed."

"Partner?" Nelson frowned. "She went in alone."

"Aw, shit." Johnny spread his arms in a gesture that denoted frustration. "Well, there ya go. She lied about that too 'cause she was bein' used like a goddamn puppet, and you people had no idea there was anythin' wrong. You still wouldn't have a clue if Lisa and I hadn't taken this case on our own to find out y'all are sleepin' on the goddamn job!"

Lisa touched his elbow. "Okay, Johnny."

Nelson smoothed his hair away from his forehead. "How could we let this happen?"

"I don't know, Nelson. You tell me."

While the bounty hunter liaison stared at the table and tried to process the new revelation, Agent Holmes cleared his throat. "I have a few more questions if you don't mind."

"I do, to be honest, but I ain't fixin' to come back here 'cause you forgot to check all the boxes. So shoot."

Lisa closed her eyes and took a deep breath.

Johnny glared at the feds as they played another round of Q&A, this time for minor details that were highly insignificant in the larger scheme of things. But at least he had an answer for every question, no matter how flippant they were.

Whoever gets to transcribe this is gonna have a hell of a laugh over it. Or shit themselves.

When the questioning finally ended, Director Zimmerman nodded. "Thank you. Agent Nelson, you can end the recording now."

The device clicked in Nelson's hand, and he dropped it on the table like he'd picked up a burning coal instead.

"Great." Johnny thumped his palm on the table and stood. "Now y'all can get to cleanin' up the mess you didn't even know you had."

"One more thing, Mr. Wa—Johnny." The director spread his arms in a conciliatory gesture. "I appreciate what you've said about the state of the department you've been working with off and on for the last few decades. I think also it applies to the Bureau as a whole."

"That's no surprise."

"I'd like to hire you, Johnny."

The conference room fell completely silent except for the heavy snores from Rex and Luther in the corner.

The dwarf scowled. "I already told you I'm done takin' federal cases."

"Not a federal case." Zimmerman glanced briefly at the aide beside him and shook his head. "I want to hire you as the independent contractor you are for an internal investigation within the Bureau. I want you to find out where the hell things went wrong."

"Uh...no." He pointed at him. "I ain't steppin' into Internal Affairs for y'all. No fuckin' way."

"I understand your hesitation." The director folded his hands on the table and for the first time, looked like he knew what he was doing. "But think about it. You're perfectly suited for the job."

"And why's that?"

Nelson caught the director's meaning and pinched the bridge of his nose briefly with a sigh. "Because you won't let anything slip through the cracks, Johnny. This would be your chance to turn the Bureau upside down. With permission."

Johnny stared at the federal employees who stared in return, their expressions expectant.

Bounty Hunter Division was all fun and games when they started it. Now they're gettin' lazy. The whole damn FBI's gettin' lazy.

He sniffed, turned away, and rolled the executive desk chair back to finally leave the table. "I'll pass."

"Item number four on your list, Johnny," the director added. "If you do this for us, we'll pay you with that."

The dwarf froze. *Yankin' my chain. That's all this is.*

"And now y'all are suddenly willin' to give me the one thing you couldn't?"

"The circumstances have changed."

He looked at a wide-eyed Lisa and grunted. "Naw. I got everythin' I want. But I'll think about it. Maybe."

His loud whistle pierced the conference room. Rex and Luther snorted, whipped their heads up, and blinked sleepily before they settled their gazes on their master.

"Come on, boys. Meetin's over."

CHAPTER THIRTEEN

Although Johnny had refused Nelson's offer to drive him anywhere while he was in DC, he couldn't pass up the opportunity to let the Bureau pay for a hotel suite for him, Lisa, and the hounds. It was nicer than the one they'd shared before and after the dwarf had stormed into FBI headquarters and delivered his list of demands.

Lisa sat in the armchair opposite the suite's kitchen while he flipped the sizzling bacon and scrambled a huge pan of eggs for their breakfast. "You're at least considering it, right?"

"You want me to consider playin' PI for the feds inside the feds? I ain't fixin' to be a part of that, darlin'."

"So what's the plan, then?" She set her tablet on her lap and looked at his back as he moved the spatula across the pan. "We've been here for two days already and even I don't know what you'll decide."

"I ain't decided yet."

"Well, how much longer do you need?"

He froze, then turned to look at her over his shoulder. "As long as it takes to make them squirm in their fancy desk chairs."

"Johnny…"

"Come on, darlin'. We're set up in this fancy suite on the federal dime. Hell, the Bureau paid for the eggs and bacon. I aim to enjoy it while I can. With you."

With a smirk, she stood and retrieved the stacked plates and silverware laid out on the kitchen counter. "I'd be lying if I said I wasn't already enjoying this a little."

"Good."

She set the table and he set the pans of breakfast in the center, followed by two glasses and a pitcher of orange juice. They sat and stared at each other for a moment before he gestured at the spread. "Help yourself."

"Johnny. Hey, Johnny." Luther slunk toward the table and his tail twitched from side to side. "You sure did cook a lot of bacon."

"Yeah, you have any grease left over?" Rex added and slid forward on his belly until his front paws stretched under the table. "We'll take anything at this point."

"Even a crumb."

With a smirk at Lisa, the dwarf took two pieces for each of the hounds and fed them from the table.

"You're the best!"

"It's still hot, Johnny. You know how to—"

Neither hound could talk while they devoured the bacon strips and began to sniff the floor around the table.

"That's all y'all get," he muttered. "You had your breakfast first thing this mornin'."

Lisa swallowed her mouthful of eggs and glanced at them. "I thought feeding dogs from the table was generally frowned upon."

"Not when it's me and mine, darlin'." He snapped his fingers and pointed to the living room of their suite.

"A little more, Johnny?"

"We're starving."

"Go on, boys. I'll get y'all somethin' else later."

"Yeah, yeah. You always say that."

"But he does follow through, Luther."

"Yeah, when we're already withering away."

The hounds trotted into the living room and looked over their shoulders at their master before they admitted defeat and curled together on the floor and licked their muzzles.

"So you don't know what answer you'll give them?" Lisa asked before she swallowed half of her orange juice.

The dwarf shrugged. "I'll find the right answer when it's time. So let's talk about somethin' else, huh?"

"Sure." They ate in silence for a moment longer, then she squinted at him. "What's this item number four Director Zimmerman mentioned?"

He choked on his eggs and washed them down with juice. "Somethin' else."

"Oh, come on, Johnny." She laughed and handed him a napkin as he brushed clumps of scrambled eggs out of his beard. "The Bureau gave you a giant tank of satellite radio tech—or whatever Margo is."

He smiled crookedly at hearing her call his newest machine by name.

"And a private jet with flight staff."

"And your continued salary while you get to be my partner, darlin'." He pointed at her. "Don't forget that one."

"I haven't. I also can't imagine what else you'd ask for that the director wasn't willing to give you the first time around. So come on. Spit it out."

"Naw. It ain't important."

Lisa placed her fork on her plate and leaned back in her chair. "If it's something you wanted, there's no way it isn't important to you."

Johnny looked at her and sniffed a little uncomfortably. *Now she has me all worked out and cornered. I can't say no to that look, either.*

He shoveled a forkful of eggs into his mouth to buy himself

more time, then mumbled around the mouthful, "It's a pipedream from a long time ago."

"Well, that's a start." She grinned at him. "Keep going."

Shit. And if she don't like the answer I give, I'm diggin' myself a deeper hole.

"You don't wanna hear about it in detail, darlin'."

"Why not?"

"It goes too far back. And I ain't fixin' to step down memory lane when the damn feds are tryin' to hold it over my head. Leave it alone." The words came out of him as a growl and he regretted the tone instantly.

Lisa stared at him for a moment longer, then began to finish her breakfast in silence.

Great. Now I done screwed this up too. Fix it, Johnny.

It took him until they were halfway through washing the dishes to drum up the courage. Or maybe it was Lisa's rigid back and the way she scrubbed furiously with the sponge and almost flung the plates at him to be dried that made the elephant in the room too big to ignore.

Johnny grunted. "Fine."

She remained silent.

"I'll tell ya, darlin'. Only 'cause I ain't fixin' to be murdered in my sleep before I get the chance to tell the feds to suck it." He thought that would have at least made her laugh, but she handed him the last dish and stepped away to dry her hands.

Quit tryin' to be funny or she might seriously try to kill you.

He put the last of the dishes away and ran a hand through his hair. "Item number four's another boat. Kinda."

Lisa raised her eyebrows. "And it's that hard to tell me about a boat?"

"Aw, hell, darlin'. It ain't only the boat part. It's the reason I wanted it in the first place." The dwarf scrunched his face up and couldn't look at her. *Now I sound like an idiot.*

When he didn't say anything else, Lisa nodded toward the

living room. "I'll sit with my tablet and read a book, Johnny. If you're ready to tell me what's going on with you, let me know."

She left him standing in the kitchen with a dishtowel dangling from his hand. He slapped it on the counter and strode after her to join her on the couch.

"I'm sorry I snapped at ya, darlin'."

Lisa shrugged and turned her tablet on.

He took it slowly from her hands and she didn't stop him. Carefully, he placed it on the coffee table. "I have a hard time talkin' about this with anyone, especially you."

"Why me?"

"'Cause whatever you and I got goin' on between us, I like the way it's headed." She finally looked at him and he shrugged. "It ain't somethin' I've thought about for a long time, you understand? Not since before my life got twisted up and torn apart."

"Johnny, I don't know how much clearer I can make it that whatever you did before we started working together doesn't matter."

Great. She's keepin' it about business. I already pissed her off enough.

She pulled her legs onto the couch and crossed them beneath her as she shifted to face him. "Whatever it is, you can tell me."

He didn't want to but he knew that if he didn't, whatever had developed between them over the last few months would change. Johnny rubbed his mouth and beard. "Shit. It wasn't only my pipedream, darlin'. I shared it with someone else."

Lisa raised her eyebrows. "Dawn's mom?"

"Letta. Yeah." He closed his eyes and sighed heavily. "We had plans to sail around in it, spend some time out in the Gulf, and take life slow like that. And we were close to gettin' it but it ain't been on my mind for years."

"Until you listed it as number four on the list of demands you slapped on Director Zimmerman's desk."

"Yeah…" Johnny scratched the back of his neck. "I wrote that list a long time ago and didn't go over it again. I only added the parts that concerned you."

Lisa laughed. "You didn't bother to read your blackmail terms?"

"Hell, don't call it that."

"I'm not saying you shouldn't have done it, Johnny. The Bureau owed you big time. They still do after what we found in New Mexico. But you blackmailed the FBI. That's the only word for it."

He couldn't hold back a small smirk. "I guess I did."

"And then you thought I'd be mad because you asked for something you'd wanted…what? Twenty-five years ago with the mother of your child?"

"I guess." He scowled at the couch and shook his head. "It sounds ridiculous when you put it like that."

"It's not ridiculous. I get it."

"Huh?" *If she's screwin' with me, I have no idea how to handle this.*

"You never said what happened to her and if you don't want to, that's fine. But it might be good to get it off your chest with the rest of it."

"Oh, boy…" He clicked his tongue. "Nothin' happened to her, darlin'. Or if it did, it happened too slow for me to see it."

She raised her eyebrows and waited for him to continue.

This ain't the kinda fun time I imagined havin' in a suite paid for by the feds.

"I guess Letta realized what she had wasn't what she wanted," he continued. "After Dawn was born, it got worse. I woke up one day with her gone and Dawn still in the crib, and a note sayin' she couldn't do it anymore."

Lisa sucked in a quick breath. "She left you both?"

He nodded slowly. "And I let her. I didn't even try to go after her, and it wasn't 'cause I didn't love her—"

"No, I know, Johnny." She caught his hand and squeezed it. "It's because you did love her. Trust me, I get it."

He froze. "Now that there don't make any sense."

"What? That I understand why you'd let someone go out of love instead of trying to cling to them forever?" Lisa chuckled. "Okay, sure. It might be hard to understand if I'd never had to do it myself but that's not the case."

"If this is the part where you tell me about some beau of yours you let run off into the wind, darlin', we ain't gotta go there."

"Beau?"

"Yeah. It means—"

"I know what it means, Johnny." She released his hand and lowered hers into her lap. A light flush crept into her cheeks and the tips of her ears. "It's not what you think."

"It ain't?"

"No. And you're not the only one who's made mistakes they regret."

"Well, I know that." He cleared his throat. "It sounds like you wanna tell me somethin' else that ain't all wrapped up in confusin' riddles, darlin'. So go ahead and—"

"I have a kid, Johnny."

He stared at her and for some reason, couldn't decide whether to widen his eyes or narrow them into slits. "Say what now?"

"A son. Hamish."

Johnny studied her warily. "I assume you ain't gonna tell me he's still little, but I can't get over you lookin' younger than twenty-seven."

Lisa snorted. "That's a nice round number—and wrong. He's grown now and has been for a while. About…oh, six years ago, he left. The last I heard from him, he seemed to be doing well."

"Where did he go?"

"To Oriceran."

The dwarf clicked his tongue and leaned away from her. "No shit."

"Yep. He wanted to 'see where he came from.' At least, that

was the reason he gave me. But he's more from Earth than I am. Still, I had to let him go to do his own thing."

"All right, now wait a second." The dwarf did the math in his head and couldn't make the pieces fit together. "How old are you, darlin'? 'Cause I can't tell if you're blowin' smoke or givin' it to me straight."

"Nice try." She batted her eyelashes at him and gave him a coy smile. "But you'll have to try harder than that to get my age out of me. I'm not lying to you, Johnny. The point is, I understand what it's like to let someone go when they no longer want to be around you. Or they'd rather be somewhere else. And I blame you for your boat-dream with Letta as much as you blame me for having a kid I don't talk about."

"Naw, darlin'. I'd never hold that against you."

"That's my point."

He patted her knee a few times, then turned away. "It's a helluva day for airin' dirty laundry, ain't it?"

"Which leads us to the Bureau's dirty laundry, Johnny." She grinned. "A perfect segue."

"Aw, hell. I thought we were havin' a moment."

"We were. It was great. Thank you."

The dwarf snorted.

"And now we need to have a different kind of moment, where I remind you why it's a good idea to take on this internal investigation and find out what's going on within the department. And maybe even beyond it."

"It ain't my job to clean their messes up, Lisa." Johnny removed his hand and folded his arms. "I've already spent too much time doin' that and it ain't payin' nearly enough."

They stared at each other before she leaned toward him with wide eyes. "Do you know why I became a federal agent in the first place?"

"It sure as shit wasn't for the fame and glory."

She fought back a laugh. "I'm serious, Johnny. I took this job because I wanted to be a part of keeping this entire planet safe along with everyone on it. Because I believed a government agency that could pivot with the reveal of magic and bring magicals on board to work together would make a difference."

"It does, darlin'." Johnny wrinkled his nose. "But maybe not the kinda difference any of us were hopin' for."

"That's the point. I've put my faith in the department for a long time—almost ten years now. And for the first time, I'm starting to wonder if I made the right choice now that I'm so closely tied up in this."

He pointed at her. "Naw, what happened in New Mexico wasn't your fault. Paulson wasn't your fault."

"It wasn't anyone's fault directly. I know. But how much responsibility do we have to use what we know?" When he shook his head, she scooted closer. "I'm not saying the way the department handled Dawn's death and the Red Boar wasn't a huge mistake. But letting their agents fall into something like the kind of control Crazik had over Ellis? With no clue what was happening? The people I've worked with for most of my career don't know what they're doing anymore, Johnny. Maybe they never did if they keep making bigger and bigger mistakes like this."

"Uh-huh." He stared at the ceiling. "And you're sayin' I do?"

"I'm saying we do. Come on. I've watched you operate the same way over the last four months. You're not the kind of guy who knows what has to be done but looks the other way." She chuckled. "And you're certainly not the kind of guy who passes up a chance to say, 'I told you so.'"

Johnny sighed. *This Light Elf's gonna be the end of me.*

"Hell, darlin'. You know I can't argue with that."

Her smile widened. "I told you so."

"Yeah, I know you been itchin' to let that one out for the last two days."

"Admittedly, it was hard to keep in until the right moment."

"Well, that's the only one you get." With a scowl, he removed his phone from his back pocket and pulled Nelson's number up. "Let's get this straight, though. If I do this, you're doin' it with me."

"I am your partner, Johnny."

"Uh-huh. Which means you'll have my back however I decide to handle this whole internal investigation bullshit."

Lisa stared at his cell phone and bit her bottom lip. "I have to draw the line at blowing HQ up, though. So promise me that won't be part of your methods."

With a snort, he activated the call to Nelson and lifted the phone to his ear.

CHAPTER FOURTEEN

Two days later, Johnny walked into Agent Tommy Nelson's office feeling like a million bucks. *It had better last. If Nelson don't come through with this one, I'm walkin' out.*

The man looked up from his desk when he barged in with the hounds at his heels. Lisa walked slowly through the open door behind them. He snatched a folded sheet of paper off his desk and waved it at the dwarf. "Do you know how many hoops I had to jump through to get this for you ahead of time?"

"Not enough to prevent you from doin' it." He snatched the paper and waved it in the agent's face in return. "Does it have everythin' on it?"

"Why don't you take a look for yourself?"

"Naw. I wanna see you tell me to my face this right here has all the specs, buildin' requirements, and a team to start workin' right now already signed off on."

Nelson glanced at Lisa, who shrugged with her hands in the pockets of her light zip-up sweatshirt. "Yeah, Johnny. You made it perfectly clear what you wanted. Three times. And Director Zimmerman signed off on the whole thing."

"Good." Johnny slid the paper into his back pocket and

nodded. "If I find anythin' fishy about the way y'all are carryin' out your end of the deal, y'all are on your own."

"I understand how agreements work. Thanks."

"Don't mention it." He turned away from the desk and gestured with a smirk for Lisa to join him in the hall again. "And don't let any of your guys get in my way. This is what y'all wanted."

Nelson tapped his fingers on the desktop. "As long as the building's still standing at the end of it, you have free reign."

"I ain't interested in the buildin', Nelson. Only the dirt caked in it." The bounty hunter strode down the hall without another word.

Rex and Luther growled at Nelson and bared their teeth in snarls. "Better not screw this one up, buddy."

"Yeah. If Johnny says the word, I'll bite a hole in your other ass cheek."

Their master snapped his fingers and both hounds turned to trot obediently out of the man's office. Lisa stayed long enough to nod at the agent, but she didn't have anything to say to him now. No one bothered to close the door behind them, and once he was alone in his office, Nelson slumped in his chair and ran a hand through his thinning hair.

"This is either the worst mistake we've made or the best choice," he muttered.

Out in the hall, Lisa caught up to Johnny. "What was that?"

"What was what?"

"That paper. Tommy looked like he was about to keel over when he handed it to you."

The dwarf smirked and shook his head. "I'll explain it all to you later, darlin'. It ain't important right now. We have some interrogatin' to do."

"You mean investigating."

"Sure. If that's what you wanna call it."

She stopped in the hall and stared after him. "Johnny? Johnny, tell me you're not serious. Hey."

"We're independent contractors, Lisa. We do this our way or that's it. Game over."

With a heavy sigh, she nodded at a woman who passed them in the hall with wide eyes when she saw the dwarf, his two alert coonhounds, and the explosive disks and utility knife strapped onto his belt. *He means his way. This will certainly be interesting.*

Director Zimmerman had a list waiting for them—every single agent and federal personnel even remotely involved in the Department of Monsters and Magicals, including the Bounty Hunter Division, of course. Johnny thought it perfectly fitting to start with Agent Clifford Holmes, who'd sat in on their debriefing turned hiring opportunity with the FBI Director.

"This wasn't an invitation to storm into my office," the man grumbled as the dwarf and his hounds arrived unannounced.

"Ain't no one exempt from this investigation, Holmes." Johnny grunted and took a handful of books from the heavy, expensive-looking shelves before he rifled through them. "I might as well start at the top, understand?"

Holmes looked at Lisa for reassurance—or maybe he expected her to tell him the bounty hunter was joking—but he found no comfort there. She folded her arms, leaned against the doorway, and let Johnny do his thing.

They found nothing with Agent Holmes and moved on to the next top-level special agent in the Department, then the next, and the next. Johnny battered them with questions. How long had they worked here? Where were they before they joined the FBI? What were their daily tasks? He asked for lists of criminal informants, most recent cases marked as solved, and open cases with high-level clearance—which, of course, he'd been granted access to for the investigation.

The seventh agent who became the subject of the investigation, a wizard named Carlyle Maldonair, became a little mouthier with the dwarf than he should have and was shoved against the wall in the break room. The huge jug of the water dispenser wobbled on its stand when the agent's flailing hand smacked against it. It responded with a burbled grumble as a huge bubble rose from the bottom and the container rocked even more violently.

"You don't get to tell me how to do my job," the bounty hunter told him forcefully and the man stared at him with pure hatred. "I'm callin' the shots on this one, understand?"

"You're not one of us," Maldonair snapped.

"Damn straight, I ain't—and proud of it. Now, are you gonna hand your active case files over or do we need to do this the easy way?"

The wizard stared at him in confusion. "I think you have the whole interrogation process backward."

"Naw." He thumped him against the wall again. "I meant easier for me. Way harder for you, pal."

The agent provided a stack of his four open cases twenty minutes later before he scuttled out of the conference room the dwarf had commandeered and turned into his private office. Johnny smirked when Maldonair closed the door behind him and he pulled the case files toward him across the table.

Lisa tapped her pen against the notepad she'd carried around and watched him rifle quickly through the cases. "You're not doing yourself any favors by roughing up federal employees. And you're certainly not making any friends this way."

He snorted. "I never had any real friends in this agency anyhow, darlin', 'cept for you. And I ain't tryin' to make more." He slapped the last case file closed and nodded at her. "All these chumps are as meatheaded as Nelson. They are completely clueless and that makes 'em useless. None of 'em has the balls to be a mole. Who's next on the list?"

She sighed and gave him the next name. *And here I am, playing secretary for the bounty hunter hell-bent on turning the department inside out.*

Two more agents in the next two days had a particularly difficult time answering the questions and cooperating by putting whatever they had at the dwarf's disposal. Johnny thrust one of them over the edge of the table and drew his utility knife on him. The second agent—who'd stepped into the makeshift office as the interrogation was getting heated—tried to intervene.

Both ended on the floor with bloody noses but they told him everything he wanted to know after that. Unfortunately, none of it was useful.

By the end of the fifth day, the bounty hunter had used his personal brand of questioning on every single agent in the Department of Monsters and Magicals, the cleaning crew that came in at night after office hours, the three interns—one of whom ran away afterward and almost didn't make it to the bathroom—and the Hispanic woman who arrived every Tuesday afternoon with her wheeled cart of homemade tamales sold by the half-dozen.

"Was that necessary?" Lisa asked and frowned in concern as the woman scampered down the hall and cast terrified glances over her shoulder.

"I ain't lettin' anythin' through the cracks." Johnny grunted and opened the thin paper wrapper of a tamale he'd paid for after the woman had told him everything she knew in broken English. He took a huge bite, chewed thoughtfully, and nodded. "The only thing she's guilty of is makin' a damn fine…whatever this is."

"They're tamales, Johnny."

"Sure. Want one?"

She stared at him and shook her head.

"Suit yourself."

"Johnny. Hey, Johnny. Those smell good." Rex and Luther sat at their master's feet and licked their muzzles.

"Yeah. We've done a great job of interrogating. Come on."

"Sorry, boys. I'm sure there ain't a single type of Mexican food that don't have onions in it." He shoved the rest of the tamale into his mouth, jiggled the plastic bag filled with the other five, and stepped into his office. "Who's next on the list, darlin'?"

"Well, I..." Lisa ran her finger down the last sheet of the stapled pile. "You haven't talked to the IT team yet."

He snapped his fingers and tossed the bag on the table. "That's right. Let's go. IT guys callin' themselves techies oughtta be hidin' somethin'."

"Johnny, they work with computers all day—"

"And update the systems and enter information. Hell, I bet they have private recordin's of every conversation comin' in and out of the phone lines here. Huh. I shoulda maybe started with them." He hurried past her and left the conference room, the hounds at his heels.

With a sigh, Lisa stood and prepared herself for another round of his unique investigative skills. But when she entered the hall, she knew immediately that something was wrong.

Agents and personnel ran past them down the corridor toward the large room almost like a lobby that served as the space for department-wide meetings. Phones rang off the hooks. The federal employees who'd learned over the last five days to avoid Johnny Walker and his low-growling coonhounds didn't pay them any attention as they hurried past, answered their cell phones, and shouted at one another.

"We gotta get our people on the ground out there now!"

"Get Emergency Response on the line."

"O'Malley! Where the hell's O'Malley? He was supposed to have his eyes on the location."

A woman in a pantsuit and loudly clicking pumps stormed past the dwarf and he stepped aside with barely enough time to avoid being run over while she focused instead on her tablet and snapped orders through a Bluetooth headset. He turned and raised his eyebrows at Lisa. "That ain't good."

"No. Come on."

They followed the wave of agents moving through the halls until they reached the open central room. Nelson was there amid the sea of chaos and ringing phones, his cell phone pressed to his ear as he scowled and listened to whoever had called him. Johnny reached him as the man ended the call. "What's all this?"

"We have a serious issue." He glanced at Lisa and cleared his throat. "We've been attacked."

The dwarf pointed at him. "I'm tellin' you right now, Nelson, I ain't had nothin' to do with it—"

"Not HQ, Johnny. I know. One of our engineering labs in Saltsburg, Pennsylvania, was the target—they were assaulted with serious firepower."

"An engineering lab in Saltsburg? Why the hell didn't I know about this?"

"Because it's in Saltsburg. And we're not investigating the Engineering Department."

"Well, now you are, ain'tcha?" Johnny folded his arms and scowled at the FBI personnel who raced around the room and tried to gain control of the situation any way they could. "Who was it?"

"We have no idea, Johnny." Nelson gestured toward the chaos. "That's what we're trying to find out. But we need to get a team out there ASAP and I..." He grimaced and finished with a frustrated hiss. "I have a bad feeling about this."

"Oh, yeah? Someone blowin' up your top-secret gear lab? Go figure."

"It's not only the attack." He grasped the dwarf's shoulder, led him away from the center of the action, and lowered his voice. "I know it's impossible but this looks like Omar."

The bounty hunter slapped the man's hand off his shoulder and stabbed a thick finger in his face with a scowl. "Don't fuck around with me like that, Nelson. Omar's dead."

"Do you think I don't know that? Listen, the way the lab was attacked has Omar's signature all over it. He didn't come back from the dead, no. But I think we might have a copycat on our hands."

"Goddammit, that's even worse." Johnny snarled in disgust.

"I know." Nelson looked at Lisa as she approached. "And we need—"

"Johnny!" Director Zimmerman stormed through the mass of scurrying, talking, shouting agents. "What have you found?"

"Besides your labs gettin' blown up? Nothin' yet, Director."

"Agent Nelson, do you have a team out there yet?"

"No, sir." Nelson glanced at Johnny. "I just got the first-response details. This looks like a copycat."

The dwarf grimaced at the word. *Who the hell would be copyin' a dead guy and blowin' up FBI sites?*

"Copycat of whom?" The director scowled at all three of them.

"It looks like someone knew Omar as well as we did," the agent muttered.

"I have no idea who that is."

"Johnny and I knew him."

The director pointed at Johnny. "Then that settles it. Johnny, I want you and Agent Breyer out in Saltsburg right now."

"You wanted me to dick through your payroll list," the dwarf protested.

"And now I've changed my mind. Get him out there, Agent Nelson. We need to move on this yesterday." Director Zimmerman glanced warily at the hounds before he turned on his heel and strode away to make more decisions elsewhere.

"He doesn't like us, Johnny," Luther said with a growl.

"I don't think anyone likes us right now," Rex added. "Good."

"Just like that?" Johnny gestured toward the retreating director and grunted. "The independent contractor gets shucked around from one unfinished job to the next?"

"You're the one who knew Omar best, Johnny," Nelson

replied. "And this isn't the first time we've encountered something that looked like Omar twenty years after the fact."

"Are you tellin' me this copycat's been workin' y'all for a while and you ain't done nothin' about it until right now?"

Nelson swallowed thickly. "Yep. You could say that."

"What the hell's goin' on here?"

"Listen, Johnny. The last few places were nothing huge. We thought whoever it was, they were blowing off steam. We tried to follow the guy quietly to see where he was headed next—"

"And y'all failed big-time on that one, didn't ya? 'Cause now, the asshole blew up your biggest location for makin' all the junk that passes as tech around here."

"I know." Nelson sighed heavily and pinched the bridge of his nose. "And it's a good thing you're already here because no one else in the Department knows more than you do about how Omar operated. We need you on this."

Frustration etched on his face, the bounty hunter scratched the side of his face through his thick beard and finally rolled his eyes. "Fine. Get me everything you have on that lab in the next twenty minutes. Then we're headin' out to Saltsburg, of all places."

"Right." Nelson reached out to shake but quickly lowered his hand when the dwarf turned away from him and snapped his fingers for the hounds to follow. The agent yanked his phone out to get the info he needed.

Lisa stepped around a group of agents who all but ran down the hallway. She rejoined Johnny, her face set in a frown. "Who's Omar?"

"Someone else from the past."

"Like another old bounty coming after you?"

"Not quite, darlin'."

CHAPTER FIFTEEN

Two hours later, they were in the air again on the private jet en route to Saltsburg, Pennsylvania. Johnny pored over the detailed information Nelson had printed for him. The agent had known he wouldn't be bothered to read up on the engineering lab in question on any kind of device whatsoever. Instead of his usual four fingers of whiskey that stood on the tray table, he drank from a Perrier bottle that had also been stocked on the jet.

"Okay, Johnny." Lisa scanned the papers he'd set aside after he'd read them. "We'll go in together to catch the guy blowing up high-security federal labs. I think now would be an excellent time to tell me what we're looking at."

"We're lookin' at a bastard who thinks he's bein' cute."

"This Omar guy?"

He shook his head. "No. Omar's been dead almost twenty years."

"Hmm. That's where the copycat part came in." She ran a hand through her hair. "Who was he?"

"It don't matter, darlin'. He's gone. We're lookin' at someone else."

"But if Nelson and Director Zimmerman both think this perp

is following in Omar's footsteps, it's kind of important for me to know about the original, don't you think?"

"Not really."

"Johnny." Lisa placed her hands on the stack of papers and forced him to stop reading. "Hey. I can tell when you're avoiding telling me something, which means it is important. And it doesn't help either of us for me to go into this blindly while you know exactly what we're up against. Right?"

He sighed heavily and leaned back in his seat. "Fine. You ain't gonna like what you hear, though, and I ain't gonna like sayin' it."

"Okay. I've officially been prepared now."

"Uh-huh." He glared at the back of the seat in front of him, ran a hand through his hair, and sipped his bottled water slowly. "All right. Omar was an old CI of mine when I first started workin' with the department way back when. He was half-wizard, I think. Anyway, he outsmarted me a few times before I finally got him to make a few deals. They would get him off the hook so I could nail a bigger jackass runnin' all over to avoid a bounty on his head."

"Yes, Johnny. I do know how informants work."

"Right." He sniffed. "We got to know each other well after a while. I could count on him for almost anythin' I needed. You might even say we got to be friends. He wanted out of the crime life so I helped him and took the guy under my wing. I taught him everythin' I knew about bounty-huntin'. Even Nelson took a likin' to him and after that, Omar was with me on every case."

"He was your partner."

"Unofficially, yeah." With a grunt, Johnny shifted uncomfortably in his seat. "I ain't had to dig all this up since it happened, darlin'. Now, I'm lookin' an Omar copycat in the goddamn face and it's all blowin' up on me."

Lisa studied him and gave his arm a gentle nudge. "What happened?"

"He died and I'm the one got him killed." He gritted his teeth and stared directly ahead. *If I look at her now, I think I'll lose it completely.* "We went on a case together—a regular job that was supposed to be easy. But we stepped into the wrong minefield at the wrong time and that was it."

Her eyes widened. "Not a literal minefield, right?"

"That's a figure of speech, darlin'. We got caught up in this case way over our heads. Omar wasn't anywhere near prepared enough to handle it, and I wasn't on top of my game enough to help him at the last minute. It's my fault he's dead." Johnny swallowed thickly and cleared his throat. "I knew he wasn't ready but I needed help and I pushed him into it anyhow. Omar's the one who paid for it."

"Johnny, I'm so sorry."

"Naw, it's my damn fault." He finally looked at her, his fist clenched tightly around the green glass Perrier bottle. "I kept goin' backward and forward over whether I did the right thing by helpin' him or if I should have left him where he was as a CI and called it good."

"You helped him out of a life of crime. That's something to be proud of."

"Is it? When it turns out that everyone I try to help or to teach how to be better turns up dead or hurt or skippin' out on me entirely?"

Her mouth opened but the words hitched in her throat and she studied his jaw muscles as they worked tightly. "This is about more than Omar, isn't it?"

"Damn straight it is." He shifted again in his chair. "Now, I'm wonderin' whether or not I made the right choice with Amanda too. I did the same thing with her, you know—took her under my wing and showed her the ropes."

"You don't take Amanda with you on high-priority cases, Johnny. She's in school—the school you built for her. And don't try to pretend you would still have done it if Amanda wasn't part of the picture."

"Huh. I guess you're right about that one, darlin'. I don't know what I'd do with myself if I made the same mistakes with her. If I pushed her so hard that she thinks she's invincible now or if I steered her the wrong way."

"You did more for Amanda than anyone else could have." Lisa took his hand and interlaced their fingers. "The Bureau wanted her, Johnny. I can't imagine what life would be like for her now if you hadn't stood up for her."

"Yeah, well. I did that with Omar too, didn't I?" The dwarf met her gaze for a moment, then snorted. "And now you know what I do to partners, darlin'. They all end up in a gutter somewhere."

"You won't get rid of me that easily." With a smirk, she released his hand and returned her attention to the hastily compiled writeup of the FBI engineering lab that had been attacked and the analysis of the event. "So how is this guy copying whatever Omar used to do?"

"He was something of an explosives dabbler." Johnny smirked. "It might be why we got along so well from the start."

"You don't say."

"There's a pattern here. It's the type of explosives—magi-tech related like mine. But the combo of that and the order in which this new copycat detonated the explosives..." He waved a hand over a quickly reconstructed image of how the department assumed the attack had progressed. "We're gonna go in there and find this same pattern, I think. A strike in the back first to catch everyone's attention and give anyone inside time to get out. After a set amount of time, all the exits are targeted next. Finally, the central explosions on the real meat of the site."

"The meat?"

"The important stuff, darlin'. The thing is, whoever did this wasn't lookin' to hurt anyone only to give 'em a warning to get out before he destroyed the gear and tech and probably all the computers and server systems. He was essentially wipin' the whole lab clean so there's nothin' left."

Lisa responded with a low whistle. "I hope they used backups."

"Well, it's the FBI's high-security engineering lab. It could go either way."

She snorted. "I guess we'll see. And you honestly think this guy will be easier to apprehend once we confirm it was a copycat attack?"

"I sure do." Johnny rubbed his mouth and beard. "Anyone who can't get creative enough to make their own brand of trouble ain't creative enough to give us the slip either. We'll find him."

They didn't even have to step out of their rental car in Saltsburg and investigate the engineering lab to see the damage. It was obvious from a mile down the frontage road leading to the high-security site, and the guards stationed in the gate towers looked pale and worried when they let the two partners through.

He parked at the far end of the lot between two emergency response vehicles and the shredded chunks of asphalt that lined the other side of the area. The federal lab employees wandered around and were examined by medical personnel, and some still wiped dust and blood off their clothes.

Johnny got out and opened the back door for the hounds, who headed immediately to the destroyed site. When Lisa closed the passenger door, he nudged her arm gently and nodded at the two brutish-looking guys who approached them. "And this is the part where we get crap from the muscle 'cause word don't travel fast enough."

"They can't stop us." Lisa moved toward the destruction zone and one of the bulky men in a suit jacket and jeans held his hand out to stop her.

"I can't let you go past here, folks."

She retrieved her ID badge and flashed it at him. "We were sent here to take a look at the damage."

The second guard nodded at Johnny. "You got an ID too?"

"No. I have a license and Director Zimmerman's blessing."

The dwarf muscled past them and pointed ahead to Rex and Luther. "And no one touches the hounds. They're with me."

Lisa shrugged at the men and followed Johnny toward the piles of rubble—all that was left of the once long rectangular building that housed the engineering lab.

They negotiated a careful path through the destruction and their shoes crunched on broken glass, tiny pieces of metal, and a considerable amount of plaster and charred debris. Some of the building's structure remained in the places left almost untouched by the explosions, and they passed in and out of sections where the roof and walls had been left intact.

Johnny snapped his fingers. "We're lookin' for magical leftovers, boys. Anythin' you can sniff out that ain't gear and fire, got it?"

"Yeah, Johnny. We're on it."

"No problem, Johnny. Magic and tech." The hounds sniffed enthusiastically and a moment later, Rex raised his head with a sharp yip. "Hey, Luther. I think this used to be the lunchroom."

"Ooh. Bet they stocked it up pretty well—"

Johnny's whistle cut them short. "Trackin', boys. That's it."

"Yeah, yeah. Right. Tracking."

They disappeared behind more piles of broken beams and shattered stone walls. The bounty hunter stopped to examine one of the blast points where a bomb had been detonated and had taken six feet of the ceiling and the entire outer wall with it. He stooped to look at the charred remains and shook his head. "What'd I tell ya, darlin'? Look here."

Lisa joined him and frowned at the rubble. "It's all destroyed. What was this room supposed to be? An armory?"

He picked up what could have been the broken end of a firearm and flicked a metal badge that had been welded to the side of it in the explosion. "It says right here, *Laser Projectile – Mach 1.* I assume these were prototypes."

"Laser projectile?" She frowned as he tossed the destroyed

metal hunk onto the pile of crumbled walls and shelving. "Like what Chiron and the magicals from Philly used to fight that worm?"

"It looks like it." Johnny snorted. "What did I tell ya? The feds ain't never been at the front line of invention and ingenuity. They're still tryin' to get somethin' to work that's already been perfected by someone else. I only wish I'd thought of it first."

"Johnny!" Luther uttered a wild bay from what would have been the hallway outside the prototype room. "Found something!"

"Smells awful, Johnny," Rex added with a bark.

"Yeah, and not the kinda awful we like."

"Definitely magic. And something else."

Johnny nodded at Lisa. "The hounds found somethin'."

"What?"

"Dunno."

They scrambled carefully over the debris and leapt aside when a few damaged electrical wires sparked and hissed at them. Unscathed, they reached the hounds, who were both huddled over a dark puddle on the ground, their tails sticking up in the air.

"What's this now?" Johnny asked.

"No idea, Johnny. But it's gross."

"Kinda smells like blood," Rex added and sniffed it warily. "Or gasoline?"

"What?" The dwarf snapped his fingers and shooed Luther away from the puddle. "Boy, if you start tryin' to eat this, I swear I'll be at the end of my rope. Then you're goin' to the vet."

"Crap." Luther whined and took two steps backward. "I only wanted to see what it is, Johnny."

"Yeah, I know. That's what we're doin' here."

Lisa stopped beside him and squatted in front of the dark pool that looked like blood and oil combined. Opalescent swirls traced through it but the coloring was more red than black, and when she stuck a broken piece of drywall into it, she had to tug especially hard to free it again. "It's like tar."

"Uh-huh." Johnny sniffed and crouched beside her to get a better look. "And that there—that ain't like the rest of the tech blown up in this place."

A glittering piece of segmented metal parts was half-submerged in the substance and it glowed with a faint, flickering silver light.

"I think this is the bomb itself."

"Johnny, don't touch it. You don't know—okay. Fine. Go ahead and touch the weird substance and the glowing tech. If you blow up, don't say I didn't warn you."

"It ain't gonna hurt me, darlin'." He removed a plastic baggy from his back pocket and opened it to drop the piece of abandoned tech inside. "But it is evidence."

"Since when did you start carrying evidence bags with you?"

He shrugged. "Since your bosses put me on interrogation duty."

"Huh. I'm not so sure they're my bosses anymore," she muttered.

"Well, think of it this way. You still have a fed ID to flash at boneheads tryin' to get in our way." The dwarf sealed the baggy and held it up to inspect the contents more closely. Finally, he stood and sniffed the black-red sludge that coated his fingertips. "Ugh. Yep. Engine oil and blood. What else does this smell like to you?"

Lisa was completely unprepared to have evidence-coated fingers thrust under her nose, and she almost fell backward when she jerked away. "Jeez. Don't put that in my face. I have no idea what it is."

"Humor me, darlin'."

She took a tentative sniff. "I don't know. It kinda smells like… raw meat?"

"See, Johnny?" Luther tried to sneak back toward the puddle

but backed away immediately when his master gave him a warning glance. "It smells awful with something kinda good in there underneath."

"And magic," Rex added.

"Kinda like meat, huh?" Johnny wiped the sludge onto a pile of crumbled bricks and nodded toward the front of the destroyed lab. "If this has any bio components as the actual bomb, we're lookin' at somethin' I ain't never seen before."

"Okay. Do you know someone who would recognize it?"

"I probably do. But first, I wanna talk to the folks here who saw a hell of a lot more than either of us did."

CHAPTER SIXTEEN

It was harder than they imagined it would be to find one of the engineering lab's employees who was willing to talk to them—or who had seen anything remotely helpful.

The most responsive group of employees stood away from the medical personnel vehicles, huddled together, and held a meeting in low conversation while they glanced occasionally at their destroyed workplace.

"Hey, folks." Johnny stopped in front of them, jerked his chin up, and folded his arms. "Did y'all see anythin' go down here before it all blew up?"

"Who are you?" A woman adjusted her glasses and scrutinized him suspiciously.

"Agent Breyer and Johnny Walker," Lisa said quickly. "Director Zimmerman sent us here to find out what happened."

"We don't know anything about what happened. And I can't understand why no one will let us go home. We've been out here for five hours already."

"It might be 'cause they wanted y'all to stick around until Agent Breyer and I are done here." Johnny tugged his beard. "Did anyone get hurt in these explosions?"

"A couple but so far, only Paxton was killed." A man with dirt and blood smeared across the front of his white lab coat pointed at a black body bag on the ground beside the emergency vehicles. "He lost his cane after the first blast and couldn't make it out."

"I'm sorry," Lisa said.

"We weren't supposed to operate in a high-risk facility. Not this high-risk."

Johnny wrinkled his nose at the body bag. "Well, that changed today, folks. I'm sorry to be the one to tell you that but y'all already know, I guess. So what happened?"

"Our lab blew up!" The woman shouted so forcefully that her glasses slipped down the bridge of her nose and she fumbled to right them again. "What else do you need to know?"

"Anything you can remember would help us considerably," Lisa said gently. "I know it's been an awful day. But the more we know now, the better chance we'll have of finding the person responsible for this."

The woman turned away and muttered angrily and almost inaudibly.

Two other technicians moved closer to the partners. "The first explosions came from the back of the building. It's a storage area, mostly, and one of the old locker rooms no one uses anymore."

"All right. That's a good start." Johnny nodded. "Do you remember how many?"

"Two."

"N-no," the bloodied man interjected. "I think it was three. Two before the guards went to investigate. Then another one and we were all told to get out so we did."

The short, stocky man beside him shook his head. "We should have tried harder to make sure everyone was out."

"That wasn't your job and y'all can't go blamin' yourself for what happened to Paxton, understand?" Johnny glanced at each of them in turn. "Y'all might not have made it out otherwise."

"Jennifer wanted to go back for him," the guy in the lab coat said and lowered his voice as he gestured to the agitated woman with the glasses who'd stepped away. "She almost made it inside but then the front of the building blew up."

"Is that right?" Johnny glanced at Lisa, who seemed to know exactly what he was thinking. *This is definitely a copycat. First the back as a distraction, then the front to keep anyone else from headin' inside again.* "About how long was it before the second round of explosions?"

"Oh, I don't know. It's all…fuzzy."

"Maybe fifteen minutes," the stocky guy said. "Enough time to do a general head-count, I guess."

"Uh-huh. Then what?"

"Then the rest of the lab was blasted to smithereens!" Jennifer shouted. "You two don't know how to do your jobs very well, do you? All it takes is one look at the building to know. All our research was destroyed! Every single prototype. All models. Years of research stored on private servers out here. Millions of dollars in technology, experimental equipment, stored plans for future projects. It's all gone!"

She burst into sobs and the guy in the bloody lab coat excused himself to go comfort her.

The dwarf nodded at the rest of the group who'd gathered to talk to him. "Do y'all back up your servers?"

A man with chunks of rock and a few metal pieces stuck in his long gray ponytail sighed heavily and rubbed the back of his neck. "I sure hope so."

"Thank you for your time." Lisa handed him a business card. "I'm so sorry you guys had to go through this today. If you can think of anything else, give us a call, okay?"

"Yeah, sure. Okay." He pocketed the card. "Hey, when are they gonna let us off the property?"

"We'll tell 'em to open up when we're done here." Johnny

snapped his fingers and returned to their rental car. "Come on, boys. Time to—"

"Let go of me!" The desperate shout came from one of the emergency response vehicles parked in the lot where it blocked most of the exit onto the frontage road. "I'm telling you what I saw and none of you are listening!"

"Well." The bounty hunter raised his eyebrows at his partner. "It sounds like someone might have a little extra insight."

"Okay, a reminder to go easy on him," she replied as she hurried after the dwarf toward the emergency vehicles. "These people have been through enough already."

"Me? Come on, darlin'. I can do gentle. As long as he cooperates."

When they rounded the side of the first emergency vehicle, a man in a shredded, tattered lab coat with a giant hole in the toe of his boot struggled in the grasp of two medical personnel who tried to restrain him. "There's nothing wrong with me, I tell you. I know what I saw. We have to get everyone out of here right now and submit a report. They have to understand what this is."

"Hold on a sec, fellas." Johnny nodded at the medics, raised a hand, and gestured for them to cease trying to control the crazed victim. "I only want a minute if you don't mind."

"Go for it." They released the engineer and stepped back. "He's been getting worse over the last few hours—head injury."

"Yeah, I see that." He peered at the guy's blood-smeared head, wrinkled his nose, and stepped closer to the engineer. "You say you saw somethin' in there?"

"And I barely escaped with my life." The man studied him intently, then did the same with Lisa. "Who are you?"

"HQ sent us. Agent Lisa Breyer." When she extended her hand, the engineer recoiled like she'd offered him a rabid squirrel instead. "HQ sent a dwarf?"

Johnny spread his arms in a placating gesture. "The one and only on this job, sure. What's your name?"

"Phillip Gendrick." The man tried to regain some of his dignity as he straightened the collar of his lab coat, even though it was barely a garment anymore. "I run the weapons engineering part of the lab. Or...I did."

"Yeah. You will again. Now listen, Gendrick." Johnny waved toward the parking lot where the man's coworkers milled around, still in shock and grief and wanting to be released from the site. "We heard you shoutin' here about seein' somethin' inside. Do you wanna tell us about that?"

The man's eyes widened. "It was awful. Horrible. Explosions detonated seemingly everywhere and no one paid attention to anything else but fleeing the scene. But not me. I was looking."

Great. It sounds like he hit his head real hard.

"All right. What did you see?"

The man shuffled toward Johnny and leaned forward until their faces were almost touching. "A cyborg," he whispered.

"A what now?"

"Huh. Director Zimmerman sent you and you don't even know what a cyborg is?"

"No, I know what it is just fine." He scowled and leaned away from the guy's horrid breath.

"What do you mean by cyborg exactly?" Lisa asked.

"Exactly what I said," Gendrick shrieked. "Half organic life form, half machine. That's who did this. Glowing eyes lurking in the hallways. That whirring creak and click as the thing walked on the walls. I saw it planting the bombs! I saw it watching us!"

"Yeah, okay." Johnny rolled his eyes and turned away. "Thanks for your time—"

"No, you have to listen to me!" The man leapt at him and grasped fistfuls of the dwarf's collared shirt. "This isn't a figment of my imagination."

"Naw, I think it's a figment of the concussion you have there, Gendrick." He pulled the man's hands off his clothes. "Get some rest, huh?"

"I'm serious. No. No! Get your hands off me!" The man struggled against the medics who tried again to get him under control —if not to dress his wounds, then at least to sedate him if they had to. "You're missing the bigger picture. It was a cyborg, I tell you! Ask Ricardo. He knows—he saw it with me!"

Lisa frowned at the man as he was guided forcefully toward the open door of the emergency vehicle. "What do you think?"

"I think the guy's batshit crazy. He's lost his life's work. That's it."

"But think about it, Johnny. Organic life form and machine. It fits if we look at that goo-covered tech you have in that plastic bag."

"This?" Johnny lifted the evidence. "Sure. The cyborg he saw was a bomb."

"Maybe we should talk to Ricardo?"

He stopped, rolled his eyes with a heavy sigh, then turned and shouted, "Where's Ricardo?"

"Y-yeah?" A man who couldn't have been older than his late twenties shuffled around the corner of the second emergency vehicle, wringing his hands. "What's...w-what's going on?"

"My name's Johnny. Gendrick was tellin' us you saw a cyborg inside too? Before everythin' got blown to bits."

"A...a cyborg." Ricardo's lips moved rapidly, although no sound escaped him. "I saw...I-I saw the explosion. And t-the fire. And then...I...I..."

"It's all right, man." The bounty hunter clapped a hand on his shoulder and immediately pulled away when he flinched. "Sorry. It's all good, brother. Don't worry about it. The next crew to get out here will see you get home safe and sound to get some rest."

"Rest. I saw...I need rest..." Ricardo shuffled vacantly behind the vehicle again.

Johnny shook his head. "Yeah, I ain't puttin' stock in this cyborg crap."

"Well, it's traumatizing to narrowly escape being destroyed

with your work and the entire building." Lisa took a final glance at the ruins of the engineering lab.

"Yep. No one's makin' sense here. I reckon none of them has seen a thing that can help us."

"So we find out what that stuff is." She nodded at the evidence bag in his hand.

"Next step, darlin'. Without a doubt." When they reached the rental SUV, Johnny opened the back door for the hounds and dropped the evidence bag on the floor before he retrieved his phone. "This will be much easier if we don't have to hop to Florida to get it done."

"Yeah, that'd be nice." She slipped into the passenger seat and waited for him to get behind the wheel as he made his call.

"Hey, Wallace. It's Johnny."

"Johnny!" The gnome sounded genuinely happy to hear from him. "What's going on? Usually, I get your face at the jeweler's, not a phone call."

"Yeah, listen. I'd come to you for somethin' like this if I was in town but I'm out East."

"Okay."

"Do you know anyone near Saltsburg who can help analyze leftover magical goo for me? I ain't fixin' to fly all over the place to get a read on this."

"Hmm." Wallace took a minute to rifle through something and the shuffle of papers came over the line. "What kinda magical goo?"

"The explosive kind."

Lisa stared at Johnny as he strapped himself in and started the engine, holding the phone between his tilted head and his shoulder.

"Yeah, Johnny. I know someone out there. I'd call him more of an acquaintance than a friend but you can tell him I sent you. And he'll get the job done. The last I heard, he was in Pennsylvania's kemana."

"In Pittsburgh, right?"

"That's the one. He goes by Mr. Steel and is something of a grumpy bastard, so you two should get along fine."

He snorted. "Thanks."

The dwarf hung up, dropped his phone into the console slot below the dash, and pulled away from the destroyed parking lot.

"I take it we don't have to get on the jet again?" Lisa stared at the ruins of the engineering lab as they turned and drove toward the gate towers.

"Nope. It's not far to go at all, darlin'. Only beneath the streets of Pittsburgh."

"Oh. Fun."

CHAPTER SEVENTEEN

The only entrance to Pittsburgh's kemana Johnny knew of happened to be through the basement of the Andy Warhol Museum. The dwarf grumbled the whole time about having to pay full-price tickets to get inside when he didn't even plan to enjoy the museum itself.

"You say that like you'd ever come here to look at Andy Warhol art," Lisa muttered as they headed to the back of the building on the ground floor. "Or any art."

"I can appreciate art, darlin', but not this pop-and-copy crap. I don't get it."

They passed a large display in bright colors and she frowned. "Yeah, I never got this kind of art, either. To each his own, right?"

"Sure. And to us the kemana entrance." He pulled on an unmarked door at the end of the hall. It didn't budge at first but at his second tug, it screeched loudly and jerked open.

"Are you sure this is the way in?" Lisa turned and scanned the hall, waiting for them to be called out for their mistake.

"Sure I'm sure. At least, last time I was in Pittsburgh, this was the way in." He nodded and held his hand out for the hounds' leashes she'd been holding for him. "Now that I think about it, though, this was technically the back way in. The bounty I was after at the time had eyes everywhere."

"Oh, good. So we might not even get down there."

"'Course we will. I always find a way in. Come on." He took the leashes from her, let her walk down the stairs first, then scanned the hallway again before he jerked the door shut behind him with another grating shriek.

"Johnny, I don't think I like being a bomb-sniffing hound." Luther sat on the top step as his master unhooked the leashes from both collars. "Everyone stares at us."

"Y'all are already bomb-sniffin' hounds," Johnny muttered and shoved the leashes into his pocket. "We simply gave you a title that fits."

"But you had to tell that two-legs at the front that we were hers?" Rex added. "I like her and everything, Johnny, but we're not her hounds."

"Yeah, and we don't work for the FBI."

"Hush up, now." With a smirk, he followed Lisa down the short staircase as the hounds' claws clicked behind him. "Y'all are doin' fine. The leashes are off and we're in."

Luther snorted. "You never used to put leashes on us, Johnny."

"Yeah, it's not like we're gonna eat any of the paintings upstairs."

"Hey, but did you see the one with the soup cans? Was it painted with actual soup?"

Johnny ignored their brain-numbing art critiques in order to focus on finding the right door in the museum's basement. The only one that wasn't locked was the door he wanted, and he led them all into Pittsburgh's kemana.

After half a mile of walking through the dimly lit tunnel, the noise hit them as hard as it would have if they'd been driving through the heart of the city at rush hour.

A group of pixies at somewhere between miniature and full-magical size zipped past and left a stream of glittering color in their wake. "Outta the way, dwarf."

"Move it!"

Johnny tilted his head to the side to avoid being clipped by one of their outstretched hands and snorted. "What is it with pixies all of a sudden, huh?"

"I heard there are many of them here," Lisa replied and moved her foot away from a Willen who scrambled around the corner, rolling a chrome hubcap on its side.

"Why? What's so special about Pittsburgh for pixies?"

"Hey, but that sounds good, Johnny." Luther laughed. "Pittsburgh for pixies."

"You think they run the place down here, Johnny?"

The dwarf shook his head. "Keep an eye out for anythin' that says Mr. Steel."

"Is that the name of his shop?" Lisa asked.

"Maybe. I dunno. But he runs the same kinda tinkerin' and testin' that Wallace does in Florida or at least somethin' close to it."

"And that's all the information he gave you?"

"Yep." Johnny scanned the few signs mounted outside the storefronts at the heart of the kemana. In the next moment, something tugged on the evidence bag dangling from his hand. "What the—"

"Hey, dwarf!" A Willen smiled at him with dangerously sharp teeth and poked the bag. "Watcha got there?"

"Nothin' for you."

"Hey, but it's shiny. And glowing."

"And covered in sludge."

"I don't care about that, man. I can clean anything. What do you want for it?"

The bounty hunter looked at Lisa, who barely managed to hold back a laugh as the Willen continued to poke and prod at the evidence bag.

"Nothin'." Johnny snatched it away and tucked it under his arm. "I'm lookin' for Mr. Steel."

"Uh-huh. Uh-huh." The Willen sucked his teeth and studied Lisa. "What do you got?"

"Oh, uh…" She patted her pockets, then pulled out a handful of loose change. "Clean these and they'll shine like gold."

"Huh. Nothing shines like gold, lady." The creature sneered at her, but his beady eyes didn't leave the small pile of US coins in her palm. "All right, what the hell? Give it."

She handed over all of two dollars and thirty-five cents and the Willen tucked it into the folds of his skin.

"Right over there on the other side of the crystal. Hard to get in with Mr. Steel, so if you don't have an appointment, good luck."

"All right. What's the—" Johnny grunted when the Willen scurried away and darted between the feet of the other magicals who moved around the kemana on their business before he disappeared. "Great. He was a big help."

"Well, I did pay for information with less than a decent cup of coffee would cost."

He looked sharply at her and scowled. "You're gettin' your joe in all the wrong places, darlin'. Come on."

"He said we needed an appointment."

"Naw. If we did, Wallace woulda mentioned it. I'll drop his name instead and see where it gets us."

"That's an excellent idea—with no Plan B."

"You know that's the way I like it, darlin'. Plan B is makin' it up as we go."

They moved across the kemana toward the giant crystal at the center that powered the magic for the whole city and surrounding areas. A low, humming vibration emanated from the huge crystal mounted into the floor. Luther sneezed as they moved closer. Then Rex sneezed. In the next moment, both hounds scampered after Johnny and Lisa with a constant barrage of sneezes and snorts while they shook their heads vigorously.

"Are y'all all right?" the dwarf asked and paused to look at his hounds.

"That big glowing rock shouldn't be—achoo!—down here, Johnny."

"Yeah, for real. Talk—achoo!—about all the hounds getting—achoo!—messed up by magic. Hey, Luther. Did you even know we could—" Rex sneezed so violently, he stumbled into his brother and set them both off on a grunting, snorting fit.

"Well then, stay away from it. We'll walk around next time." He continued toward the low building on the other side of the kemana's crystal, where the only sign above the shop's front door was a printed image of two sheets of corrugated steel. "I assume this is the place here."

"Oh, good. Well, that was easy." Lisa turned to watch the dogs regain their balance before they trotted forward to catch up with their master.

The door to Mr. Steel's shop opened with a jingle, and Johnny strode across the room toward the counter at the back. "Hello? Is anyone in here?"

A thump and growl issued from behind the thin wall divider on the other side of the counter. "Appointment only! And I don't have any appointments right now which means you don't belong here. Get lost."

"So how do we make an appointment?" Lisa asked.

"Naw, forget that." Johnny thumped a fist on the back counter. "Wallace sent me, Mr. Steel. He told me you'd be able to help with some analysis I need done."

"Wallace? Who the hell is that?"

"Wallace Fine Jewelers out of Cape Coral. He makes magical bombs for me."

"Oh, sure. You think you're such a bigshot, huh? Who the hell are you?"

Lisa covered her mouth with a hand and tried not to laugh when Johnny hunched his shoulders and sighed with exaggerated patience. "Johnny Walker."

Another thud rose from behind the wall divider, followed by several more as a stack of something fell over. "Aw, shit. Dammit. If I wanted all this to fall on me, I would've built a giant Jenga set instead. Did you say Johnny Walker?"

"Yep."

A huge silhouette grew on the divider as Mr. Steel shuffled toward it. A moment later, it slid aside on a set of wheels and the two partners stared at a Kilomea with eyeteeth as long as Johnny's middle finger and a giant bald patch covering the side of his face where thick hair should have been. He trundled toward the counter and peered at Johnny with one eye squinted almost completely shut. "Johnny Walker?"

"Have you heard of me?"

Mr. Steel laughed and slapped a meaty hand on the counter. "Of course not. Why would I have?"

The dwarf ignored the blow and placed the evidence bag on the counter. "Wallace told me—"

"Yeah, yeah. You already said that. And you're hoping dropping his name like that will get you in at the head of the line, huh?"

"Will it?" Lisa asked.

"Hell yeah, it will. So watcha got?"

"I need to have some analysis on that sludge." Johnny pointed at the bag. "And anything you might be able to pull up on that little gadget in there. I guess I can pick it apart myself if I have to. But I ain't in the know when it comes to magical substances."

"Uh-huh. Sure, sure." Mr. Steel lifted the bag in both hands and held it up to the low light. His hint of a smile disappeared. "Well. I can tell you simply by looking that I have no idea what this is."

The dwarf narrowed his eyes at him. "But you've seen it before."

"What makes you say that?"

"You're frowning like I handed you a pile of dog shit."

"Hey, what gives, Johnny?" Luther snorted.

"Yeah. That's more than a little insulting, you know."

The Kilomea growled, set the bag down, and slid it toward him. "Yeah, I've seen it before. I don't like seeing it again."

"Why not?"

Mr. Steel glanced briefly at the hounds who sniffed around his storefront, then tilted his head at Lisa. "Because you're the third stranger this week to walk into my shop and ask about—"

An explosion rocked the store from the back and debris was hurled in all directions. The owner jolted forward against the counter, wide-eyed, and he snarled as pieces of tech peppered his back.

"Get out! Now!" Johnny snatched the evidence bag and turned to run only when he saw the Kilomea vault over the counter in one leap. He caught Lisa's hand and pulled her out into the central square of the kemana. The hounds darted through the front door after them two seconds before Mr. Steel barreled out as well with another explosion hot at his back. He roared and staggered forward before a series of smaller detonations followed in quick succession in a pattern from the back of the shop toward the front.

Finally, the front doors exploded and a huge cloud of thick black smoke churned and rose to the top of the kemana's underground ceiling.

"Dammit." Johnny ran a hand through his hair and stared at the destruction as magicals scattered away from the store, screaming and shouting at each other while they tried to regain their bearings.

"Great." The Kilomea shucked a chunk of shattered wall and brushed his hairy arms off. "That's why I don't like looking at something in my shop I don't recognize. Too much confusion, too many questions, and I don't have any answers."

Johnny couldn't reach the hulking proprietor's shoulder, so he gave Mr. Steel's burly, hairy arm a reassuring pat instead. "Yeah. That's why we're here. I'm sorry about your shop."

He grunted. "I'm only glad I didn't go down with it."

CHAPTER EIGHTEEN

The two partners made their rounds through the closest area of the kemana, and while they helped magicals settle and regain their equilibrium, they asked if anyone had seen anything or witnessed any suspicious activity. Finally, Johnny nodded at Mr. Steel. "I'd like to take a look inside if it suits ya."

"Go right ahead. There's much less to see than there was half an hour ago."

Lisa joined him at the destroyed shopfront and they went inside to inspect the damage. "You don't think this was a random attack, do you?"

"Not even a little, darlin'." He scanned the broken shelves and scattered pieces of machinery and blasted tech parts. "In the same moment that the Kilomea's tellin' us we ain't the first to bring in this kinda sludge in a bag? Naw. This was intentional and it's the copycat's MO too—a warning blast in the back, time to get everyone outside, then bam."

"Yeah, bam's right, Johnny." Rex yipped on the other side of the counter. "Over here, Johnny. I found more of that bloody meat-oil goo."

He snorted and headed around the counter—half of which

had been blown to pieces—to join his hound. Sure enough, the animal had found a much smaller splatter of the same substance with a few scattered pieces of glowing silver metal.

"Hey, Johnny!" Luther called from the back. "More sludge. Much more. In a trail."

"Yeah, that's a nice lead. Come on, darlin'."

Lisa hurried over the rubble to follow him and his hounds into the back of the shop. "What's going on?"

"Luther found our perp's trail."

"I did?" The hound wagged his tail furiously when they reached him in the back room. "Hey, yeah. I did. Johnny, it goes that way!"

A huge hole had been blown through the back wall of the shop, but the splatters of thick, viscous red-black sludge tripped in an obvious trail away from Mr. Steel's store and on into the kemana. "On the trail, boys. Let's go!'

The hounds bayed mercilessly and darted away, following their newest lead.

Maybe a cyborg ain't so far outta the question. If that's what this bastard is and he's bleedin', we'll catch him faster than a one-legged man in an ass-kickin' competition.

"Whatever this is," Lisa muttered and drew her service pistol as they hurried after the hounds, "it's dripping off the guy like blood."

"You took the thought right outta my head, darlin'. We'll catch him."

The goo trail led them toward the other side of the kemana and a series of branching tunnels. Johnny drew his utility knife and flicked it open as he raced after the hounds. "You see him, you take him down, boys!"

After two more minutes of running in the semi-dark tunnel, Rex barked sharply. "Shit. Luther, where did it go?"

"Why are you asking me? I was following it like you."

"Johnny, it's gone!"

"What do you mean it's gone?" he snapped as he jogged to catch up with them.

"It's gone, Johnny."

"Yeah, look. Drippy goo right here and then nothing."

The hounds sniffed around the tunnel floor, pressed their noses against the walls, and finally returned to their master. "Nothing, Johnny. It's like he disappeared."

"That ain't possible."

Lisa holstered her weapon again and sighed as she studied the walls and floor. "I assume the dogs are saying what I'm thinking. That this guy vanished into thin air."

"Yeah. I'd say he stopped his drippin' somehow but this old tunnel's a dead end." The bounty hunter stalked toward the end of the tunnel that had been blocked off and sealed tightly. "It looks like it's been shut down for a long time so how the hell did this guy up and disappear?"

"Well…teleportation is a possibility."

"Uh-huh." He sniffed and glared at the evidence bag in his other hand. "It takes a hell of a lotta juice to teleport, though. Someone usin' an organic-magic-tech-combo bomb simply to shut Mr. Steel up don't seem like the kinda magical who'd be able to handle teleportin'. That leaves enough of a mess on its own if it ain't done right."

"Well then, we're right back where we started."

"Uh-huh. 'Cept for now, we ain't got someone to run analysis on this shit for us. Damn."

"We should talk to Mr. Steel again, though. Ask about who else walked into his shop with this same substance."

"I guess that's the next best step for now. Leave it, boys. We're headin' back."

"I don't like this at all, Johnny." Luther sniffed furiously and uttered a low whine. "Since when do trails go cold, huh?"

"Maybe there's something wrong with us, Johnny." Rex

glanced constantly over his shoulder at the end of the trail. "I don't get it."

"There ain't nothin' wrong with y'all. This copycat bomber's gonna get what's comin' to him sooner or later. I ain't worried."

They spent another half hour in Mr. Steel's shop, questioning him and doing what they could to help him pick up the pieces of his destroyed store. Or, rather, Lisa did most of the questioning, and Johnny rummaged about in the debris, examining pieces of machinery and tossing aside what was nothing more than junk at this point.

There was no immediately obvious connection between the three other magicals who'd come to visit the Kilomea about the sludge. The only common denominator seemed to be the fact that they'd all been close to an explosion site over the past two weeks and couldn't find out on their own what had happened.

"Beyond that," the proprietor finished, "I can't help you. I didn't even have the right machines to strip that down the first and second time. It broke my gear on the first attempt. I thought I'd modified it enough when the second guy arrived but I was wrong. By the time the third stepped through those doors, I was sick of looking at that slime, whatever it is."

"Uh-huh." Johnny sniffed. "Now it looks like whoever did this was sick of folks comin' to you with questions."

Mr. Steel looked affronted. "What happened to meeting face to face and asking nicely in person first, huh?"

"That ain't on the agenda when someone's tryin' to hide their face and their involvement." The dwarf paused, stepped back, and made a quick mental inventory of all the broken tech pieces that littered the floor. "Mr. Steel."

"Yeah."

"Would it bother you if I took a few things with me?"

The Kilomea scratched the side of his head and shrugged. "Go ahead. It's all useless now anyway."

"Maybe for what you were fixin' to do with it. Do you have a bag?"

Mr. Steel squinted at the dwarf, then shuffled across his ruined store and pulled a canvas tote from beneath a pile of shattered glass. "Will this work?"

Johnny wrinkled his nose at the flowery wreath printed on the side of the bag. "Is that all you have?"

"This isn't a purse store, dwarf. You want it or not?"

"That'll be great," Lisa said and forced a smile. "Thank you."

"Aw, hell." The bounty hunter scowled at her in exasperation, snatched the bag from the Kilomea's hand, and shoved a pile of wreckage he'd set aside into it. "When we find the asshole who did this, Steel, we'll let you know."

"That's Mr. Steel, Johnny," the Kilomea hollered in response as the team stepped outside "Don't you forget it!"

"Yeah, I'll tell all my friends."

The proprietor chuckled wanly in the slanting doorway, then turned toward the mess and set to work with the cleanup while he muttered under his breath.

Lisa glanced at the tote decorated in colorful flowers and vines slung over the dwarf's shoulder. "I'd love to hear why you're leaving that magical's shop with a haul of broken junk."

"You know what, darlin'? For the first time, I reckon the Willens have the hang of this. They might even have it down to a science."

"Oh, no. Don't tell me you hit your head too running away from the last explosion."

He snorted and snapped his fingers at the hounds, who were busy sniffing at a witch's table of magical street food across from the kemana crystal.

"Aw, come on, Johnny."

"It smells so good."

"Y'all can eat at the hotel with me and Lisa. We're gettin' outta here."

The hounds obeyed reluctantly —but not before they snatched up pieces of food dropped by a passing Wood Elf in a baseball cap—and Lisa chuckled. "I get using the dogs as an excuse to not answer my question—"

"I ain't hit my head on nothin', darlin'."

"So what's with all the Willen talk, then?"

"All I'm sayin' is they have this all worked out." He jiggled the flower tote on his shoulder. "One magical's trash is another's treasure, ain't that the way of it?"

"Wow." Lisa glanced over her shoulder at the front of Mr. Steel's shop, but there was no sign of the huge Kilomea. "You should have offered to pay him for that."

"Why? He thinks it's useless."

"Johnny…"

"Yeah, yeah, I know. If this works, I'll return it all. With interest. Maybe."

CHAPTER NINETEEN

They found a hotel in Pittsburgh's Cultural District, reluctant to stay too close to the kemana in case the copycat bomber saw them. Johnny didn't waste any time getting to work on the new project he'd made out of Mr. Steel's not-so-useless machine and tech parts.

After an hour and a half, Lisa was fed up with having to sit silently and wait for him to finish. "I'd love to know what you're doing."

"I'm almost finished, darlin'. Gimme a little longer." The dwarf constantly pulled pieces out of the flower tote and shaped them with a pair of needle-nose pliers and other random tools and supplies in a plastic bag he'd purchased at the home improvement store on the way.

A little longer turned into another two hours, and he didn't stop in his makeshift hotel workshop even when the fried-chicken takeout Lisa brought filled the entire suite with its aroma. The hounds, however, weren't about to let that go.

"Hey, lady. Hey. How about some of that chicken, huh?"

"Hey, come on. We've been great hounds. You can't deny it."

She chuckled and shooed them away as she plated dinner for

her and Johnny. "Go on, boys. You know I'm not allowed to feed you anything. I'll get in trouble."

"No, you won't." Luther sniffed the floor beside her shoes. "Johnny's not even paying attention."

"Come on, lady. He won't be able to tell the difference. Watch." Rex barked once. "Johnny! You stink!"

"Yeah, you're the worst two-legs to ever throw a bomb!"

"Whoa, bro. Go easy. That was harsh."

"What? He didn't even hear—"

"Y'all need to hush up in there," Johnny grumbled and his tools clinked and clanked on the table. "I'm tryin' to focus."

"Oh, shit." Luther crouched low and looked at Lisa. "You think he heard us?"

"Dude, she can't hear us. What are you asking her for?"

"I don't know. Look at her, Rex. I think she can understand us too. Or at least part of it."

Lisa tore a smaller chunk of fried chicken slowly in half as she stared at Johnny's back hunched over the built-in desk at the far end of the suite's living area. Crumbs of breading spilled onto the floor and the hounds licked it up in seconds.

"Well, at least she doesn't care about dropping food."

"Holy crap, lady! This stuff is good!"

She glanced at them and lowered the two pieces of chicken slowly toward the hounds.

"Wait, what is she doing?"

"Hey, shut up! You're gonna ruin it for us if you don't— Oh man, that's delicious."

"Yeah, yeah, yeah! You're the best."

Lisa dusted her hands off and stared at the dwarf. "Johnny? Are you okay over there?"

The hounds licked their muzzles, finished eating the crumbs off the floor, and froze. "Bro, he didn't even notice."

"Johnny?" Rex crouched and uttered a low whine as he

stepped slowly around the corner of the kitchen. "Uh...hey, Johnny. You feelin' okay?"

"Come on, y'all. I'm almost done."

Lisa pressed her lips together and stared at the kitchen. "Okay, then. I assume you're super-engrossed. I'm gonna eat without you because I'm starving."

"Uh-huh." His tools clicked and clacked.

With her plate in hand, she looked at the hounds again before she moved to the small dining table against the wall. *I fed Johnny's hounds and he didn't say a thing. Whatever he's doing had better work the way he wants it to.*

The rest of the chicken was cold by the time he finished creating his new gadget but he snatched the plate off the counter anyway and brought it with him to the desk. "Are you busy, darlin'?"

Lisa looked up from the book on her tablet and raised her eyebrows. "No, I'm not. That's been you."

"Uh-huh. I need your help here for this last piece."

"Okay..." She stood slowly and joined him for the first time since he'd sat when they arrived. "What am I supposed to do?"

"Only the last part, and then this will be workin' like a charm. I need a little extra juice first."

She sighed. "Please don't tell me you're asking me to make a booze run for you."

"What? Naw. I meant magic...juice."

"Um...I don't quite follow."

"Listen, I need you to power this. With your magic."

Lisa folded her arms and stared at the small, misshapen box of metal parts and odd wiring with a little window in the center where Johnny had mounted the piece of glowing silver tech covered in the biohazard blood-slime. "I don't wanna be your battery."

"Come on, darlin'." He licked the chicken grease and bread crumbs off his fingers, then dusted his beard over his plate. "I'm not big on magic and castin' spells. You know that. I need you to help me out a little."

"Okay." She leaned on the side of the desk and frowned at him. "Any suggestions in particular for how to go about doing this, exactly?"

"Simply hit it with magic, Lisa."

"That's not how it works."

He snapped his fingers and grinned at her. "What you did in New York. On the bridge, when the thugs almost had Amanda and you kept the hounds from getting' blown to bits. Use that."

"An energy shield?"

"Yeah, yeah. But aim it at this here device and we'll get her powered up."

"Johnny, I don't even understand what this does."

He snorted. "It's basically like a projector for organic memory. Yeah. I had the idea after Grady gave me that little somethin' to hook the worm up to Margo. Look. Everyone has memory written into their DNA. Blood holds it particularly well. Water makes the best for reading, but the guy we're after ain't a river sprite. Magicals? We're even easier to read this way. But it takes a lotta magical juice to get something like this turned on so we can use it and I ain't fixin' to waste any more time by runnin' round to shops for what I need only to get them blown up too—"

"Okay, okay! I'll do it." Lisa rolled her shoulders and drew a deep breath. "I have no idea what you said, but I'll do it."

"Excellent." Johnny rubbed his hands together and leaned away to give her space to work. "Let her rip."

Lisa frowned, ignored his over-enthusiastic comments, and extended both hands toward the device he'd built. A bright white light appeared at her fingertips and shimmered with opalescence before it moved in a concentrated stream into the center of the device. The cobbled-together metal box flashed, emitted a croaking beep, and went silent.

"All right. All right." Johnny stroked his chin and stood. "That was a good start but we need more."

"More?"

"Yeah, I know what you can do. Make it powerful, darlin'. Come on."

"More," she whispered and shook her head before she tried again. *He's gonna have me break this damn box instead.*

The light bloomed on her hands again.

"Yeah, hold it steady. It has to last long enough for the charge to catch and hold, understand?"

"No, Johnny. I honestly don't."

"Keep blastin' it nonstop!"

"Jesus, okay." Lisa focused on the device and let her magic flow in one continuous stream of energy. Johnny's device illuminated again and dozens of small, randomly placed lights blinked to life.

"Yeah. Keep goin', Lisa. More!"

"Johnny, I'm gonna break it—"

"No, you ain't." He looked quickly from her hands to the organic-memory reader. "Turn it up, darlin'. Come on! More!"

"Johnny, this isn't—"

"Goddammit!" The dwarf pounded a fist on the desk. "Are you gonna pussyfoot around like this all goddamn night? Quit bein' so scared of yourself and hit the fuckin' thing with some power!"

Something inside her snapped and she unleashed her full strength of magic on the tiny device that had taken him three hours to put together and looked like it wouldn't last another ten minutes. The entire hotel suite filled with the blinding white light, sparks erupted from the box, and a low whirring hum rose from it as her magic faded.

"Yes! Hot damn!" Johnny rapped his knuckles on the desk and grinned as he stared at the buzzing device that had flared to life with the magical power source it needed. "Now that's what I'm talkin' about."

Lisa glared at him, breathing heavily. *This is the part where you bite his head off for talking to you like that.*

She was about to but Johnny punched a makeshift button on the side of the device and tapped the little window that showed the red-black gooey sludge left after the explosion. The window widened, then filled with a projected image.

Although she had no idea how any of this was working, she couldn't look away from the blue-tinted vision that played out on a magical hologram Johnny Walker had made out of mystery slime and destroyed machine parts.

Still grinning madly, the dwarf pulled his phone from his back pocket and prepared to video what they saw.

The projected image was of the back of the FBI's engineering lab from outside. Lisa didn't recognize it until she saw the gate tower at the end of the road in the distance. They were looking at the lab building before the explosion and from the back corner. In the next moment, a voice played through the device.

"The mission's almost complete, sir. Yes, I took care of it. No one at HQ will ever find out about this one. You have my word. I already know how they'll react and I'll be ready for them."

The image changed slightly when the owner of the voice stepped toward the corner of the building and glanced at something in his hand.

It was a case file stamped *Classified* across the front. An FBI letterhead on the corner of a page poked out from the rest of the documents.

"What the fuck?" Johnny stared at the projection until it flickered and finally ended. He stopped his video recording and replayed it to take a look at what he thought he'd seen. "Did you see that? The goddamn Bureau left their sloppy fuckin' signature all over this. They blew up their own goddamn lab!"

"Asshole," Lisa muttered.

"Yeah, tell me about it. Nelson has some kinda goddamn nerve, I tell you what. He's hidin' even more secrets from me and still sendin' me out to do his dirty work while he gets to sit back and laugh in my face at the whole—"

The door to their hotel suite opened and slammed shut with a loud bang.

"Lisa?" Johnny turned to face the door, but she was gone.

"She walked out, Johnny," Luther said from beneath the large desk. "She looked pissed."

"Smelled pissed too, Johnny." Rex sniffed the floor for more fried-chicken crumbs. "You should probably do something about that, right?"

"Yeah, well, I'm pissed too. These bastards had no idea I'd find what they're hidin', and the hammer's comin' down this time, boys." Johnny texted the video to Nelson—which was surprisingly easy given that he'd never attempted to send a video before —then immediately called the agent without waiting for a reply.

The man answered immediately. "What am I looking at, Johnny?"

"You tell me, asshole," he snapped into the phone.

"I have no idea. But I assume you're about to—"

"The son of a bitch who blew up your engineering lab is a goddamn fed, Nelson! Or at least connected enough that he might as well be. Did you think I wouldn't find out? Huh?"

"Hey, you need to cool it—"

"Don't tell me what I need, Nelson! If you ain't got a hand in this, you know good and well who the hell does. Director Zimmerman's gotta be behind this. Watch the goddamn video and tell me I'm wrong. It has his name all over it! And when you decide how to tell me what the fuck is goin' on without tossin' a lie in there 'cause you can't help yourself, then we'll talk!"

He hung up before Nelson could get another word out and almost hurled his phone across the suite. Fortunately, he stopped himself and dropped it on the desk instead, then clutched the edge of the wood laminate tightly in both hands and glared at his impromptu device.

Sendin' me on a wild goose chase and wastin' my time.

"Um…Johnny?" Rex lowered his head to nip the underside of his rear leg, then stood and circled his master. "You're gonna go after her, right?"

"After who?" he shouted.

Luther scoffed. "Yeah, I think that's why she left."

"What? Lisa?" The dwarf stepped back to look at his hounds. "Naw. She can take care of herself."

"Johnny, for real, you should listen to us." Luther trotted toward the front door and paused to wait for his master. "You need to go apologize."

"For what?"

"Being an asshole." Rex joined his brother and sat to nip his leg again. He uttered a low whine and licked his muzzle. "That's what she said, anyway. I wouldn't exactly argue with her on that point."

"You screwed up, Johnny. She's the best lady two-legs you've ever set eyes on. Don't let her get away."

He snorted and glowered at the door. "She ain't my prisoner."

"No, but your life is screwed if you let her walk out of it. Trust us, Johnny."

Luther padded toward the door and his tail wagged slightly before it stilled. "For real. We can smell things before they happen. And if you don't go after her, I smell failure in your future."

"Huh." With a glance at his device, Johnny snatched his phone up, shoved it in his pocket, and hurried the door. "Fine. If y'all are so convinced I gotta do this, you're helpin' me find her."

"Duh. That was the whole point."

As they headed down the hall toward the elevators, the hounds hung back a little.

"That was probably the best speech you've ever given, bro," Rex muttered.

"You think so?"

"Uh-huh."

"I wasn't going for a speech. But cool. Hey, Rex. We can't smell things before they happen, right? 'Cause I was making that part up—"

"Shh. Of course we can't. But he doesn't know that. Good thinking."

"Right, right, right. Our secret. Gotcha."

Johnny smirked as he pressed the elevator call button. *Yeah, their hearts are in the right place. I'll give 'em that. Here's to hopin' Lisa's is too after this.*

CHAPTER TWENTY

The hounds had no difficulty following Lisa's trail through the city, even though the evening nightlife at the end of summer started to kick up and the streets were filled with pedestrians. "She went this way, Johnny."

"Yeah, yeah. In a hurry, too."

Damn. I'm usually the one doin' the stormin' off.

The hounds stopped in front of a real gem of a dive bar called The Ambler and looked at their master with wagging tails and canine smiles. "She's in there, all right."

"Yep. Smells as pissed as when she left. And boozy. Kinda like you, Johnny."

"Y'all sure it ain't only the ambiance?" Johnny snorted as he opened the door and stepped into the crowded bar with Guns 'N Roses playing in the background.

"Well, sure." Luther licked his muzzle and scuttled out of the path of a drunk man who stumbled toward the front door. "But it'd be weird if everyone in here smelled like her too. Like actually her. Then how would you tell you found the right lady two-legs?"

Rex sniggered. "Might even get back to the hotel only to find out you didn't come home with a lady two-legs at all."

The hounds cracked up laughing and Johnny shushed them with a hiss.

These damn hounds are gonna drive me to doin' somethin' I regret. Where is she?

Lisa was seated at the opposite side of the bar with one elbow propped on the counter while she stirred her gin and tonic with a cocktail straw. Her other hand tapped the stained wood and she tilted her head when the man beside her leaned closer to continue the conversation.

The asshole's tryin' to make a move.

Johnny clenched his fists and gritted his teeth as he watched.

Lisa glanced at the stranger who was laying it on thick and shook her head but she didn't look pissed. She also didn't say or do anything to put the guy out of his misery immediately.

She doesn't wanna let him down hard. And she sure as shit doesn't want me to storm over there breakin' hands that wander way too far in all the wrong places.

"Johnny, I see her." Luther yipped but the sound was lost beneath the music. "Right there. Sitting there by herself."

"Get over there, Johnny," Rex urged.

"I'll hang back for a minute, boys." The dwarf's fists clenched even tighter. "I need to see what I'm walkin' into."

The stranger who attempted to hit on Lisa chuckled, slid off the barstool, and moved down the bar to get the bartender's attention.

Johnny growled. *She's into that kinda ugly bastard? Are you kiddin' me?*

With the boneheaded creep out of the way, Lisa now had a clear view of Johnny standing in the center of the room, his fists clenched at his sides and both hounds whipping their heads from her to their master. She met his gaze, bit her bottom lip, and frowned before she turned to her drink.

Yeah, she can take care of herself. But it don't mean I ain't here to help if I gotta.

He strode toward her and wove through the bar patrons as the hounds did the same behind him.

"Okay, Johnny. This is the part where you start with, 'I'm sorry.'" Rex ducked a guy's foot as he uncrossed his legs. "That's it. Nothing else."

"Yeah, what else do you need?" Luther stopped to lick experimentally at a puddle of spilled beer on the sticky wood floor. "The answer's nothing, Johnny. Say you're sorry and you'll stop being an asshole."

"Or maybe that you'll stop being that big of an asshole." Rex stopped to paw at his ear. "Gotta make it believable."

"Yeah, I heard lady two-legs can see a lie like hounds see farts."

That last one made the dwarf pause for a split second and he glanced at an oblivious Luther before he shook it off. *It ain't worth my time to try to get to the bottom of that one.*

Finally, he reached the bar and slid onto the stool beside Lisa that had previously been occupied by the creeper who thought he could get anywhere with her.

She shook her head and continued to fiddle with her drink. "I just wanted to be left alone, Johnny. Hence me storming out without telling you where I'm going."

"Yeah, or answerin' your phone. That ain't playin' fair."

"Fair?" She gestured toward the hounds without looking at them. "You tracked me with your coonhounds. What's the point of answering your calls?"

"Huh." He folded his arms on the bar and darted her a sidelong glance. "Oh, come on. You can't be mad at me for followin' you, darlin'. You don't leave me alone when I want a little privacy."

"No." Lisa took a huge sip of her gin and tonic and cleared her throat without batting an eyelid. "I don't leave you alone to brood all day about something when you have other options. I stop you locking yourself in your hotel or your house or your toolshed for ungodly amounts of time. It's not the same."

"Yeah? And how's that?"

Finally, she looked at him, her eyes slightly glassy after she'd downed most of her drink. "I've only been gone for twenty minutes."

Johnny looked at the hounds, who seemed oblivious to the conversation happening above them. *Why do I listen to two zipper-head canines? She was fine here on her own.*

"All right. I get it, darlin'. I ain't givin' you enough space. Do you want me to leave, then?"

For a moment, he didn't think she would give him an answer, but she shook her head. "No. You can stay." She nodded at the bartender when his attention centered on her and semi-playfully slapped Johnny's shoulder with the back of a hand. "Have a drink with me."

"Only one, huh?"

"I don't know, Johnny. I guess we'll have to play it by ear."

"Uh-huh."

When the bartender approached, Lisa raised her empty glass toward him. "Hendricks and tonic, double. And a Johnny Walker Black Label, neat." She looked at the dwarf and shrugged. "You'd better make that a double too. And put it on my tab."

Johnny bit his lip and scowled at the bar. His nose twitched as he tried to stay calm and make her feel like he was there to mend things, not make them worse. But what he wanted to do was sweep her off her feet and out of the bar. *It might be the sexiest damn thing I ever heard come outta her mouth.*

As it turned out, "only one drink" devolved into as many as they could throw back before the trouble started. Lisa swayed on her barstool and raised her glass toward Johnny's for what had to be the sixth toast at least since they'd started.

"And to all the bastards who think they can screw with the perfect team," he roared.

"Perfect, huh?" Their glasses clinked and she grinned at him.

"Sure, darlin'. Hell. Think of what we been through together in the last five months. I ain't felt this on top of the world since…shit."

"Four and a half."

"What's that now?"

She shrugged and tilted her half-full glass from side to side as she considered it. "Somewhere between four and a half and five months. I think."

"Oh, look who's keepin' score!" He laughed and shook his head. "I like to round up."

"Yeah, I bet you do."

"You're killin' me with that, darlin'." He leaned toward her, smirked through his beard, and studied her face lazily from his booze-glassy eyes. "What are you up to?"

"Do you think I'm hiding something?" She batted her eyelashes at him. "Honestly, Johnny, there's only one thing I'm up to right now and that's getting Johnny-Walkered with Johnny Walker."

"Huh?"

Lisa threw her head back and exploded with laughter before she raised her glass for another toast. "To letting loose with the best damn bounty hunter on two worlds!"

He chuckled, toasted with her, and sipped his drink. "I wouldn't call me the best, darlin'. One of 'em, mind. Sure, but not *the* best."

"That's not the way I see it." She held his gaze the whole time while she swallowed the rest of her drink and thunked her glass on the bar. "Are you ready for another?"

"Ha! You ain't gotta match me drink for drink, you know. It might not be a good idea for you."

"Oh, shut up." She smacked his arm with the back of a hand

and raised two fingers at the bartender, who'd been on top of their drinks all night. "Just because you haven't seen me drink like you doesn't mean I don't know how to."

Lisa's coy smiles and sidelong glances were driving him up the wall. *I can't tell if she's comin' onto me or the gin's comin' onto her even stronger.*

Below the overhanging lip of the counter, the two hounds had found themselves cozy spots to curl at the foot of their masters' barstool. Luther lifted his head and chuffed. "Hey, Johnny? It's great that you guys are having fun and everything, but I think you got incoming now."

"Yeah, maybe a lot," Rex added. "Honestly, it's hard to tell which one of you they are pissed at."

"Yeah, all right." Johnny waved the hounds' warning aside and tossed the third twenty-dollar bill of the night on the counter as the bartender slid the next round toward them.

"I appreciate it, man." The guy nodded at Johnny and pocketed the twenty. "You guys come back whenever you want."

"You been takin' care of us." He nodded in return and watched Lisa dive into her fourth or fifth double gin and tonic. *She ain't lyin' about knowin' how—*

"Johnny," Rex insisted. "These dinguses look like they want somethin'."

"It's dingusi, bro."

"No, it's not."

The dwarf grunted and scowled as he sipped. He'd caught occasional glimpses of the asshole who thought he could hit on Lisa from the second she'd walked into the bar. The guy had given him the stink-eye and he had felt his glare on his back for the first half-hour, then he'd seen him mumbling into his cell phone. Now, it seemed, the chump's friends had come to start a fight.

He focused on Lisa instead as the dingus and his dingus

buddies finally found the balls to approach them. *I ain't doin' shit this time. She can take care of herself.*

"Hey, asshole."

Lisa turned on her stool and raised her eyebrows at the guy who'd been hitting on her and now brought three of his friends—presumably to hit Johnny with their fists instead. He ignored the guy and sipped his drink.

"I'm talking to you, bud." The angry drunk shoved his shoulder, and the dwarf turned slowly to look at him.

"So talk."

All four idiots' eyes widened and two of them stepped away from the bar.

"I was here first," the chump muttered and it seemed like he realized he'd made a big mistake but couldn't back down in front of his friends.

"Yep." Johnny raised his glass to his lips and paused to add, "And I've been here for hours. Tough."

The third friend brushed one side of his open button-down shirt over a white undershirt open to flash the hilt of a knife on his belt.

The bounty hunter glanced at it and sniggered. "Cute."

"You're not even from here, man. Do you have any idea who I am?"

"A moron?"

The drunk guy sneered and shoved a finger in his face. "You're messing with the wrong guy, asshole. You need to leave."

"I think you have us confused, pal."

"Are you trying to get your face beaten in?"

Johnny drew his utility knife in the blink of an eye and flicked it out. The idiot and his chums leaned away as he waved the blade tip from one to the other and pointed it at each of their faces in turn. Then, he picked a line of dirt out from under one nail. "I ain't tryin' to do nothin' unless the lady here says so. Y'all should follow suit."

Lisa glanced at the dangerously sharp blade he used as a nail file and chuckled. "Do you mean that?"

"'Course I do. You do what you gotta do, but I ain't liftin' a finger unless you want me to."

"Wow." She grinned. "That's a big change."

"What can I say, darlin'?" He turned his back to the angry assholes with one cute little knife between all four of them and gave her a crooked smile. "I'm maturin'."

"I said it's time for you to leave!" The drunk douche reached for Johnny's shoulder, but the dwarf had his blade at his hand in a split second.

"You can strut all you want, pal. Don't touch."

"You motherfucker—"

"Hey." Lisa turned fully on her barstool and spread her arms in a placatory gesture. "We're here minding our own business. You should mind yours. And you were never gonna get anywhere anyway. Your pickup lines suck."

The moron's goons sniggered until he turned and glared at them. He sneered at Lisa and pointed at Johnny. "I'm warning you—"

"All right. Go warn someone else."

"Come on, man." The man with the knife clapped a hand on his friend's shoulder and tried to drag him away. "It's not worth it. Let's get outta here."

Lisa grinned at them and wiggled her fingers in a mocking wave. "Have a good night."

The crew of idiots drew slowly away through the crowd, although the guy who'd set his sights on her threw heated glances over his shoulder and tried to remove his friends' hands as they guided him away.

"Truly, Johnny." She smirked at him. "That might have been the most impressive thing I've seen you do in a bar."

"What? Scare off a group of puffed-up roosters by cleanin' my nails?"

"Showing restraint."

"Yeah, well, you done told me the first time we met that you could take care of yourself—"

Luther and Rex barked once simultaneously. "Johnny, watch out!"

The dwarf didn't even have to move. In an instant, Lisa snatched the empty stainless-steel shaker off the end of the bar and spun in her chair. The douchebag trying to blindside her companion shrieked and stumbled back, clutching his hand as the shaker clanged onto the bar and rolled off the other side.

"What the fuck, lady—" Lisa slapped him so hard, the loud buzz of conversation over the classic-rock background dimmed for a second. The guy stumbled into his buddies and his eyes rolled back in his head.

His friend sneered at her and drew his knife. "It's like that, huh? Fine. You'll go down with the short guy."

He lunged at her with the weapon. Lisa dodged the swipe and side-stepped around him before he could make another attempt.

"Hey, hey, hey!" The bartender shouted. "Not inside!"

Her boot cracked squarely against the chest of the third drunken idiot and he thunked against the bar before she grasped the back of the knife-wielder's open button-up at the hem and jerked it up and over his head from behind.

The suddenly blinded man slashed wildly backward with his knife and she hammered his wrist with hers to pin it painfully against the edge of the bar. Something crunched in his hand, he squealed, and the weapon was dislodged from his hold. It clattered on the bar and spun on its side.

"You fucking bitch!" His scream was muffled through his shirt still pulled over his head so it lifted his shoulders by the tightened sleeves. "You broke my fucking—"

The sharp right hook she delivered into his fabric-covered jaw knocked the jerk out cold and he dropped. She shook her hand out with a hiss and glared at the last man who stared at two of his friends who'd been whipped by a woman. "You can be the guy who cleans them up or the guy who gets cleaned up by someone else. It's your call."

The idiot raised both hands in surrender and shook his head. "We're cool."

"Not really."

As the drunken buffoons moaned and tried to rise to their feet, Lisa returned to the last barstool at the end, downed the rest of her drink, and set the glass down with a heavy sigh. "That felt good."

Johnny beamed at her. "It felt good to watch, darlin'. I tell you what."

"You're welcome."

CHAPTER TWENTY-ONE

The bar was completely silent now except for Led Zeppelin playing through the speakers, and all the patrons stared at the fools who'd tried to take on Johnny Walker and ended up meeting Lisa Breyer instead. With a sigh, she nodded at the bartender. "I'll close out now."

The bounty hunter set down another twenty as she settled her tab, then slid off the barstool and stretched. The hounds rose from their place on the floor and stared at Lisa as the other customers returned to their regular nightly activity. Some of them laughed at the drunken idiots who cradled their heads, chests, and hands as they stumbled toward the other side of the bar.

"Johnny." Rex looked at his master and licked his muzzle quickly. "If you don't keep her around for the rest of your life, you're a dumbass."

"Yeah, she's one of a kind, Johnny." Luther sniffed Lisa's ankles and his nose moved up her leg. "I knew that from the very beginning. And if you don't do something about it, I will—"

Johnny snapped his fingers. "Down, boy. For Christ's sake."

"I didn't do anything, Johnny."

"Bro, she's not for you."

"I know that."

The second Lisa tossed the pen on the bar, she turned and took Johnny's hand to tug him across the room toward the front door. The hounds skittered after them, wove around the other patrons, and sniffed spilled puddles of booze and random ankles and shoes in their direct path.

"Man, I miss Boots," Luther whined.

"Don't take it out on her, bro. Leave that for Johnny."

"Well, it's about time, don't you think?"

The dwarf whistled for the hounds to catch up as Lisa thrust the door open and dragged him out into the night. "Y'all need to hurry!"

And shut up. It's none of their damn business what happens next.

It was easy to imagine Lisa was like this all the time, but her occasional stumble as they hurried down the sidewalk to the hotel reminded him that she was as liquored up as he was. Watching her fight four morons, one of whom carried a knife, had only sobered him long enough to appreciate everything he realized he didn't know about the half-Light Elf who'd become his partner—and something more.

She ran a hand through her long brown hair and took a deep breath of the night air before she finally released his hand. "So. I'm guessing you called Nelson and ripped him a new one after I left."

Aw, shit. Why did she have to bring Nelson up now?

He forced a cough and hooked his thumbs through his belt loops. "Yep."

"What did he say?"

"Nothin'. He's useless."

She snorted. "Yeah, I've thought the same thing lately. Now what?"

"Well..." Johnny glanced at the hounds who padded along silently beside him and shrugged. "We can go to the hotel and wait for the copycat bomber who disappears into thin air to strike again. Or for Nelson to cough up whatever extra info we could have damn well used before we left HQ."

"Great. Back to the hotel, then." Lisa looked at him, smirked, and pointed at the liquor store's red neon sign at the next street corner. "Why don't you grab a bottle of whiskey? I think I get why you like drinking at home more often than not."

He squinted at her. "Or in a hotel room."

"Exactly. And I'm not done unwinding."

"Uh-huh." *What the hell is she tryin' to pull?* "All right. Gimme two minutes."

Johnny held two fingers up and walked backward toward the liquor store, grinning like an idiot. She stayed on the sidewalk with her arms folded and watched him disappear into the liquor store.

"You got him smiling, lady," Luther muttered as he sniffed her feet. "You have no idea what a big deal that is."

"Yeah, listen. You better get it right with him." Rex sat on the sidewalk and thumped a rear leg as he scratched behind his ear. "And seriously, don't drag it out any longer than you have to, huh? It's getting ridiculous."

Lisa looked at them, swayed a little before finding her balance again, and chuckled. "I wish I knew what you were saying right now."

"Ha! Careful what you wish for, lady."

"Yeah, I bet Johnny wishes you could too." Luther sniggered. "Or that he hadn't made these collars. It's one of those."

"Don't confuse her, bro. She's had way too much to drink."

"But not enough, I don't think. Hey, there's Johnny!"

"Johnny!"

The hounds yipped and the bounty hunter raised the bottle of whiskey in the brown paper bag before he nodded down the street toward the hotel. "Ready?"

"Always." Lisa grinned and hurried to join him.

When they stumbled through the door of their hotel suite, the bottle of Johnny Walker Black was out of the bag, the lid gone and lost somewhere along the way, and the first fifth of the bottle gone with it. Johnny thumped a hand against the slowly closing door to keep it open for the hounds, who rushed inside and headed to the huge bowl of water on the kitchen floor.

"Hey! Come on, Rex. I'm thirsty!"

"Wait your turn." Quick, splattering lapping came from the kitchen as the dwarf shut the door with a click. "They're so drunk, it's making me dehydrated."

The bounty hunter snorted and turned with the open whiskey bottle held high. "I ain't complainin', darlin'. But if the truth be told, I didn't expect you to get on board with whiskey like this."

"I guess I'm full of surprises." Lisa spread her arms and emptied her pockets onto the kitchen counter—a small set of keys, her cell phone, and the second room key.

"No truer words…" Johnny took a swig from the bottle as he walked toward her, then held it out. "You gonna keep drinkin' this with me? Or do I gotta—"

She threw herself at him and a spray of whiskey sloshed over the top of the bottle onto the floor. He grunted and gaped at her with wide eyes as she ran her hands through his hair and covered his face with kisses.

"Whoa. Now…now, hold on…"

Lisa didn't stop.

"Wait a minute." He pulled away and scowled at her but realized that his other hand had already settled in the small of her back.

With a laugh, she shook her head. "Now what's wrong?"

"I only…you…" The dwarf glanced at the whiskey bottle in his hand and shrugged. "I thought you wanted a drink."

The bottle slid easily from his grasp when she snatched it away and placed it on the counter. "Don't be an idiot, Johnny. Not tonight."

He didn't have a chance to say anything else because her mouth was on his and her hands in his hair again, and she pulled him with her toward the closest bedroom of the two-room suite that shared the living space.

"Oh, shit, Johnny!" The hounds raced out of the kitchen, leapt around the two of them wrapped in each other's arms, and stumbled across the suite.

"Damn. Look at that!" Rex barked sharply. "This is finally happening!"

"Go, Johnny!" Luther uttered a warbling howl and jumped onto the couch before he bounded off the other side after his master. "And all it took was for you to do nothing. Who knew?"

"Yeah, yeah. Look at him, bro. He has no idea what's going on."

"Don't worry. He'll learn eventually. You got this, Johnny!"

The hounds laughed and ran in tight circles around the living area, barking and yipping.

When Lisa shoved the bedroom door open and pulled him inside, he reached out to grasp the doorway and paused. *Goddammit. I ain't drunk enough to not check.*

He studied her face as she gazed at him with hooded eyes. "Yeah?"

Lisa didn't say anything but she didn't have to when she stepped away from him and tugged gently on his other hand with both of hers.

"Do it! Do it! Do it!" the hounds chanted.

Luther raced forward with another sharp bark. "You need some help or something, Johnny? 'Cause you look a little frozen—"

The dwarf kicked the door shut behind him with the heel of his boot and the hound backed away with a snort.

"Yeah, yeah, okay. If you need anything, we're right out here."

Rex burst out laughing. "Yeah, try not to need anything, Johnny. You're on your own now!"

"Right? I mean, finally."

"Yeah, it took him long enough."

Shoes thumped to the floor on the other side of the bedroom door, followed by both Johnny and Lisa's soft laughter.

"Hey, Rex. I bet there's still some chicken bones in the trash."

"Forget the trash, bro." Rex leapt up to place both paws on the large desk that served as Johnny's temporary workshop and took the side of the plate in his teeth. It slid off the desk, clattered onto the floor, and spilled half-eaten fried chicken and bones all over the carpet. "Tonight, we feast!"

CHAPTER TWENTY-TWO

Johnny rolled over in the king-sized bed that had been designated as Lisa's and scowled fiercely. She was gone.

He sat with a grunt and rubbed his face vigorously before he leaned toward the nightstand. Beside her shoulder holster and service pistol, the alarm clock blinked its green digital numbers at him—7:34 am.

Huh. I thought I would have slept past eight, at least.

"Come on, lady. A little taste, huh?" Luther's voice filled the bounty hunter's head, and he whipped the covers off before he slid to the edge of the bed.

"Hey, you can't expect us to ignore everything," Rex added. "You had your fun last night. Time to share."

It took him five minutes to hit the head, splash water on his face, and get his boxers and jeans on but his shirt was nowhere to be found. Scratching his chest, Johnny opened the bedroom door and shuffled barefoot into the shared living area. The aroma of coffee, bacon, and toast hit him hard and his stomach growled.

"Yeah, yeah, yeah." Luther panted hopefully.

"Only one little piece."

With a smirk, he walked through the living area until he saw Lisa on the other side of the counter. She faced the stove and wore his black button-down shirt and nothing else.

Unaware of his presence, she took two pieces of bacon off a plate beside the stove and leaned down quickly to offer one each to the hounds.

"Yes! You are the best, lady!"

"Yeah. If Johnny doesn't tell you enough, we sure will—"

The dwarf cleared his throat. "Mornin'."

Two pieces of bacon landed on the floor.

"Shit, Luther. Grab it and run."

"Hey, wait up!"

Both hounds scuttled out of the kitchen with bacon strips protruding from their jaws before they raced through the other bedroom door and disappeared.

"Into the bathroom, bro."

"Yeah, he'll never think to look for us here."

Lisa turned partly away from the stove but continued to scramble the eggs on the burner. She grinned at him. "Morning."

"Now here's the thing, darlin'. I wake up, step out here, and find you—"

"Whatever you think you saw, I had nothing to do with it." Her failure to completely wipe her smile off when she glanced at the plate of bacon made him chuckle.

"I was talkin' about you wearin' my duds."

She glanced at his black shirt that reached barely past the tops of her thighs and shrugged. "Do you want it back?"

"Not even a little. You wear it better than I do." He rapped his knuckles on the counter as he stepped around it to enter the kitchen. "How you doin'?"

Lisa snorted and turned fully to look at the eggs. "Better. You?"

"Sure. Better. That's one way to put it." He approached her slowly and frowned in confusion at her easy smile and how straight she stood over the stove as she finished scrambling. *It took me years to not get hungover after a night like last night.* "And you were up and at 'em this early, huh?"

"It's almost eight, Johnny. That's not very early."

"Uh-huh. And your…head's okay?" He stopped behind her, put a hand on her waist, and stared with wide eyes at the pan of eggs.

"If you're asking me whether I'm hungover, the answer's no." Lisa looked slyly over her shoulder at him. "I do know what I'm doing most of the time."

"Oh, I'm sure you do, darlin'. You made that very clear last night." She snorted and elbowed him playfully, and the dwarf pursed his lips, on the verge of laughing out loud. "How about those knuckles?"

She turned her spatula hand so he could see it. Her blow to the side of the knife-wielder's face at the bar had broken the skin slightly and now a red-purple bruise had already come through. "It's nothing I can't handle."

"There was never a doubt in my mind."

"The coffee is over there. I'll be done with these in a sec."

"Uh-huh. I appreciate it." Johnny turned slowly toward the other end of the counter where the coffeemaker was still on and still hot. *I got no damn clue what to do now.*

He shuffled to the pot and stared at the empty counter.

"It looks like you seriously need it." With a light chuckle, Lisa opened the cabinet over the coffeemaker and pulled a mug out before she placed it on the counter. She paused, caught Johnny's face with both hands, and gave him a hell of a good-morning kiss. He stared dumbly when she pulled away. "Get out of the kitchen, Johnny. I don't wanna burn the eggs."

The bounty hunter grunted a laugh, poured himself a cup of coffee, and snuck glances at her in his black button-down as she cooked them breakfast.

Right. I guess it's okay for everythin' to be okay, ain't it?

The coffee helped kill most of his confusion and he took it with him to the small dining table against the wall. The hounds slunk through the open bedroom door behind him but didn't dare to look their master in the eye.

"Morning, Johnny."

"Hey, what's up?"

"You sleep okay?"

"You sleep at all?"

They sniggered and went to curl beside the couch, licking their muzzles.

Johnny sipped his coffee slowly.

I could get used to mornin's like this. Sure.

His phone buzzed in his back pocket and he pulled it out as he watched Lisa. The lazy smile beneath his mustache disappeared when he saw Nelson's name on the screen. "Aw, for cryin' out loud."

"What's wrong?" She pulled two plates down from the cabinet and served the eggs.

"Nelson. Talk about a buzzkill." He answered the call with a voice that was almost a growl. "What?"

"Whoa. Rough night, I take it?"

"It ain't none of your business, Nelson. Neither is my mornin'. You'd better be callin' me with somethin' useful."

The man cleared his throat. "Yes and no."

"I don't do riddles." When Lisa paused halfway toward the table with their breakfast in hand and a questioning frown, he shook his head. "You have twenty seconds to tell me why you interrupted my breakfast. After that, I'm turnin' my phone off."

"Okay, I get it. Listen, I went over that video you sent me with a few of my guys. The Bureau letterhead was disturbing, yeah, but it wasn't a federal case file the perp had in his hand. Not entirely. It's part of a CIA operation."

"You gotta be shittin' me." Johnny slumped in his chair as Lisa put their plates down and sat across from him.

"Nope. I wish I were, Johnny. Truly. But we reached out to a few contacts and it's all been confirmed."

"You're tellin' me the goddamn CIA's wagin' war on the FBI? Whatever you're smokin', Nelson, it needs to stop."

"Please, hear me out. Nothing's active right now and this isn't the CIA aiming a weapon internally. I know that much." The squeak of Nelson's desk chair came clearly through the line. "The CIA ran a program for creating tech-enhanced magicals—wartime stuff when we all still thought that kind of thing was viable or even necessary. But it was shut down sixteen years ago. The subjects didn't take very well to the treatments—or experiments, I guess. And there were too many major flaws."

"No shit." Johnny slurped his coffee and made sure it was loud enough for the agent to hear through the phone. "Lemme guess. Major flaws like these subjects gettin' out where they weren't supposed to be, terrorizin' civilians in public, and fixin' to blow up federal assets like…oh, engineering labs?"

"Yeah, Johnny. That kind of flaw. Look, I'm sending you the details of a contact I have out where you are now. She's expecting you but do us both a favor and let her know you're coming before you show up, huh? She has more details about this program than anyone in the Bureau and I don't feel like playing the middle man on this one."

"So you're finally givin' it up, huh?"

"Call her, Johnny. Then let me know what you need after that. Is Lisa there with you?"

"Yeah."

"Let me talk to her."

"No." Johnny hung up and dropped his phone on the table beside his plate.

"It sounds like useful information." Lisa shoveled a forkful of eggs into her mouth and waited patiently for an explanation.

"Yeah. Useful." He crunched a strip of bacon into his mouth

and chewed noisily. "The damn scientist with a concussion was right all along."

"What?" She lowered her fork to her plate again.

"Yeah. We're goin' after a damn cyborg."

CHAPTER TWENTY-THREE

Former CIA Deputy Director Annette Bristol lived in a quiet, clean, tree-dappled gated community in Brookline. Fortunately for the two partners, it wasn't a very long distance from their hotel.

"It looks like retirement's been good to her," Johnny muttered as he pulled up to the curb.

"Yeah, it works for some people." Lisa turned away from the window to wink at him. "Not you, though."

He squinted at her. "Cut it out with the winks while we're on a case, huh? You're killin' me."

With a laugh, she got out of the car and opened the back of the rental for the hounds to leap out.

"Hey, nice place." Luther sniffed the sidewalk. "Lots of critters running through here, Johnny."

"We can hunt in Pennsylvania, right?"

"Not today, boys." Johnny joined them on the well-maintained stone path that cut across the yard to the front door. *Not game, at least. We're huntin' CIA cyborgs. And that's the weirdest thought I've had all month.*

Lisa reached the front stoop first and knocked on the door. There was no answer. "She said it was fine to come over now, right?"

"'Course she did." Johnny joined her and hooked his thumbs through his belt loops. "You heard me talkin' to her before we left. She said she'd be back by noon."

"Yep." She glanced at her watch. "We are a little early."

He knocked on the door this time. "Annette? Johnny Walker and Agent Breyer. We spoke a few hours ago."

Only silence followed his greeting.

"Huh. Her car's in the driveway. Maybe you should call her again."

"Uh...Johnny?" Luther yipped from the side yard. "I think he beat us here."

"What?" The dwarf scowled at his hound who stuck his nose into the rustling bushes of the front garden. "Who?"

"The cyclops."

"Cyborg, bro," Rex corrected and sniffed vigorously the edge of the front stoop. "He's right, though, Johnny. I found the goo."

"Oh, yeah. Me too!"

"Dammit." The bounty hunter pounded on the door, then jiggled the doorknob but found it locked. "Annette! Open up. It's important!"

"What's going on?" Lisa asked. "Johnny!"

"The hounds found the same damn slime. The bastard's been here already. Annette?"

"Back away." Lisa drew her firearm and stepped back. Johnny barely had enough time to move out of the way before she fired at the doorknob and shot it out of its setting.

"That's one way to do it," he muttered as he readied his foot to kick the front door open.

"Wait, wait, Johnny." The hounds darted toward them and barked a warning. "You might wanna plug your—"

The door burst inward with a puff of dust and splintered wood. Johnny and Lisa covered their noses and mouths instantly as the same smell of the goo from the other explosions filled Annette Bristol's home—iron, meat, engine oil, and ozone.

"Aw, shit." Johnny cleared his throat and marched through the house. "Annette?"

"The chair." With a scowl as she tried to breathe only through her nose, Lisa leveled her firearm across the dimly lit living room. She nodded at an armchair that faced away from them. A thin, wrinkled hand dangled over the side of the armrest.

"Damn." He trudged forward, scanned the hallway at the other end, and found it empty. "Annette? It's Johnny. We're here to—"

He stopped when he rounded the chair and saw exactly what he expected to find but hoped he wouldn't.

The woman in her late sixties with white hair lay slack in the armchair, her eyes wide and mouth open in surprise. In the center of her chest was a hole that looked like it had been punched and seared through her. Mixed with the blood and charred flesh that stained the hole were thick splatters of the same red-black slime. It could have only been blood and guts from such a gruesome death or it could have been the murder weapon.

"No..." Lisa lowered her pistol by a few inches when she joined him in front of the armchair. "We were early and still too late."

"It might not be too late to pin the bastard down, though," Johnny muttered through clenched teeth. He snapped his fingers. "Rex."

"Yeah, Johnny." The hound stepped around a pile of shattered china and trotted toward his master.

"Tell me if you smell anything here besides...dead Annette." Lisa glanced at him in exasperation and he shrugged. "I'm only callin' it like it is."

"Same stuff as outside, Johnny," Rex said with a snort.

"Are you sure?"

"Yeah, I'm sure. I don't even have to get close."

"All right." He nodded at his partner and lowered a hand to the explosive disks on his belt. "He was inside."

"Was or is?" she whispered.

"We're about to find out."

"Johnny?" Luther uttered a low whine and sniffed the bottom of a door in the living room wall. "You might wanna check this out. There's something weird in here."

"All right, boy. I heard you loud and clear." He pointed at the door and nodded at Lisa. "You wanna call this in, darlin'?"

"Yeah. I can do that." She caught his meaning immediately and stepped slowly and carefully toward the hound and the door, following the dwarf's lead.

They could call in the murder of former CIA Deputy Director Annette Bristol later—after they dealt with the immediate threat.

Luther whined again and scratched the door. "For real, Johnny. I don't know why you're going so slow, but whatever this is, it's not good."

"Seriously?" Rex took a final look at the dead woman in the chair, then padded across the living room to join his brother in sniffing. "Whoa. Johnny, it's—"

The floorboards above them on the second story creaked, and everyone stopped to look up. Johnny drew an explosive disk and yanked the door open at the same time. He didn't smell anything new coming from the dark basement but he was a dwarf, not a coonhound.

Lisa glanced at the hounds. "What's down there?"

"Don't ask us, lady. How are we supposed to know?"

"Yeah, we're here to sniff out the weird."

Johnny translated by shaking his head. "I think we oughtta—"

"Stop now before you can't get out again," a low voice warned behind them.

They spun and Lisa raised her pistol at nothing but an empty living room. "FBI! Show yourself!"

"You're in way over your heads already." A black light strobed at the far end of the living room and a moment later, the intruder appeared out of thin air.

"Shit!" Luther scuttled back. "Johnny, where did he come from?"

"That's the guy, Johnny! Right?"

That's him, all right.

Cyborg was an accurate description, although the wizard who stood in front of them looked more like he'd been strapped inside a machine made to fit his body. An unmatched, crooked collection of wires and metal bars crisscrossed over his chest and back and the ends of two rods jutted over the backs of his shoulders.

He was missing his left foot, which had been replaced by a mechanical version. His left arm was strapped into some kind of hydraulic casing that moved when he moved, but his right arm ended a little above the elbow. A machine extension had replaced the rest of the limb and ended in five mechanized fingers. The arm itself was hollow as if it had been created only from a blueprint of a skeleton.

The metal parts that completed the cyborg glowed with the same silver light as that on the tech piece Johnny had taken as evidence. The thick, viscous red-black sludge dripped from his mechanical hand and marked him as exactly who they'd been looking for.

"Who are you?" Johnny snapped.

"That's what you're trying to find out, isn't it?" The wizard tilted his head with a whir and click of his machine parts. "You're not gonna find out."

"Don't move," Lisa shouted, her weapon trained on his head. "Hands up."

"Lisa, wait—"

"You mean like this?" The wizard sneered and raised both

hands. The mechanical arm fired a blast of electric-blue magic, a spray of the same oily sludge, and fire. It struck the doorway into the basement with a rocking explosion and hurled shattered wood fragments in every direction.

Lisa dropped to one knee below the blast and fired three rounds at their attacker.

The wizard cackled wildly and disappeared.

"What?" Breathing heavily, she stood and swung her weapon around the living room.

"I think he has some kinda illusion built into that getup," the dwarf muttered. "Watch for footsteps."

"Footsteps?"

"It ain't really teleport—"

The black light strobed again two feet in front of them and the wizard's mechanical arm sailed through what looked much like a teleportation portal to catch Johnny squarely in the jaw.

"Stop!" Lisa fired but her target was already gone.

The bounty hunter staggered back and wiped the red-black sludge and his blood off his split lip. "Bastard."

"Where'd he go, Johnny?" Rex barked madly.

"He could be anywhere, right?" Luther crouched low and snarled at the empty living room.

"How do we fight someone who doesn't follow the laws of physics?" Lisa demanded.

"It ain't physics, darlin'. It's magic." Johnny stepped away from the top of the basement stairs and scanned the living room. "That's how we do it."

She took his meaning and holstered her weapon. "As long as we find him."

"He'll come to us." Johnny started a slow circle around the living room. "And when I find him, make sure you hit him with—"

The black light reappeared beside him and he ducked. He

stabbed the button at the top of his disk and tossed the device into the circle of black light. It sailed through and what could be called a portal winked out.

"Behind you!" Lisa shouted.

He had enough time to drop into a crouch and spin before his detonated disk sailed over his head toward the foot of the staircase to the second floor and exploded.

Johnny staggered sideways, his ears ringing as the hounds barked madly at every little sound.

Tricks and new gear ain't gonna work on this bastard. We gotta go old-school.

The cyborg stepped out of another portal and strode toward him with a grin. "I bet you've never seen tricks like this, huh?"

The dwarf whirled and put the whole force of his momentum into a swing at the wizard's gut. His fist pinged off hollow metal that sure as hell looked like it was flesh beneath the guy's shirt. He roared and shook his fist out. His adversary laughed and swung his mechanical fist toward the bounty hunter's head.

"Johnny!" Lisa launched a huge fireball at the attacker. It glanced off his metal arm like she'd tossed a bucket of water at him instead.

Johnny took the cyborg's next blow to the jaw and lurched sideways before he bent over to spit a mouthful of blood onto the wood-chip-scattered floor.

"There's nothing you can do," the wizard snarled. "Pathetic."

He swung again, and the dwarf straightened at the last second to catch the metal fist that rocketed toward him. It smacked into his palm and he grasped a handful of wires coiled around the glowing forearm to yank them free. Red-black ooze and sparks erupted. He shoved the cyborg's arm to the side and pinned them together in a reverse arm-wrestle and the machine limb screeched and clicked. With his free hand, he took hold of the metal straps crossing the wizard's chest and pulled him closer.

A sickening crunch resulted when Johnny cracked his head against his opponent's completely organic face. The cyborg staggered back with a howl and the dwarf ducked beneath the other swinging arm and whipped the guy's machine arm back with another screech of grating metal.

"Now!"

Lisa already had both hands raised toward the wizard's metallic chest. The brilliant white light of her energy shield darted in a thick column toward him, no longer a shield now but a powerful burst of attack magic.

The bounty hunter was too slow to release his adversary's arm and froze in the massive shock of energy that blazed across all the conductive parts. Sparks scattered from the arm and launched Johnny across the room. The wizard stood where he was and he bucked and jerked beneath the shock as his machine parts sputtered and short-circuited. None of his limbs would move. Crackling threads of electricity snaked across him and he sneered at Lisa.

"Nice...trap." He snarled in fury. "You'd better think of something else clever before I—"

She drew her pistol and cracked it against the side of his head. More sparks shot from his short-circuited parts as his eyes rolled back in his head and he dropped to the floor with a heavy clank and thump.

The bounty hunter coughed. "I guess that was clever enough."

"Johnny." She raced to where he'd landed at the base of the couch and dropped to her knees. "I'm sorry. I didn't mean to hurt you with that—"

His laugh turned into a cough and made her stop and he waved her off as he pushed to his feet. "Do you think after all the years I spent buildin' my gear, I ain't used to a little shock now and then? Come on, darlin'. It tickled."

"Uh-huh." She glanced at the unconscious cyborg. "Are you sure?"

"Listen, he's the one still sparkin'." Johnny put a hand on her shoulder and squeezed gently. "Don't you worry about me. We ain't done here."

"Right. Now I'll call it in."

"Good idea."

As he dusted himself off, Lisa pulled her phone out to make the call. The department would send out a cleanup crew and hopefully someone from the CIA who knew Annette Bristol and any next of kin who needed to be notified.

"I tell you what, darlin'. Don't mention this asshole yet."

A metallic thump made her turn with the phone pressed to her ear. Johnny had his hands hooked under the cyborg's metal back braces and hauled him toward the open doorway into the basement. "What are you doing?"

"Gettin' ready for another interrogation. And yeah, I know the difference." He stepped down the first few stairs and pulled. The body was dragged over the edge of the landing. "Trust me. This won't be nothin' like HQ."

"You got him now, Johnny!"

"Throw him down!"

The hounds bayed and howled as they darted forward to snap at the cyborg's metal and organic feet.

Johnny stepped around the unconscious wizard and climbed the stairs again. "Heavy motherfucker."

He kicked the closest leg with a metallic ping and the body slithered completely over the top of the stairs, then clanked and thumped down step after step.

"All right!"

"That'll teach him, Johnny!"

The hounds raced down the stairs and howled and barked when the body finally thumped at the bottom in a heap.

Johnny turned slowly to meet Lisa's gaze, his eyes wide, and she shook her head. "Yeah, hi. This is Special Agent Breyer. Connect me to…"

With a shrug, the dwarf reached around the doorway to switch the basement light on before he hurried down the stairs after their copycat bomber. "It's time to make the cyborg squawk."

CHAPTER TWENTY-FOUR

The wizard groaned and regained consciousness to see two coonhounds standing in front of him. They snarled with their hackles raised.

"Watch it, asshole." Luther snapped at the guy.

"Yeah, one wrong move and you're toast."

He tried to stand and realized he was chained to the metal poles that served as legs for the workbench built into the wall of the basement.

Johnny walked into the wizard's field of vision and shook a small black device slowly at him. "Now we're gonna have us a little chat. Understand?"

"You can't hold me here forever." The prisoner coughed and strained against the double round of winter tire chains strapped across his chest to bind him in place. "What's that, huh?"

The bounty hunter smirked. "It's a shock collar. Annette must have had a hound or two back in the day and never got around to clearin' things out."

The wizard scoffed and tried to look at the dog collar fastened around his neck. "I heard you were smarter than this, dwarf. I won't even feel that."

"Not the way it was made, sure." He tossed the hand-held remote for the shock collar and caught it again. "But I like to tinker."

He pressed the button for two seconds and the cyborg erupted in a blaze of sparks from his mechanical joints. His legs jerked against the floor and the metal foot clinked repeatedly until the bounty hunter released the button to end the shock.

His captive groaned, breathing heavily, and spat.

"Did you feel that? Or should I play around a little more?"

"You have no idea what you stepped into." The wizard sneered.

"All right. So why don't you enlighten me?" Johnny moved forward and pressed the button again.

"Whoa, Johnny." Luther backed away and stared at the cyborg's electric fireworks display. "Look at him go."

"That's a lotta juice, Johnny." Rex looked at his master as the shock ended and the prisoner grunted with relief. "Does it go higher?"

The dwarf snorted at his hounds and stepped close to the wizard to grab the metal frame of the machine parts surrounding the guy's chest. He gave him a little shake. "Who are you workin' for?"

The cyborg laughed and finally focused his gaze on him. "You haven't worked it out yet?"

"You ain't doin' this for the feds or the CIA." Johnny lifted the remote in warning. "Otherwise, they would have put you down a long time ago for goin' rogue. So tell me why you're blowin' up federal labs and kemana shops and killin' little ol' retired ladies in their homes."

After staring at the remote, the wizard licked his lips and grinned. The steady patter of the oily sludge that dripped from his machine parts was the only sound in the silence in the basement for a long moment before he chuckled. "I didn't get it at first."

"Get what?"

"Why Omar couldn't shut up about you." His smile widened into a crazed grin and his head seemed a little unsteady as he stared at the bounty hunter. "He fucking worshipped you. Did you know that?"

Johnny stepped back and gritted his teeth. "You don't get to talk about him."

"Sure I do. Man, I can't tell you how many times I wanted to wring his scrawny neck for gushing constantly about Johnny Walker. Like you're some kinda god. And then—" A shriek of laughter burst from the wizard's lips. "And then you went and got him killed 'cause he was trying so hard to please you!"

He thumbed the remote's button again and the cyborg lit up with another flare of sparks as electricity jolted through him. This time, he made no effort to ease the flow of power that coursed through his prisoner.

"Johnny." Lisa stepped closer to him and placed a hand on his shoulder from behind. "Maybe take it easy." He grunted, irritated by both her intrusion and the fact that he hadn't heard her enter the basement.

"You want me to take it easy on this jackass?" He gestured toward the bucking, sputtering cyborg caught in the electric shock.

"Okay, easier. It won't help us if you kill him. I know you want to."

With a grunt, he took his thumb from the button to cut the flow of power and let the wizard catch his bearings again. He folded his arms. "So you thought you'd pick up where he left off, huh? Copy him and try to throw anyone who knew him off your trail? Or on it? It seems to me that you're itchin' to get yourself caught with how sloppy you've been with the attacks on the lab and the kemana."

The wizard sucked in a rattling breath and exhaled sharply in a whoop of laughter. "You think I'm a copy."

Johnny gritted his teeth.

"You moron. I'm the original!" The wizard spat a glob of oily-looking phlegm at the dwarf and missed by a foot. "Omar was copying me. He always did since we were kids running around naked in the yard."

Damn. This is a family thing now.

"Don't get me wrong, I hated listening to him gush about you every chance he got. But you know what I hate even more?"

"You're about to tell me, ain'tcha?"

"You, Johnny Walker. You killed my brother and I decided it was time I got in on the action myself. It was only a matter of time before you realized you couldn't get away with his blood on your hands forever." The wizard laughed again and fell into another coughing fit.

"The guy's lost his mind," Rex muttered through a snarl. "Johnny, he's crazy."

"I don't even understand half of what he said," Luther added.

He stepped toward the cyborg, lowered into a crouch, and waited for him to catch his breath and look at him. "This ain't all about me. You didn't throw yourself at a CIA cyborg project over sixteen years ago to blow me up or you would've done it already."

The wizard sneered. "No. I heard about you and your failure at retirement, Johnny. It was the best place for you, honestly. I'm surprised you didn't do it right after Omar. Who else had to die to make that happen?"

The shock collar activated again for another three seconds and when it was over, the prisoner hung his head and chuckled.

"It's on all of you. The whole government—FBI, CIA, it doesn't matter. You're all gonna pay."

"You're tryin' to destroy the same agency that did all that to you." Johnny gestured toward the dripping, sparking cage that couldn't be separated from the wizard's body. "You realized you made a mistake and shouldn't have blended yourself with tech, huh?"

"Ha! Wrong again, Johnny Walker." The wizard's laughter was shrill. "You truly are merely another fallible bastard like all the rest of us."

"Yeah, and you're chained to a table with a shock collar around your neck. Why are you doin' this? What's in it for you?"

"They shut the program down!" the cyborg yelled and strained against the chains. "They simply stopped halfway through, told everyone it was over, and tried to get rid of us. I wanted more! Don't you get it? All this..." He gazed lovingly at his twitching, malfunctioning arm that still dripped with sludge. "This was all me and now, I'm better than anything they tried to make us in those fucking labs."

Johnny stepped back and shook his head. "You made yourself into a machine and lost your damn mind."

The wizard lurched against the restraints and cackled. "And I'll take it all down with me."

"What's that supposed to mean?"

"You'll find out soon enough. Ha!" Spit dribbled down the cyborg's chin and his eyes blazed with madness. "You're out of time."

"Shit." Johnny spun and pointed at Lisa. "Upstairs."

"What's going on?"

"Now!"

"Johnny!" Rex howled at the far corner of the basement. "He put something under these boxes. Smells like the same goo."

Luther raced toward his brother and together, they pulled down the stack of boxes to reveal a small metal sphere hidden against the wall. Its silver light glowed with increasing brightness as it flickered and dripped with the oily red-black slime.

"Oh, shit. Johnny, is this a bomb?"

"Upstairs!" The dwarf caught Lisa's hand and yanked her toward the staircase.

With a scrabble of paws on concrete, the hounds scurried

after them, and the cyborg howled with laughter as a high-pitched whine rose behind them from the basement wall.

The bomb detonated two seconds after they reached the top landing. Lisa was catapulted forward but managed to stop herself on the armrest of the couch.

"That ain't the only one. Move!" Johnny slid an arm around her waist and hauled her away from the couch toward the front door. The hounds raced outside, and both partners were hurled forward by a quick series of three larger explosions that erupted from the basement. Another exploded at the front of the house and a huge chunk of the roof ripped away and careened over them. It missed the rental SUV by two feet but damaged shingles pinged off the front grill.

The bounty hunter huddled over Lisa where she'd sprawled on the grass in the front yard. He lowered his head between his raised arms to shield them both. A final explosion came from what was most likely the kitchen at the back of the house, and a column of flames flared into the sky. Metal, glass, and drywall rained in the aftermath but the bombs had at least all gone off.

He sat back on his heels and stared at Annette Bristol's burning house. When his partner pushed slowly off the grass, he pulled his gaze away from the flames to study her. "Are you all right?"

"Yeah."

"Is anythin' hurt? Broken?" He prodded her and checked her arms, legs, and the back of her head.

"Johnny, I'm fine. Honestly."

"Boys?"

"We're good, Johnny."

"Yeah, right here. We got out before you."

"Maybe you should work on your cardio."

With a snort, he scratched both hounds behind the ears when they moved in front of him, and the partners simply sat and watched the blazing house together. The already broken door fell from its hinges and kicked up a spray of sparks and more thick smoke. "Damn."

"This wasn't what I'd expected to find."

"Tell me about it, darlin'."

Lisa snorted and he looked at her in surprise. "It's funny, right?"

"I ain't followin'."

They helped each other to their feet and she gestured at the burning shell of a house. "Things are still getting blown up and making a mess but for the first time, you're not the one doing it."

CHAPTER TWENTY-FIVE

The fire department arrived at the house with surprising speed, followed by two squad cars from the Pittsburgh PD. The fire didn't last much longer after that and fortunately didn't spread to any of the neighboring homes.

Once the partners had told the police as much as they could without divulging classified FBI and CIA information, the officers finally agreed to let them examine the drenched, charred wreckage of Annette Bristol's house before they went in to conduct their investigation.

"But everything stays where it is," one officer said and pointed firmly at them as they headed toward the house. "We're the ones who have to deal with the rest of it once the FBI picks it clean."

"Fine." Lisa nodded at him and stepped carefully inside the house with Johnny.

"Hey, uh...Johnny." Rex picked his forepaw off the front step of the stoop and whined. "Maybe we'll stay out here."

"Totally," Luther added. "You know, keep an eye out in case the cyclops escaped while we were all running away."

"Cyborg."

The dwarf snorted. "There ain't no way he survived the explosion. And I had him trussed tighter than a hog on a spit."

"Well, all the same…" The hounds backed away and scanned the outside of the decimated house. "We'll stay."

"Honestly? After all the places we've been, y'all are scared of a wet house?"

"I mean, maybe we should've been scared of it before it got wet."

"Or before it blew up, Johnny."

"All right. Don't go anywhere." With a smirk, he stepped through the ruined doorframe and offered Lisa a hand to help her over the pile of rubble, the broken front door, and the clumps of ashy frames and burnt upholstery that had once been the furniture.

"Have you considered the part about this guy being able to teleport out of the basement?" she asked as they descended the stairs carefully.

"Sure I considered it." Johnny sniffed and scrambled over more debris at the base of the staircase before he extended his hand again to help her do the same. "But that lunatic wasn't interested in gettin' outta this one."

"What do you mean?"

"He wanted to blow himself up with the rest of it."

"There's no way to know that, Johnny."

"Sure there is. It was there in his eyes."

Lisa pulled her phone out to use the flashlight app and it seemed that he had been right. The charred metal hull of the wizard cyborg's body was still wrapped in chains. The poles supporting the workbench, however, had been uprooted from the floor by the blasts, and what was left of the wizard lay halfway buried beneath what remained of the wooden planks.

Johnny gestured toward the remains and raised an eyebrow.

"Okay, fine. You get points for that one but we need to make sure he's still in there."

"Oh, he's in there, all right." He slid one of the broken poles out from beneath the wreckage and used it to poke at the burned remains of the crazy wizard. When he pulled it away, a thick string of the same oily slime pulled away before it plopped onto the floor.

"Oh, jeez." Lisa covered her mouth. "It's even worse now."

"What? You don't like the smell of barbequed cyborg?"

"That's so not funny."

"Maybe a little funny." He squatted beside the body and nudged it again with the pole. "Nope. There's no way he's comin' back for another round after this. I think he knew he was at the end anyway, what with all that slime drippin' off him at every turn."

"What are you doing?" She scowled as he poked around with the pole. "Oh, come on. Johnny. Don't touch it."

"Hold on now." Johnny leaned closer to the body and reached into a hole in the metal casing around what was the wizard's chest. When he withdrew his hand, the same strings of sludge clung to his fist and he shook them off with wet splats.

"Johnny—"

"Do you think the Pittsburgh PD are gonna throw a fit if we take a tiny souvenir, huh?"

"What is it?"

He opened his hand. "Some kinda chip. If it is, this might be how we find the others."

"There are more? Great."

"'Course there are, darlin'. You heard it straight from the cyborg's mouth. The program ended and all these half-tech magicals had the rug yanked out from under 'em. There's no way he is the only one." He pulled another evidence baggy out and dropped the slime-covered chip inside.

Lisa folded her arms. "Did you bring an unlimited supply of those with you?"

"Sure. I have a box of 'em in the jet too just in case."

She rolled her eyes and looked at the staircase. "It's time to go."

"Yep. Then we run this through a couple of tests and I'll bet you anythin' it brings us closer to who's runnin' this show."

"He said he was doing it on his own."

"Darlin', he was talkin' to someone in that first livin' memory we recreated. We saw him followin' that someone's orders and all this was an attempt to take all the credit for himself when he thought it was the end."

"Okay. So we're looking for someone who filled the void of this cyborg program after the CIA shut it down."

"That's what I think but I can't tell how much of what he told us was true and how much was his mechanized brains all scrambled into mush." Johnny wiped his slime-covered hand on the wall as they climbed the stairs and made sure to shove every inch of the evidence bag into his back pocket so the police wouldn't see it.

At the hotel—after a shower and a fresh pot of coffee—the bounty hunter sat in front of his living-memory projector on the desk and set it up to read the last memory from the wizard before he'd died. He inserted the chip in the device too in case it gave them anything extra, but he wasn't counting on it.

"All right, darlin'." He turned in his chair and nodded at Lisa. "Now, I ain't fixin' to repeat the way things went last night. I know you already used that super-spell to fry a cyborg once today, but we need your skills again."

She approached the desk with pursed lips and stared at him as she placed her hand on the top of the device.

He cleared his throat. "Please?"

Her hand blazed with bright white light, and she didn't look away from him until her magic had supercharged the living-memory reader so its tiny lights blinked and the mechanism hummed and a few sparks erupted from the back. She removed her hand and shrugged. "Asking nicely goes a long way."

"Uh-huh. I get the point." He rubbed the back of his neck, cleared his throat again, and pulled the video app on his phone up as the projection illuminated through the enlarging window at the front of the device.

So this is the next level of our relationship, huh? Where I start askin' nicely and she starts to get scary.

His urge to laugh at that died immediately when the projection clarified and he saw himself looming over the prisoner, the hounds growling at his sides, and Lisa standing six feet behind him with her arms folded.

It's on all of you. The whole government—FBI, CIA, it doesn't matter. You're all gonna pay."

"You're tryin' to destroy the same agency that did all that to you."

As strange as it was to see and hear himself talking in a blue-tinted magical movie, he focused on angling his phone correctly to capture the best view.

"You realized you made a mistake and shouldn't have blended yourself with tech, huh?"

"Ha! Wrong again, Johnny Walker." The wizard's laughter was shrill. "You truly are merely another fallible bastard like all the rest of us."

Johnny rolled his eyes and let the living memory go on as long as it needed to. Which, conveniently enough, was at the point where the hounds uncovered the bomb and he shouted for all of them to get upstairs. "Shit. I thought that was never gonna end."

The device powered down and he shoved his phone into his pocket before he slumped in the chair.

Lisa rested a hand on his shoulder. "You should probably send that to Tommy too."

"Not yet. I aim to hold onto it a little longer. I have a feelin' we might have to use some leverage sooner or later."

"Against someone in the Bureau?"

He shrugged. "I can't rightly say yet, darlin'. It's more than likely we'll be up against someone connected to the CIA if they're not an active part of it. This ain't exactly a simple case either."

"Well, you did look incredibly bored with all the simple local cases taken in your front yard—I mean,…uh, office." Lisa chuckled and leaned against the edge of the desk. "The complicated cases are the ones that suit you the best."

"Huh. Is that so?"

Her smile faded. "What's wrong? And don't tell me that's your thinking face, Johnny. I can tell the difference by now."

"Aw, hell." The dwarf ran a hand through his hair and tugged the end of his beard. "This one's way closer to home than I was prepared for, is all. Omar. *Omar*. I'd be lyin' if I said I didn't think about him some days, but to have his brother show up in my face like that? Twenty years later?" He clicked his tongue and shook his head. "How the hell did it pan out like this?"

"Hey." Lisa slid along the edge of the desk until she stood between it and his rolling desk chair. "None of this is your fault—not Omar, not his brother, and not anything the Bureau or the CIA can and can't do. Now or however long ago. You didn't make him what he was. That was all him."

"Sure, and he was damn clear about that from the start, wasn't he?" He cleared his throat, looked slowly at her, and squinted. "I gotta be the one pulled into all this like a goddamn time loop of my own life."

"Again." Lisa bent slightly to put her hands on both his shoulders and look him in the eyes. "None of this is your fault."

"I know." He patted one of her hands. "But it will be if we don't find out what the hell's goin' on and stop it before every government agency in America blows up its own damn self."

CHAPTER TWENTY-SIX

Nelson called a total of six times before Johnny finally answered simply to shut him up. "Normally, when someone doesn't pick up, Nelson, it means the guy you're tryin' to talk to don't wanna talk."

"I get that, Johnny. But we have bigger problems."

"Yep. I'm workin' on it." He placed his phone on the table and stabbed the speaker button so Lisa could listen from her seat in the armchair.

"I heard Annette was dead when you found her. Is that true?"

He narrowed his eyes at the dead cyborg's weird chip clamped between his needle-nose pliers and snorted. "I know none of it makes sense, but we ain't lyin' to you. Some of us have learned how to move past that tactic."

"Okay, fine. I'm sorry I asked." The sound of a door closing came over the line. "Johnny, things are getting very tense here at HQ and at all the other hubs and safe houses. I've received calls like crazy from mutual contacts between us and the CIA. No one over there wants to reach out to us themselves but it sounds like they're taking it personally. Annette was a big deal, even in retirement."

"Uh-huh. I heard that happens sometimes." The small flare of the mini welding torch he activated to use on the new device in his hands illuminated his face with an orange glow. "I suppose they wanna talk to us, then."

Nelson sighed. "Who knows what they want?"

"Lemme rephrase, Nelson. We need to have a meetin' with someone who was involved in their cyborg program."

"Johnny, I don't think that's what it's called—"

"It don't matter what it's called. That's what it is. And it ain't dead, neither."

"What?"

The dwarf focused on the precise line of the welding torch and a buzz and sparks filled the hotel room.

"Are you...are you using power tools during this conversation?"

He snorted. "Nope."

Lisa stood and approached the desk. "Tommy, can you get us into a meeting with the CIA? Preferably someone who was in on the program when it was operational if it's possible."

The agent released a long, drawn-out sigh. "I should be able to set something up with you two as liaisons. Honestly, though, it'll probably end up only being you, Lisa."

"Forget it," Johnny grumbled. "If she goes, I go."

"Sure, Johnny. You can try. The CIA isn't exactly fond of bounty hunters—or magicals, as a general rule. They think they're too good for magicals. You strike out two for two on that one."

"Go ahead and set the meeting up," Lisa said and leaned over the phone. "We'll take care of the rest."

"And by take care of, I assume you mean muscle your way past any CIA operatives who try to stop you. And maybe blow down a few doors and bash in some heads while you're at it?"

The dwarf chuckled. "The things you come up with, Nelson. I don't know where they come from."

"Right." The man cleared his throat. "Yeah. I'll set the meeting up."

"Thanks, Tommy." Lisa ended the call and frowned as Johnny continued to tinker with his mini welder and the chip he'd pulled out of a burnt body. "You know, I want to ask what you're doing with that but I don't think I'll understand a word of it until you show me."

"Yep." He grunted and picked up a different tool to bend, twist, and pry at the device. "You and me both, darlin'."

"Oh, good. So all this focus is merely a shot in the dark, huh?"

The welder flared to life again in his hand and he grinned and wiggled his eyebrows. "That's all part of the fun, ain't it?"

Lisa raised both hands in mock surrender and stepped slowly away from the desk. "You'd think we've had enough of magicals grinning like complete lunatics before they're about to do something truly insane."

"Aw, come on. This ain't nothin'."

"Yeah, and I think that's what I'm afraid of."

The sound of the whiskey bottle opening and two glasses clinking together made Johnny set his tools down and swivel in the desk chair to face her. "Are you sayin' you're scared of me?"

"Certainly not. Only of the fact that I know you have several more levels of crazy until you've finally lost it and I have no idea what they look like." She poured them each half of what Johnny normally poured himself and brought him a glass.

He wrinkled his nose. "That's it?"

"You can have more when you put the incendiary devices and conductive materials down, Johnny. This is called a compromise." She tilted her head challengingly and held the glass out.

"Huh. While we wait for our secretary to set up a meetin' with the assholes who made the cyborgs."

They clinked their glasses together and drank.

"Wait. By secretary, you mean…"

"Nelson. Who else."

Lisa grinned. "Good answer."

Their meeting the next day with the CIA's Head of Development and Engineering was near Fowlerville, Michigan. When they received the info from Nelson, Johnny couldn't help but grumble, "They did that on purpose."

"What? Arrange a meeting? Yes, Johnny. That was the point."

"They made it out in Fowlerville. Annette still lived here, close to whatever she was doin'. They're simply tryin' to bust our balls by pickin' a place and time they don't think we'll be able to make."

She wrinkled her nose at his choice of words but brushed it aside. "Well, it's a good thing the Bureau bought you a private jet, Johnny. Now we have a chance to…bust their balls in return?"

He snorted. "It still needs work, darlin'. Let's get movin'."

It took them three hours to reach the designated location, which was way farther in the middle of nowhere than Johnny had first expected. Still, they exited their rental vehicle two minutes before the agreed-upon time and found the man waiting in front of what looked like an old barracks building that should have been on a military base.

Mac Cardum looked as old and washed-out as Nelson, although admittedly more disappointed to see a dwarf, a half-Light Elf, and two coonhounds moving toward him. He scowled, double-checked his wristwatch, and rolled his eyes. "Oh. I had begun to think you wouldn't make it."

"Are you sure you weren't hopin' that was the case?" Johnny stopped five feet from the department head and studied him with narrowed eyes. "'Cause you look like we're already wastin' your time. And we're early."

"You are wasting my time."

"Lisa Breyer." She held her hand out but the man didn't take it.

"You two blew Annette Bristol's house up."

"Naw, someone's gettin' their facts scrambled. The cyborg blew her house up." Johnny hooked his thumbs through his belt loops and regarded the man with a steady stare. "And killed her before we had a chance to talk to her."

"You arranged the meeting with her!" Cardum stabbed a finger at Johnny's face. "That asshole wouldn't have known to expect you otherwise. This whole thing's on you."

"Now, I dunno about all that." The dwarf cocked his head, his expression unreadable. "You're workin' for the agency that created the damn monster in the first place."

"What the hell do you think gives you the right to—"

"I'm sorry. Director Cardum, I know tensions are high, but we came here to see you for a reason. Right now, it's to take a look at the site." She nodded at the man and raised her eyebrows. "But our end goal is the same as yours."

"That's what you think." He sneered.

"To find out who was behind these attacks and stop them before they can do it again. So if you don't mind…" Lisa gestured toward the front of the building, and Cardum took a moment longer to glare at Johnny.

"No one said anything about the mutts coming along. Put them in the car."

"The hounds stay with me," the dwarf stated and seethed inwardly.

"If they get into anything they're not supposed to—"

"Yeah, yeah. Then you can wrap your twitchin' fingers around my neck and call it even. Let's do this."

Lisa glanced warningly at him and he rolled his eyes before he snapped his fingers. "We're goin' in, boys. Don't touch anythin' without my say so."

"Uh, wasn't planning on it, Johnny." Luther caught up quickly and padded at his master's side. "This place already smells funky."

"Like mold and dust."

"And fried wires."

"Not the kind you wanna eat, Johnny."

"Not the kind we wanna eat."

He snapped his fingers again and the hounds fell silent.

"So you two think this mad wizard who performed one too many modification surgeries on himself was a part of our Living Augmentation program, huh?" Cardum didn't bother to hold the door open for them or even turn to face them when he spoke.

"It ain't a matter of thinkin' it." Johnny made a point of holding the door open for Lisa. "We have proof."

"Bullshit."

"He told us himself," she added. "Before he blew himself to pieces and tried to take us with him."

"Do y'all have any records of the program participants goin' back more than sixteen years ago?"

Cardum looked over his shoulder to scowl at the dwarf.

"Yeah, I didn't think so."

"Living Augmentation was shut down due to lack of funding sixteen years ago."

"We heard it was because of the...side effects." Lisa scanned the bare walls covered in rust stains and traces of mildew. "The procedures didn't take with the subjects. Right?"

"How the hell should I know? It was before my time." The man shook his head irritably. "But they should have expected that kind of reaction from you people."

"Say what now?" Johnny stopped in the hall and glared at the man's back, his fists clenched.

Lisa put a hand on his shoulder and shook her head. "Let it go. It's not important right now."

"The hell it ain't."

"I don't have all day for this," the agent called acerbically. "So if you want to see the facility, I suggest you keep moving. I'm only doing this as a favor to Tommy but I can still change my mind."

"Huh. Some favor."

"Come on." Lisa tugged on his arm and he finally moved down the hall again.

"Ew. Rex. Check it out." Luther stopped to sniff the mildewed wall. "Okay, I know it's different than the tunnels in Portland and everything, but does this smell like blood to you?"

Rex joined his brother for a sniffing session. "Uh…yep. Don't lick it, bro."

"I'm not."

"This building was the main hub of Living Augmentation at its inception and during the majority of its lifespan before they killed it." Cardum sounded entirely bored by the tour he'd agreed to give. "All this here is administrative. Down that hall was the residential area, I guess you could call it. The subjects had their own rooms, exercise yard, and library. You name it. They took all their meals with the staff so the team could observe them more closely in day-to-day life."

They moved farther toward the back of the building, where the hallway T-ed off. The man gestured to the right and said blandly, "Testing rooms were down here. All the subjects were tested for physical and mental agility, not to mention whatever screwed-up special powers they had after certain procedures. None of them were tested together, as far as the reports state. Down here"—he swung his arm to the left—"were the enhancement theaters."

"They played movies in this place, Johnny?"

Rex shook himself vigorously from head to tail. "Creepy. There's gotta be better places to do that."

"Explain those," Johnny said and forced himself to not shush the hounds no one else could hear.

Cardum turned and glared at him. "Operating rooms. Is that more digestible for you?"

"You bet." Johnny nudged Lisa with his elbow and nodded toward the left-hand hallway. "I wanna see what's in those."

He didn't wait for anyone to agree but brushed past their guide. His boots thudded hollowly on the dusty linoleum floors.

"There's nothing in there," the man called. "Everything was cleared out years ago. The facility hasn't been touched since."

"It don't mean there ain't nothin' worth seein'." The bounty hunter threw open the first door on the left with a bang. Inside was a dented metal operating table, a rusted gurney, and an empty stainless-steel cart. The huge operating light hung low over the table, and only a handful of old tattered blankets dangled from the side of the built-in shelving unit. "Huh. Are all the rooms like this?"

"Only the small ones in the front. The big ones are at the very end but I wouldn't bother—"

"You know, Cardum, I sometimes can't help myself. Let's go, boys." Johnny continued down the hall and opened every door he passed to peer into the rooms that had been used to experiment on live and willing magical subjects. *At least I hope they were willin'.*

"Is he hoping to find something specific here?" Cardum snapped as he caught up to Lisa.

"I have no idea. But he'll know it when he sees it. And as soon as Johnny looks through every corner and cupboard here, we'll be out of your hair."

"Great."

"Nothing but sterile rooms, Johnny," Rex called.

"Ooh. More blood in this one." Luther trotted out of the room with his tongue lolling from his mouth. "Like a ton of it. But it's been there a long time."

"Y'all keep sniffin' around. If that damn wizard was left from when this place ran twenty-four-seven, there's sure to be somethin' else."

Finally, Johnny shoved open the swinging metal doors into what looked like an old-school operating theater, complete with the balcony inside the door that looked over the three operating tables below in the center of the half-circle. "Huh. It even has stadium seatin'," he muttered.

"For the more…informative procedures, I guess." Cardum

took two steps inside and scowled at the dust-covered floor of the room's center. "Honestly, I don't see how anything like this was even allowed to move forward in the first place. The whole thing should have been a wash from the very beginning."

"I can agree with you there," Johnny said. "The feds work with magicals, sure, but none of us are experimented on like this."

Lisa stood barely inside the door and gazed at everything with wide eyes.

"Whoa, whoa, whoa, Johnny!" Luther barked and raced down the stairs to dart through the center of the circular rows of observation seating. "There's something down here!"

"Dammit," Cardum snarled. "Get your stupid dogs under control—"

"Watch it." Johnny pointed at him. "My hounds are smarter than most bipeds and I think they're onto somethin'."

Rex darted down after his brother and stopped occasionally to sniff the air. "Uh-oh. Johnny, we're sure that crazy cyborg guy is dead, right?"

"Uh-huh." The dwarf turned to share a knowing glance with Lisa, although she didn't know what was being said.

"Oh, whew." Luther spun in a tight circle in front of a sealed steel door at the other end of the theater. "That's a relief. 'Cause I thought for a minute maybe he'd followed us here."

"What do you mean?" Johnny headed down the stairs.

"It smells like him, Johnny." Rex pawed at the door. "I don't see any sludge but it smells like crazy wizard."

"What's in here?" Johnny pointed at the door and turned toward Cardum.

The man leaned over the railing at the top and shook his head. "I don't know. Nothing. It's been sealed for—"

The door shrieked and groaned when the bounty hunter tugged on it. Finally, it shuddered free and swung open. A portion of the reinforced beam that had only been partially welded to the wall and the door came loose and clattered on the floor when he dropped it. "It ain't that sealed off."

"Well, it doesn't matter anyway. Whatever's there hasn't been used for almost twenty years."

"Oh, yes, it's down here, Johnny!"

"Yeah, yeah! The smell of crazy. And meat. Crazy meat."

"And tons of metal, Johnny." The hounds raced the narrow hallway on the other side of the door and he followed them.

"What the hell is he doing?" Cardum snapped.

"Finding what he's looking for." Lisa shrugged and jogged down the steps. "Feel free to join us. I can't say how long we'll be, though."

With a growl of irritation, the department head spun to glare at the open door into the hallway. After a moment, he rolled his eyes and marched down the steps after the two magicals who he felt had no business in a CIA facility, even an abandoned one.

CHAPTER TWENTY-SEVEN

"Oh, yeah, Johnny. This is a secret tunnel."

"Of course it's a secret tunnel. Look at it. All dark and musty and—hey. Puddle of water here."

Johnny whistled and the hounds snapped their attention to the task at hand. "Follow the trail, boys. That's all y'all need to worry yourselves with."

"Got it."

"Follow the trail, Johnny."

"And then we'll catch whatever's at the end of it."

The tunnel only branched off twice but the hounds didn't hesitate in choosing which to follow. After about a mile, they skidded to a stop thirty feet from a door toward the end of the tunnel and crouched with low growls.

"What?" Johnny whispered.

"There's someone in there, Johnny."

"Muttering to himself."

"Can we eat him?"

Johnny and Rex both stared at Luther and said, "Huh?"

"What? It's only a thought."

Lisa and Cardum caught up to them and she rested her hand on her service pistol. "Did we find something?"

"I think someone is in there mutterin' to himself." Johnny nodded at the closed door. "So we should step in lightly and see what it's all—"

"This is ridiculous." Cardum pushed past them and stormed toward the door.

"Goddammit, man. Get back here." The bounty hunter hurried after him with an exasperated curse.

"No one's supposed to be in here. These tunnels were closed for a reason." Whatever righteous fury the man possessed made him throw the door open and step inside. "Hey!"

The two partners raced after him and stopped abruptly in the doorway.

It was a secret tunnel, without doubt, and led into a secret lab under the CIA's secret lab. The room was bathed in green and orange hues that emanated from the blinking lights on the many machines and glowed within vials, test tubes, and plastic bags dangling from the walls like IV drips. A woman was hunched in the center of the room. She wore three different scarves over her stained lab coat. Her fingers flew across the laptop keyboard in front of her on the center island and she glanced up, not at the open door but at something on the other side of the room.

Luther growled at the woman. "Johnny, I don't like walking, talking rag piles."

Cardum's eyes all but bulged from his head as he took another step into the room. "Dr. Monroe?"

The woman startled and her glasses slipped down the bridge of her nose. She fumbled to right them again as she whirled toward the door. "Huh? Who's there?"

"Mac Cardum."

"Mac? What the hell are you doing here?" She hurriedly shuffled the papers scattered across the central counter and tapped repeatedly on a single keyboard key before she slammed the laptop shut. "You're not supposed to be here."

"Neither are you." If the man's face hadn't been so green-washed by the energy that hummed from so many sources in the room, he would have visibly paled. "Eveline, none of this is sanctioned."

"Oh, good. Y'all know each other." Johnny strode into the room and pointed at Dr. Monroe. "So you're the one makin' cyborgs under the table, huh?"

"Under the table? No, no, no." The woman shuffled around the center island. "This is all completely professional. By the book."

"It's not sanctioned," Cardum hissed.

"Well, it was when I started this program," Eveline retorted and leaned forward over the counter. "It was all cleared to continue and they had no right to rip it all out from under me. No right!"

Her hand smacked on the counter and she blinked in surprise at the force of her blow.

"How long have you been down here?" the CIA agent asked.

"As long as I've needed to be. Oh, yes. They tried to take years of research and application out from under my nose, lock it up, and call it useless. But it's not, you know. Not what I've discovered." The woman tapped her chest as she walked backward and glanced nervously from the three newcomers to her secret lab. "Defunded. Ha! They were scared but not me. I've handled all the modifications and research on my own. And I've perfected the warrior prototype."

"The what?" Cardum whispered.

"Johnny." Lisa pointed to the side of the room at two large metal ramps that looked like they were designed to unfold from the wall and lead somewhere else.

He noticed the magicals strapped to each of the ramps instead like they were vertical gurneys. A shifter man and a Crystal woman both hung suspended by padded clamps around their chests and waists while their arms dangled from little more than shackles bolted to the wall. Their eyes were closed and the glowing green IV bags, he realized, fed directly into them.

"So this is where you do it, huh?" He pointed at the unconscious magicals, both enhanced with different mechanical parts not unlike the wizard's. One of the shifter's eyes was augmented and the Crystal had some kind of scope or small-range weapon protruding from the flesh of her shoulder. "All the experimentin' on folks who have no idea what they signed up for."

"Oh, no, no. That's where you're wrong." The mad scientist wagged her finger at Johnny and stepped toward the back of the lab, her hands grasping sporadically behind her. "These subjects know exactly what they're getting into and so do I. The whole agency's been trying to shut me up for decades and I won't have it."

"Two more," Lisa whispered.

Johnny gritted his teeth at another two magicals suspended on the other side of the room, although he couldn't tell immediately what they were beneath the green glow. "How many more do you have holed up in here, Doc?"

"Hmm? Oh, no. Only the four. That's all I need." Eveline squeaked when she backed up against a tall, narrow machine that looked more like an ATM than anything else. "You see, I've perfected the entire process. They don't feel a thing when they're like that and they won't do anything unless I say so."

"Eveline, wait—" The CIA agent took a tentative step toward her.

"No! You're exactly like the rest of them, Mac. Always trying to shut me up. You know what the problem is? No one cares about the science anymore. You won't believe what they can do already and it's only the beginning."

The woman's startled expression morphed into a crazed grin as her wrinkled hand smacked a button on the tall machine behind her. A high-pitched whine filled the room and she gazed expectantly at the beings suspended from the walls.

"All right, now see here." Johnny stepped toward the closest cyborgs. "Ain't no one gotta get hurt in all this. Cut 'em loose, Doc. Then we can all get outta here and decide the next steps after this."

"Ha! I'll cut 'em loose, all right. Yes." Eveline whirled toward the tall machine behind her and jerked a narrow door open. When she turned again, she held a heavy-duty modified firearm. "But none of you are going anywhere."

It looks more like a shortened bazooka. With a sigh, Johnny folded his arms.

Cardum ducked with a shriek and raised his hands. "Are you crazy? You can't run around pointing that at—"

"Shut up, Mac." The woman cranked a lever on the side of the weapon and swung the barrel, not toward Johnny and Lisa but the two unidentified magicals on the far wall. "Now you'll see."

She squeezed the trigger but instead of bullets or concentrated energy or even a magical blast, what emerged from the barrel was, as far as any of them could see, nothing.

Eveline grinned like a lunatic and swept the weapon from side to side between the magicals like she was spraying them with machinegun fire in a mobster movie.

That's what happens after sixteen years in a secret lab hackin' folks up and buildin' 'em back together again. She's well and truly nuts.

"Ah! Johnny! Make it stop!" Luther stumbled forward, dropped to his belly, and pawed at his ears.

Rex threw his head back and howled. It ended in a sharp yelp. "My head's gonna explode, Johnny. It's that...the stupid gun!"

"Turn it off!" Johnny roared and stormed toward her. "Cut that shit out, Doc. I mean it."

The hounds whined and pawed at their ears as they spun in circles.

"You can't stop this." Eveline swung the weapon at his chest and squeezed the trigger again.

He looked down and of course, nothing happened. "Give it to me."

As he tried to wrestle it out of her hand, Lisa drew her firearm and backed away. "Johnny, they're waking up. Or coming online. Or whatever the hell we're calling it. It's about to get messy."

The bounty hunter finally wrenched the high-frequency bazooka from Dr. Monroe's hands and flung it away. The woman merely laughed and watched her Frankenstein's monsters rip free from the IV lines as the metal belts around their waists and the manacles popped open. All four cyborgs dropped to their feet with a metallic clunk and turned toward the two partners.

The hounds snarled and raced after the defunct weapon that had fallen and now skittered across the floor.

The Crystal cyborg cocked her head with a completely blank expression, and the small gun that protruded from her shoulder swiveled and aimed at Lisa.

"Don't even think about it!" The agent leveled her pistol at the being but the shoulder-gun fired anyway. A mini-RPG launched from the tiny barrel and streaked across the room leaving a trail of glittering orange smoke. It struck the far end of the lab and exploded.

"I seriously hope none of y'all can teleport," Johnny muttered before he lunged toward the shifter with the augmented eye and a whirling series of restructured parts where his right hand should have been.

"Luther, get it!"

"I'm trying! Do you have any idea how slippery these floors are?"

"Yes! Deal with it!"

The spin and whirl of four cyborg's different mechanized parts filled the lab.

"Get them! Get them!" Eveline shrieked and pointed at the intruders in her domain. "Do what I created you to do."

The second two cyborgs—who looked like twins with their pinched noses and ridiculously thin eyebrows—strode rigidly toward Johnny. He tried to dodge out of the way but the first guy's arms elongated impossibly and snatched his shirt collar. The other magical's fist erupted with orange light and drove into Johnny's gut.

He was flung aside and sprawled with a scowl. "See? This is why cyborgs are a bad fuckin' idea!"

The bounty hunter struggled to his feet as Lisa tried her energy-shield blast on the Crystal and the shifter. She had no time to build up enough power to thoroughly short them out and could only blast them back again by half a foot. "Johnny! I thought you had a plan!"

"I'm workin' on it!" He patted his pockets and snarled in frustration. "Shit. Where is it?"

"Rex, come on!" Luther howled. "Turn it off!"

"I'm gonna rip it apart is what I'm gonna do!"

The hounds chased the bazooka that had activated the cyborgs, and Johnny scanned the floor of the lab. Finally, he located the small box he'd spent hours crafting around the chip he'd taken from the burnt chest of Omar's brother. "Hey, boys! Hold up!"

The hounds were too caught up in their singular mission to pay attention as more magi-tech explosions—not Johnny's—wracked the lab and Eveline shrieked instructions to her mini-army of mechanically enhanced soldiers.

Luther's back paw came down on Johnny's newest invention almost in slow motion and crunched the delicate device into hundreds of glittering pieces.

"Dammit." The dwarf snatched an explosive disk from his belt and gritted his teeth. "Y'all need to pay attention."

As he punched the button on the disk, the Crystal stepped in front of him and clamped her bare hand around it. He tried to yank it away with a scowl, but she held on tightly and her deadened eyes stared through him.

"Yeah, fine. You take it." He released it and whirled as he waved for Lisa to get back and take cover.

Her eyes widened when she saw the disk in the Crystal woman's hands and she threw herself at Cardum to tackle him to the floor.

The explosion never came, however. Instead, the cyborg crushed the disk when it detonated and a shiver of electrical sparks flared up her arm and into her hair to raise it on end as if she stood in the center of a cyclone. Her eyes flashed bright blue and the disk fell from her hands in numerous pieces encased in glittering ice.

"Well, damn." Johnny scratched his head. "I ain't never seen someone take a bomb like that."

"You see?" Eveline shrieked and wagged her finger at them. "Do you see how unstoppable they are? And it's all because of me."

"Rex! Rex! Lemme have it!" The hounds snarled at each other as they fought over the frequency bazooka.

"No! I got it first! I'm gonna rip it apart."

"But I wanna kill it!"

"You can't. You're too slow!"

Eveline noticed Johnny scowl at his hounds and she turned with wide eyes. "What are you doing? Filthy mutts. Shoo! Get out!"

"Hey, Rex. You can bite the pile of walking rags. I'll take th—"

"Jaws off, bro. It's mine! Don't even—"

The cyborg control weapon groaned and snapped. The scientist screamed in horror. Rex staggered back with one end of the weird bazooka still clamped in his jaws. He snarled furiously and shook it like he'd caught a rabbit instead. Luther watched the other half sail toward the tall ATM-looking machine at the back of the room and bounded after it. "Mine! Mine, mine, mine. I'll kill it. I'll—"

The severed part of the gun made impact with the center of the thin machine, which exploded immediately in a mushroom burst of green and orange sparks and glittering magical energy.

"No!" Eveline lunged toward Luther and grasped him by the tail.

Rex gasped, and the other part of the bazooka clattered on the floor when he dropped it.

Luther twisted and snarled at the woman before he clamped his jaws on her hand and shook vigorously. "No one touches a hound's tail, lady! You went too far."

She screamed and tried to fight him off with weak blows of her other hand against his mouth.

"Luther! Drop it!"

"You saw what she did, Johnny. She grabbed my tail—"

"Boy, I'll drag you out by the tail, so help me."

He released the woman's hand immediately and stared at his master. "You wouldn't."

"He didn't mean it, bro." Rex trotted toward his brother and paused only to bare his teeth and growl at the mad scientist who cradled a bloodied hand. "You know he didn't mean it. Lemme see."

The hounds circled one another, sniffed under each other's tails, and snorted.

"Yeah, you're good."

"But I feel so violated."

The tall, thin machine sparked and hissed again with another wave of glittering light. In the next moment, it exploded in a series of sputtering bursts and flung shards of plastic and metal across the lab and into Dr. Monroe's supplies.

"You idiots!" she shrieked. "Look what you've done. Do you have any idea—oh. It's all ruined now."

Lisa helped Cardum to his feet and brushed a few stray bits of shredded metal off his shoulder. "Are you okay?"

"N-n-no, that's…" The man pointed behind her, and she spun to see the shifter cyborg only a few paces away from her. He stood with his head cocked as the lens of his mechanical eye widened, narrowed, and widened again. His lips twitched, then his cheeks, and he looked down slowly to study both hands.

"What—"

"Oh, good. They talk." Johnny pointed at the cyborg twins and scowled. "Don't get cute."

"Brandon?"

"Clint?"

The twins stared at each other and their mouths worked open and closed as words failed them.

The Crystal woman ran a hand through her ice-encrusted hair and drew a shuddering breath. "What happened?"

"Huh." Johnny stood perfectly still and glanced from one lucid cyborg to the next. "I guess y'all have been released from the doc's insanely powerful hold on you and your…uh, gear." He cleared his throat. "Boys?"

"Yeah, Johnny."

"Right here!"

The hounds trotted toward their master, their tongues lolling out of lazy canine smiles. "It's all good now, right?"

"Uh-huh." Johnny squinted at the damaged machine. "Next time I tell y'all not to touch anythin', don't listen."

"Yeah, no sweat, Johnny."

"Trust us. We have loads of practice ignoring you."

"Dude…"

"What? It's true."

Eveline screeched and leapt toward the side of the lab. Her bloodied hand knocked against cables and wires as she fumbled for something on the shelves.

"Naw. We ain't got time for this, Doc." Johnny marched

toward her, grasped her hands, and lowered them behind her back. Both her scrawny wrists fit together in one of his hands with room to spare. "You're done—no more augmentations, no more experiments, and no more sendin' cyborg wizards with no more marbles left to blow your enemies up for ya."

She struggled in his grasp and moaned piteously until the hounds growled at her. At that, the fire of fury and outrage rose in her again and she bucked against the dwarf's tight hold. He didn't budge. "You can't do this! I am a respected expert in my field. I've achieved the impossible."

"You've taken this way too far, Eveline." Cardum had regained some of his dignity. He smoothed the front of his shirt and scowled at the doctor. "You're finished and for good this time."

The bounty hunter pulled his prisoner toward Lisa, who removed a pair of handcuffs from her belt and clamped them around Eveline's wrists to replace his hand. "I can't even comprehend the list of charges you're facing, Dr. Monroe. But it's a long one."

"This isn't right. You can't do this."

"We can."

"The Bureau always gets everything, don't they?" Spit flew from the woman's mouth as she screamed at Lisa. "Sure, they can have magical agents and magical bounty hunters, but when a scientist who's been with the CIA for forty years has a breakthrough, they can't fund the most important research of the century."

"This ain't research, Doc." Johnny grimaced and studied the lab and the four stupefied cyborg magicals who had been released from the doctor's control. "I think this is more like torture."

"No. No! They wanted it! Tell them."

None of the cyborgs said a word.

"You're all useless husks, anyway." Eveline spat on the floor and stumbled when Cardum took her arm and jerked her forward.

"You're coming with me. Then I'm calling this in and all your research is going into evidence against you. Do you understand?"

She hissed at him. "Where are your balls, Mac?"

The man snorted. "Out of your reach. That's for damn sure." He glanced at Johnny and Lisa in frustration. "You got the rest of this?"

"Yeah, we'll be up in a while," Lisa muttered with a half-hearted nod.

"Uh-huh. I always knew bringing magicals on board was a bad idea." Cardum jostled Eveline until she gave in and let him half-push, half-pull her out of her secret lab and down the hall.

Johnny, Lisa, and the hounds were left with four incredibly confused cyborgs who seemed on the verge of being seriously pissed off.

The dwarf nodded at the scowling shifter with the mechanical eye. "Hey, how ya doin'? My name's Johnny."

The shifter exchanged a glance with the Crystal woman and his mechanical eye narrowed into a pinpoint. "Someone better explain what the fuck happened down here."

"Uh-huh. Yep. Why don't y'all step away from the...research, huh? We'll get y'all out in the sunshine and fresh air. I think you could use a little fresh air. We'll explain everythin' after that."

"Yeah, okay." The Crystal woman nodded and took a deep breath. "Do you mind if I burn this place to the ground first—"

"Whoa, whoa. No." Johnny pointed at her and shook his head. "We've already had too many explosions for one week, you understand? I can't cover for y'all if you go rampagin' through a CIA facility."

The magical shrugged, stormed past him, and headed out of the lab. "What are you assholes waiting for?" she called over her shoulder. "We're getting the hell out of here."

He gestured expansively and attempted a smile for the other

three cyborgs. The shifter pounded his augmented fist on the scientist's laptop and shattered it before he strode out.

Lisa winced. "Okay… There goes a piece of evidence."

"Naw, we'll call it collateral after the fact." Johnny shook his head and watched the cyborg twins scurry after the other two down the tunnel. "I think anyone who wants the story will believe whatever we tell 'em at this point."

"And what will we tell them?"

"Yeah. That's still a work in progress. Come on."

CHAPTER TWENTY-EIGHT

In the parking lot in front of the abandoned building, Johnny scowled at Dr. Monroe who screamed non-stop in the back of Cardum's vehicle. He leaned toward Lisa. "Do you have any idea how the CIA handles shit like this?"

"No, Johnny. And it's out of our hands now."

"Uh-huh."

The CIA director approached them, shuffled his feet, and stared at the asphalt. He thrust a hand out toward Johnny and cleared his throat. "I guess this is the end of our tour—"

The dwarf snorted. "How astute of you, Director."

"And…you know. Thank you." The man finally met his gaze and Johnny took the guy's hand in a crushing hold to pump his arm enthusiastically.

"There. That ain't so hard to say, is it?"

Cardum looked at Lisa and suffered the bounty hunter's grin. "Admittedly, you two managed to find what we'd overlooked in the last—dammit! You're gonna rip my arm off if you keep that up."

With a chuckle, Johnny released the man's hand, stepped

back, and raised both his hands. "I'm simply pleased, Cardum. Real pleased, is all."

"Sure. I bet you are. Listen. I have a response team on the way. They'll bag the lab up and take all of Eveline's—Dr. Monroe's research and materials away to be processed and entered as evidence or whatever the hell we're calling this. I think it's best if the two of you handled those...things." He nodded at the four cyborgs who stood in a huddle on the other side of the parking lot and scowled at Dr. Monroe, who still threw a surprisingly energetic fit in the back of the car. "You know. They're your people."

He snorted. "No, they ain't. They're CIA test subjects."

"They're magicals," Cardum replied, then remembered who he was talking to and shook his head. "Even I can tell they didn't have much of a choice in this if any. But I do know that if the response team finds them here, they won't make it through the night—if you catch my drift."

"Shit." Johnny tugged his beard, his expression disgusted. "What are we supposed to do with 'em?"

"I'll leave that up to you to decide. You know, magical to magical. I'm sure you guys have some secret way to deal with this kind of thing."

"Now wait a minute." The dwarf hurried after him but Cardum had already answered his cell phone and turned away to manage the rest of his CIA business. "Asshole. It's a damn good thing they don't work with magicals in the CIA. I'd have ripped his head off by now."

"And we can leave it at that, huh?" Lisa patted his shoulder and turned toward the silently observant cyborgs. "So we can turn our attention to these guys. What's next?"

"Shit, I don't know." He glowered and hooked his thumbs through his belt loops. "We can't simply let 'em loose."

She snorted. "I assumed that was obvious."

"I don't know, darlin'. Call Nelson about it. I ain't got it in me to play social worker."

"Wait. Hold on." She nudged him in the shoulder and nodded toward the cyborgs. "Huh. I wouldn't have expected that."

"For cryin' out loud." Johnny turned toward them and stopped when he saw the shifter on one knee, scratching Luther behind the ear.

How did I not see that comin'?

"Oh, yeah. Yeah, that's good." Luther's hind leg thumped repeatedly against the asphalt as he leaned into the attention. "Holy crap, man. Hey, Rex! Who knew a robot hand could scratch this good?"

"For real?" Rex padded toward his brother and stopped in the shifter's face. "Hey, buddy. I want a scratch too."

"Wait your turn, bro."

"No way. Without me, that mind-control machine would never have blown up."

"Hey, it was my piece that landed in the right place."

"Yeah, and you never would have thrown it if I hadn't helped you break it in half. Move out of the way!"

"Back off, Rex. I'm not done."

The hounds snarled and snapped at each other and tousled for less than five seconds before Rex nipped his brother's nose a little too hard. Luther loped across the parking lot with a yelp, his eyes wide as he raced away from the larger hound. "I hate you!"

"You too, bro. Hey, I'll let you know when I'm done." Rex had all of fifteen seconds as the object of the shifter's attention before the cyborg straightened with a chuckle and fixed his gaze—both his normal eye and the mechanical one—on Johnny and Lisa. "Aw, come on, dude. You were just getting to the good part." The hound sniffed the asphalt and stopped in front of the Crystal woman. "Hey, lady. I bet you give a good scratch. How about it, huh?"

She ignored him. All four of the cyborgs stared at Johnny

now. Their tech parts glinted in the sunlight and occasionally flashed with random lights or emitted a whirring click.

The bounty hunter grimaced and tried to look away, but he couldn't bring himself to turn his back on the small group of magicals turned war machines he'd saved. "Aw, hell, darlin'. I don't know what to do with 'em."

Lisa smiled at the cyborgs and leaned toward him. "You did say you didn't want to make the same mistakes, right?"

"Same mistakes? Are you tellin' me I made mistakes with... dammit. I don't even know his name. Omar's brother. I think I handled that damn well if you ask me."

"You did the best you could, Johnny. But I'm not talking about the wizard."

"Then what the—" His eyes widened. "Oh, no. Fuck no. I ain't trainin' science experiments. Uh-uh."

She shrugged. "The way I see it, this can only go one of two ways. You do it or the Bureau does it."

"See, that's the way it's always gonna be, though, ain't it? Me against the goddamn feds."

"Well, would you rather have these magicals under the Bureau's control?" Lisa folded her arms. "I know I wouldn't. The department won't see them as magicals and victims of a madwoman's quest for revenge. It'll see these four only as assets —more machine than anything else. They'd be treated as poorly as they were in that lab behind us and maybe even worse—most likely mishandled on every level." She gave him a sidelong glance. "Exactly like they would have abused Amanda if you hadn't stepped in—"

"All right, all right. Goddammit." Johnny ran a hand through his hair and scowled at her. "You're gonna be the death of me, darlin'. You know that?"

"You're not doing it for me, Johnny." She placed a hand on his shoulder. "But I'll help."

The bounty hunter scoffed, rolled his eyes, and stormed

across the parking lot toward the four cyborgs who continued to stare expectantly at him. *They probably have enhanced hearing and all that bullshit and now have me and Lisa talkin' about 'em on a damn recordin'. This is the last thing I need.*

He stopped in front of them, folded his arms, and gazed at each of their faces in turn. "What's y'all's names?"

The guy on the end pointed at his twin and muttered, "Brandon."

His twin mirrored the gesture. "Clint."

"Huh. Do you have any objection to me callin' y'all the twins?"

They shrugged simultaneously. Even their augmentations were practically identical but mirror images of each other. Panels of thin silver metal replaced a three-inch-squared section of flesh on the side of their neck. Long metal rods ran down the length of each arm in the center to the end of their middle fingers. Lights blinked from prosthetic ears probably made of silicone and slightly off-color from the rest of their flesh. One of them scratched a phantom itch on his belly and raised his shirt to expose another section of metal where a belly button should have been. He tugged his shirt down to cover it and stared at the dwarf.

"And y'all?"

"Leroy." The shifter nodded. "I know that much, at least."

"Huh." Johnny shrugged. "Good name."

The Crystal woman studied him warily before her gaze lingered on Lisa. "3418."

"Say what now?" He turned to look at his partner, who only raised her eyebrows in surprise and curiosity. "Naw, that'd be some kinda subject number, darlin'. What's your—"

"I'm not your darling." The Crystal cut him a scathing glance but didn't move. "Ever."

"All right. Hey. I don't mean nothin' by it. It's only a figure of speech. But I gotta call you somethin' and it ain't gonna be a number."

Her thin eyebrows drew together and she scanned the air above the bounty hunter's head. "I don't know."

"For cryin' out—"

"Then what would you like us to call you?" Lisa asked quickly and placed a hand on Johnny's shoulder again. It felt more like a warning than reassurance and he grunted.

"Um…" The Crystal shared a glance with Leroy and it lasted longer than a normal look of encouragement or anything else.

I'll be damned if they ain't talkin' to each other's brains right now. What the hell am I gettin' myself into?

"I've always liked June."

"Damn. Y'all have been down there a long time. It's almost September—" Lisa elbowed him hard in the side. "What?"

"Okay, June." She nodded at the Crystal woman. "I'm Lisa. This is Johnny."

"Yeah, he said that in the lab," Leroy muttered. "I thought Johnny Walker was a whiskey."

"Yeah." The dwarf stabbed himself in the chest with a thumb. "Mine."

"Hey, Johnny." Luther sniffed the cyborgs' feet and his tail wagged. "You gonna introduce us too or what?"

"Yeah, we're part of the team." Rex sat in front of June and hadn't taken his eyes off her. "You better tell them who we are. Two-legs are always more likely to pet a hound if they can put a name to the muzzle."

"And that's Rex and Luther," Lisa said, beating their master to it. "You guys get to come with us now, okay? We'll take you somewhere safe."

"Safe?" June scoffed and the corner of her mouth twitched into a sneer. "That doesn't exist. Not for us."

Johnny shook his head. "It does when you're with me. So come on. Hurry up. And no fightin' in the back seat, ya hear? It's a rental."

The lens of Leroy's mechanical eye spun and whirled again,

then enlarged and shrunk as he zoomed in on whatever he wanted to see.

I ain't a fan of that eye.

"Where are we going?" the shifter asked.

Lisa turned toward the dwarf and grinned. "Home."

Aw, hell.

"Well, let's get a move on, then. Come on." Johnny turned toward their SUV and whistled. "Let's go, boys. Y'all are in the way back."

"Aw, man." Luther took a final sniff at one of the twins' legs, considered moving closer, then finally turned to follow his master. "Johnny, I was just getting used to having half the back seat."

"Yeah, it's cozy back there." Rex kept looking over his shoulder at June as he trotted after the bounty hunter. "These guys are like the pup. Can't they drive themselves?"

He snapped his fingers. "That's enough now. The back seat was a privilege and now we got...guests."

Lisa waved the cyborgs after him and caught up to Johnny. "You're doing the right thing, you know. In case you were wondering."

"I ain't." He scowled and glared at their rental car. "I might change my mind once we get in the car. I'm not sure it's gonna hold up under four metallic magicals."

"It'll be fine."

CHAPTER TWENTY-NINE

It wasn't fine. By the time they returned the rental car at the Capital Region International Airport, the SUV looked like it had been folded in half over a mountain. The chassis was all out of alignment and the row of back seats had been permanently dented in their frames. Johnny managed to convince the rental company that it was all paid for and gave the guy Nelson's direct number for a bill.

When they stood beside the private jet, Johnny had a quick, private chat with the captain before he turned to the cyborgs. All four stood calmly and impassively against the whir of the jet engines. It unnerved him that none of them seemed to blink.

"Do any of y'all weigh more than three hundred pounds?"

He received only blank stares in reply.

"Shit. Felix?"

"Johnny." The captain raised a hand to shield his eyes against the sunlight glinting off the cyborg's parts.

"We'll have to load up and see. Unless you have some kinda industrial scale hidden under the cabin or somethin'."

"We'll, uh…we'll be all right."

"Yeah. I trust you."

Felix clapped a hand on Johnny's shoulder and nodded, still staring at the cyborgs. "Come on in, then. Let's get you home. Oh, and we're not…making any extra stops, are we?"

"Naw. Back to the Glades."

The man headed up the rolling stairs to enter the jet but continued to cast wary glances over his shoulder.

"Load up!" Johnny waved them all forward and ascended the steps with the hounds beside him.

"Have you guys ever been on a private jet before?" Lisa asked.

One of the twins nodded vigorously while the other shook his head. Then, they paused and did the exact opposite. June rolled her eyes.

"I assume military flights don't count," Leroy muttered.

"You're military?"

"I was. I think."

Lisa paused at the top of the stairs and peered inside the jet before she turned to the shifter. "Well, you're right. A private jet is very different. And…maybe don't mention to Johnny that you think you were military, okay? At least until I get a chance to bring it up with him first."

"The dwarf doesn't like soldiers?"

"Uh… It's more like he has a thing against authority and chain of command. And anyone else who might think they know more than he does about certain kinds of operations."

Leroy snorted and raised his right arm. "I can shoot magical bombs out of my hand."

"Yep. That's why I want to talk to him first." She winked at the shifter and stepped into the jet. When her back was to him, her hesitant smile faded completely and her eyes widened.

Johnny saw the expression and glared at the front of the plane as Leroy ducked and walked aboard. "What's wrong? What did he do?"

"He didn't do anything, Johnny. Relax."

"The look on your face says different, darlin'. I swear, if

they're fixin' to cause us any kinda trouble, I have no problem shuckin' 'em off this plane and—"

"Johnny." She dropped into the seat beside him and took his hand. "It's fine. And a little too late to go back on your promise now, don't you think?"

"Nope."

"I'll tell you later."

The jet shuddered beneath the steps of four new passengers, half-machine and half-magical. Felix stared at them with wide eyes until he finally pushed past his hesitation and pulled the door closed. He hurried into the cockpit and shut that door too.

"Hey, lady." Rex gazed at June as he walked backward in front of her, his tail wagging. "You can sit by me if you want. And scratch my ears. Just sayin'."

She ignored him completely and slumped into a seat toward the back of the jet. With her arms folded, she closed her eyes and didn't say a word.

"It hurts, doesn't it?" Luther nipped affectionately at his brother's neck as Rex uttered a low whine. "Rejection."

"Yeah." Rex slumped onto his belly in the aisle and whined. "Bitches."

"Hey, bro." The smaller hound lay beside his brother and chuffed. "Who needs 'em anyway?"

When everyone was settled and they finally had the all-clear to proceed to the runway, Lisa leaned toward Johnny and whispered, "You know we'll have to rent somewhere for them to stay. They need to lay low for a while and I don't think Tommy will keep paying your tab for much longer."

"Naw. He already has." Johnny lightly kicked the black duffel bag he'd shoved under the seat in front of him. Inside it was the agreement signed by Director Zimmerman that Nelson had handed him before this whole mess had even started. "As long as the feds still know how to make good on their end of the deal, I got it covered."

They opted for two rental cars from the airport when they touched down in Florida to avoid ruining any more vehicles by packing four cyborgs into the back seat like high-tech sardines. Johnny heaved a heavy sigh of relief and allowed himself a small smile when he reached the rise in the gravel drive and his cabin in the swamp came into view. "Now this is what I call home."

In the front passenger seat, June leaned forward to peer through the windshield. "You live in the middle of nowhere."

"That's the point. You'll see." The SUV jerked to a halt and kicked up a spray of gravel in the center of the lot. "And y'all need space to run around and get a handle on whatever…changes you're goin' through without attractin' unwanted attention, understand?"

Leroy snorted. "Changes we're going through? The last time I checked, I went through puberty decades ago."

The shifter opened the back door and stepped out and the SUV rocked violently when it was relieved of his surprising weight.

Johnny rolled his eyes. "I ain't talkin' about those kinda changes."

June shook her head and stepped out without a word.

Yeah, that's what I get for raisin' a twelve-year-old shifter out here for months.

When he let the hounds out the back, Rex and Luther bounded out and raced feverishly toward the back of the house and the swamp beyond, howling in delight.

"Better keep up, bro! I'm gonna run circles around you!"

"You wish! Hey, hey, Rex. You see that squirrel?"

"Where?"

"Ha! Too slow!"

The hounds splashed into the water behind the house, baying and barking at each other until their voices faded from Johnny's head.

Lisa joined him in front of his rental as the cyborgs meandered aimlessly around the yard and absorbed it all. Her eyes widened when she stared over the roof of Johnny's cabin and her mouth dropped open for a moment before she muttered, "Is that…"

"It sure as hell better be, I tell you what. Come on." He caught her hand and pulled her along the side of the house toward the back. "I guess she needs a good inspection anyhow."

When they reached the back yard, Lisa sucked in a sharp breath and craned her neck to stare at the top of the three-story behemoth moored in the river of the swamp and tucked behind the trees.

"Huh. At least they had the brains enough to not try to drag it onto land."

"Johnny, you said houseboat."

"Uh-huh."

"This isn't a boat."

"Hell, it has a motor."

"Or a house." Lisa swiped her hair away from her face and turned to look at him. "This is your pipedream?"

He smirked at her and shrugged. "Well, when Zimmerman said they were willin' to complete my list of demands with this one, sure. Yeah. I can admit I made a few…upgrades."

"I can't believe they agreed to this."

"The feds will agree to anythin' if you have somethin' they want badly enough. Do you wanna take a look inside?"

She was speechless for a moment. "Well, I…yeah. Johnny, what in the world were you planning to do with a mansion on the water?"

He sighed heavily and rubbed the back of his neck. "Honestly? I was fixin' to surprise you with a little getaway, darlin'. Only the two of us."

"You were?"

The dwarf glanced away quickly and cleared his throat. "And the hounds."

"Yeah, that's a given." A laugh burst out of her. "What would we do with all that space?"

"Aw, come on. Don't tell me you never stayed in a five-star resort with more room than you could handle."

"Not like that. I'm very sure it takes a full-time crew to run something that size."

"Yep." Johnny turned to see the cyborgs moving cautiously down the side yard toward them. They gazed silently around at the swamp, the thick foliage, and the giant houseboat out in the river that jutted through the tops of the trees. "I think we have a decent head start on that already."

"You brought them here to man your swamp castle?"

He snorted. "Naw. But now I have the room for 'em and the need for a crew."

Lisa shook her head and couldn't hide a disbelieving smile. "You'd better pay them for it."

"Sure. In room and board. And trainin'." He shook his head furiously and grunted. "I can't believe I said that."

With a chuckle, Lisa caught his face in both hands and planted a long kiss on his lips. "You're a good dwarf, Johnny Walker."

"Huh. It's the first time I heard it said like that." *Or any other way.*

"Okay. Inspection time. And I guess we'll have to go out and get supplies, right?"

"Supplies for what?"

"To stock the five-star resort in your back yard."

Johnny laughed. "You think I had the FBI built me this beauty and didn't include all the trimmin's on the list?"

Her mouth gaped. "You're joking."

"I truly ain't, darlin'." He tugged on her hand and pulled her toward the dock. "Hey…y'all!"

The cyborgs looked expectantly at him.

"Yeah, I need to come up with somethin' better'n that to call y'all together. Look alive, huh? I have somethin' to show ya."

"Is it the hotel on floaties?" Leroy asked. The twins chuckled. Even June cracked a smile.

"Yep. I told y'all I had somewhere safe and under the radar in mind. Before we get onto it, though, I have a couple of ground rules to lay out—"

A crackling roar burst from the group of cyborgs, and June elevated sharply when smoke and propulsive fire erupted from the backs of her calves. She sailed over the overhanging branches of the trees that shielded the swamp and five seconds later, a metallic thump came from the direction of the houseboat.

Johnny scowled and stared at the place where the Crystal woman had been moments before. "Does anyone else have jetpacks built into their damn legs?"

Leroy chuckled and folded his arms. The twins looked at the backs of each other's legs, then jostled each other in reassurance, turned to the bounty hunter, and shook their heads.

"All right. Rule number one!" He made sure to shout loud enough so June could hear. "No flyin' around or usin' whatever abilities you have now simply to make things easier for yourselves. I didn't build my house all the way out in the middle of nowhere so I could listen to jet engines and explosions all over my back yard."

With a curt nod, he led Leroy and the twins onto the dock where the flat-bottom airboat was tied to the end and gestured toward it.

"Rule number two. No one touches the airboat without my say-so. Or the truck. Or Sheila. Or Margo."

"Sheila and Margo?" Leroy shook his head.

"His Jeep and that...weird metal hut in the yard," Lisa clarified.

"Huh." Johnny stared at the airboat, then studied the three cyborgs speculatively. "I might have to make a few trips for this. I ain't fixin' to sink my boat ferryin' y'all around."

"Johnny!" Rex and Luther splashed through the swamp toward them and howled. "Johnny, did you see it? A huge bird!"

"No way, bro. It was a plane."

"It was something, Johnny. Headed right for the giant eyesore in the middle of the swamp!"

The hounds leapt onto the dock and shook themselves furiously. Leroy and the twins didn't even flinch when they were splattered with swamp water, soggy reeds, and clumps of mud.

"Hey, hey. Johnny." Luther spun in a wide circle before he trotted toward his master, panting. "We going out for a hunt?"

Leroy's eyes widened at that but he didn't say anything.

Oh, sure. I always gotta have a damn shifter around to listen to my hounds for me.

The bounty hunter turned and began to untie the docking rope from the airboat. He tossed it onto the deck, leapt aboard the vessel, and moved to the stern to get the fan started. That done, he stared at the waiting cyborgs and raised three fingers. "Rule number three. Don't feed the hounds. Now get on. I guess it's best to see whether you sink or swim. Now's as good a time as any."

It's not all fun and games with the cyborgs, but they're learning. Join Johnny, the hounds, the cyborgs and of course Lisa and Amanda as they take on new challenges (including a weapons convention) In *CLUSTER DWARF*.

Get sneak peeks, exclusive giveaways, behind the scenes content, and more. PLUS you'll be notified of special **one day only fan pricing** on new releases.

Sign up today to get free stories.

Visit: https://marthacarr.com/read-free-stories/

AUTHOR NOTES - MARTHA CARR

FEBRUARY 8, 2021

This is the tale of two Mercedes and a lesson about patience, perseverance and a sweet, sweet payoff. Or as my friend, Vince likes to say, "If something's good enough to come around once, it's good enough to come around a second time."

Even if it takes twenty years to pay off.

Our story begins in the year 2000 just after we found out that the computers weren't going to suddenly halt at the stroke of midnight. The new millennium was looking pretty good for me – at last.

I had optioned my first novel, Wired – a thriller – to Hollywood. A director was soon attached, and a splashy announcement appeared in Variety. It was my first experience with movies, agents, distribution deals, scripts. All of it was brand new and exciting.

Want to suddenly feel better about yourself? Get a movie deal and then go see your agent at his office. Everyone will cater to you like you are the most important person they ever met. The effort will be so polished, so seemingly genuine, you will find yourself wondering if maybe you are different.

Money flowed in my direction with promises of more money.

Lots more. As a single mother of a thirteen-year-old kid who was always scraping together money for something, this was life changing on a grand scale.

Somewhere in the midst of all the hullabaloo I went to look at a Mercedes sedan. Nothing too fancy but a million miles better than my old silver Chevrolet. That thing was so large that the Offspring at seven blurted out at a stoplight that we could live in it if we had to, cheerfully pointing out how the shelf in the rear window could hold most of his things. I appreciated his resilient optimism but at the time worried it could come true.

But here we were on the precipice of greatness test driving Mercedes. Ah life, how quickly things can change.

The owner of the dealership came out to congratulate me, saying he'd heard of the book. I smiled slightly, not wanting to look too taken with myself. "Take it home with you and try it out," he said. "We'll fill in all the paperwork and then you can come in when the check arrives."

I think it was the smell of the leather or that windshield wiper that came on when rain hit the window. I don't know, but for some reason I said okay in a kind of haze, leaving behind my old boat of a car and driving off in this snappy Mercedes wondering what just happened. So much of life was changing.

Until it wasn't.

Something about distribution or getting the script the way they wanted to or financing. Bottom line, Wired was getting shelved for now and any future payments were on hold. This is when I learned that what happened to me is common practice and you can't really count on a check till it's already cashed. A film could even get made and then something happens, and it's never distributed, and the last payments go *poof* and disappear. That's when your agent goes back to letting his assistant answer your calls.

After my brain calmed down and I was able to take a deep breath and realize I wasn't worse off, I realized that car had to go back. Fortunately, it had only been a couple of weeks and the trusty Oldsmobile was still sitting on his lot.

No one was very happy with me, but hey, it wasn't my idea in the first place and I wasn't very happy with the end of this story either. (For those of you wondering why a dealer would let me drive off in a car I hadn't technically bought in the first place – to this day I can only figure that things are different at the higher end and I had just gotten a taste of it, only to be escorted out of rich land and back to struggling writer ranch.)

I handed over the keys to that shiny Mercedes and crawled back into my Olds and drove off, not looking back.

Turns out that *wasn't* the end of the story. It was just going to take a while to come back around. Recently, I was online looking at Kia's or another Subaru, both good cars when that Offspring, now grown, looked over my shoulder and said, "How old are you going to be before you buy the car you always wanted."

He had never forgotten that story either. I looked at him and took in a deep breath and clicked over to the Mercedes site.

Three days later I drove off a Mercedes lot again with a GLE350 SUV with a touchscreen dashboard and seats that can massage you on long trips and a million other gadgets. But this time I already had the money and could hand it over, along with a great bunch of Fans and over 150 books with my name on them and more to come. This time the dream came true with no catches.

Like Vince says, the idea of a Mercedes was good enough to come around again. Excuse me while I go drive the two blocks to get the mail. I'll catch you all later. More adventures to follow.

Thank you for reading this story and all the way back to these author notes, as well!

So, I'm going to mention my Mercedes story since Martha mentioned hers.

(For those who prefer trucks, the top-of-the-line F150 is more expensive than my Mercedes in the story below. It's all what you want.)

I don't have a 20-year story to get a Mercedes, rather what I had done was lease two different Hyundai vehicles.

One was an SUV, the other a Genesis.

The Genesis was the second car and it felt top of the line! Smooth leather, great acceleration, an automatic braking system for when you had cruise control turned on.

In short, amazing.

Like anything, I went back and studied how the Hyundai company could build such an exciting vehicle and found out they did it the smart way.

They tore apart Mercedes, BMW, and other cars and learned how they did it. When I realized this, I started noticing that yup… My grill looked like a Mercedes.

So did other parts of the car. In fact, it felt like I was in a car that was 60% Mercedes, 40% something else.

It was cheaper, though.

So, when it came time to look at vehicles, it was the summer of 2016. I was making very good money on my Kurtherian Gambit series (I had no co-authors at the time) and wanted to know what it felt like to sit in the car that my car was based on.

So, I went to the Mercedes Benz dealer.

At first, they tried me in a four-door E350 (moving up executive model.) It was too stodgy for me.

I tried a couple of others, and then they put me in a Selenite Grey two-door E400 Coupe.

I lusted for that car. There is no other way to admit it.

I saw the price and about swallowed my tonsils.

But when checking out the leasing, it was about $400 more a month than the Hyundai Genesis.

It was my first dream car.

I was writing and working 16-18 hour days with no days off during the previous eight months. I would often fall asleep typing the next Bethany Anne adventure out at night. By July, I was earning a five-figure monthly income.

I could afford the higher lease payment so taking a deep breath I signed on the dotted line.

The ONLY regret I have over that purchase was not going for the E550 Coupe with the bigger engine.

I've had two BMW's since that car, but the MB Coupe still has a hold on my heart that won't let go.

Trust me, every time a lease comes up, you will find me looking at what Mercedes has to offer just in case the company has another Coupe that can steal my heart.

Being an Indie Author has provided myself and my family a huge number of benefits. That Mercedes was the first one of many.

If you believe you would like to write for a living, it isn't easy at all. But it *can* be profitable. Check out the 20Booksto50k™ Facebook group online and there are plenty of stories of those who are making money writing stories and what you need to do.

But first, make sure that it isn't just a dream. Because there is a lot of work in becoming successful, and it isn't all fun.

Writing stories is who I am. I didn't learn that until I was 48. Give it a shot, perhaps you might learn being an author is who you are a bit earlier in your life?

Ad Aeternitatem,

Michael Anderle

Solve a murder, save her mother, and stop the apocalypse?

What would you do when elves ask you to investigate a prince's murder and you didn't even know elves, or magic, was real?

Meet Leira Berens, Austin homicide detective who's good at what she does – track down the bad guys and lock them away.

Which is why the elves want her to solve this murder – fast. It's not just about tracking down the killer and bringing them to justice. It's about saving the world!

If you're looking for a heroine who prefers fighting to flirting, check out The Leira Chronicles today!

<u>AVAILABLE ON AMAZON AND IN KINDLE UNLIMITED!</u>

CONNECT WITH THE AUTHORS

Martha Carr Social
Website:
http://www.marthacarr.com
Facebook:
https://www.facebook.com/groups/MarthaCarrFans/

Michael Anderle

Website: http://lmbpn.com

Email List: http://lmbpn.com/email/

Social Media:

https://www.facebook.com/LMBPNPublishing

https://twitter.com/MichaelAnderle

https://www.instagram.com/lmbpn_publishing/

https://www.bookbub.com/authors/michael-anderle

OTHER LMBPN PUBLISHING BOOKS

To be notified of new releases and special promotions from LMBPN publishing, please join our email list:

http://lmbpn.com/email/

For a complete list of books published by LMBPN please visit the following pages:

https://lmbpn.com/books-by-lmbpn-publishing/

Made in the USA
Las Vegas, NV
19 December 2022

00154